Who Was

David Weiser?

Pawel Huelle

Who Was
David Weiser?

Translated by
Michael Kandel

A Helen and Kurt Wolff Book
Harcourt Brace Jovanovich, Publishers
NEW YORK   SAN DIEGO   LONDON

First published in Polish as *Weiser Dawidek*
by Wydawnictwo Morskie, Gdańsk, 1987.

Library of Congress Cataloging-in-Publication Data
Huelle, Pawel.
[Weiser Dawidek. English]
Who was David Weiser?/Pawel Huelle; translated by
Michael Kandel—1st US ed.
p.   cm.
Translation of: Weiser Dawidek.
"A Helen and Kurt Wolff Book."
ISBN 0-15-196294-4
I. Title.
PG7167.U86W413   1992
891.8'537—dc20   91-24788

Designed by Trina Stahl

Printed in the United States of America

First United States edition
A B C D E

To Juliusz

Who Was

David Weiser?

To this day I don't know how it all happened. How did we three come to be standing in the headmaster's study, ominous words such as "sworn statement" and "investigation" resounding in our ears? How had we turned from ordinary schoolboys into defendants in the dock? By what strange fate had this adult status been thrust upon us? Some investigating must have been done in advance, but we knew nothing about that. All I was aware of at the time was the pain in my left leg, because they had us standing constantly, and then came those questions repeated over and over, those devious smiles and threats mixed with sugary coaxing to "start once again from the beginning,

I

not leaving anything out, and without making anything up."

The man in the uniform wiped the sweat from his brow, stared at us with the dull eyes of a tired animal, and shook his finger, muttering curses. The headmaster, his tie loosened, drummed his fingers on the black desktop. And every now and then M-ski, the nature teacher, dropped in to ask how the inquiry was going. We watched the rays of the September sun as they entered between the drawn curtains and fell upon the dusty, wine-colored carpet, and we were sorry that the summer was over. Meanwhile they went on asking us the same questions, for the hundredth time, as if incapable of grasping the simplest things, almost as if they were the children and not we. "You're withholding information. That's a punishable offense under the Criminal Code!" shouted the militiaman, and the headmaster nodded, tugging at his tie. "What am I to do with you, boys, what am I to do with you?" he asked as he loosened again the huge triangular knot, which began to look like a Jacobin jabot. Only M-ski remained unperturbed, as if sure of himself; occasionally he'd whisper something into the militiaman's ear, and then they'd both gaze at us with renewed interest, which meant a whole new barrage of questions.

"Each of you has a completely different story,"

shouted the headmaster. "And it's never the same story twice. How is it you can't decide on one version among you?" The militiaman interrupted and said, "This is no joking matter—the joking was over yesterday. Today the whole naked truth must be put on the table!"

We had no idea what the whole naked truth looked like, yet we hadn't been lying either, we'd simply told them what they wanted to hear. If M-ski asked about unexploded shells, we admitted that, yes, unexploded shells came into it, and if the militiaman asked about a cache of old ammunition, we said that somewhere, certainly, there had been a cache, perhaps it was still there, but who knew where?—at which point he would turn red as a beet and light another cigarette. And when they asked us if we'd participated in Weiser's explosions, we were quick to answer yes, but none of us was able to say at what time of day; and then one of us would invariably add that actually Weiser did the explosions alone, only occasionally inviting Elka to join him. We knew perfectly well that there were no right answers to their questions, and even if there had been, the events of that August afternoon would remain as strange and mysterious for them as the solution of a quadratic equation was for us.

Szymek and Piotr stood on either side of me. They could get some relief by looking to the left or right, but I was marooned in the middle, having nothing to rest my eyes on but the headmaster's face and the national emblem, a white eagle in a dark frame, above his head. I thought I saw the eagle move one of its wings, as if to fly out into the playground, and I expected us all to hear the sound of breaking glass as the bird took off, but nothing like that happened. Instead, the questions and threats came thicker and faster, and we went on standing there, completely innocent, terrified, not knowing how it would all end—because everything comes to an end, just like the summer, whose dying echoes reached our ears through the open window.

"A person can't disappear without a trace," shouted the militiaman. "Yet you tell us, Korolewski," he said, turning to Szymek, "that Weiser and your friend"—he could never remember Elka's name—"left home together that day and went off toward Bukowa Hill, and you never saw them again, when in fact the three of you were seen together on the railroad embankment that afternoon."

"Who saw us?" asked Szymek timidly, shifting from foot to foot.

"You're not here to ask questions, you're here to answer them!" bellowed the militiaman, his eyes flashing.

Szymek gulped, and his protruding ears reddened. "But it wasn't that afternoon we were seen, it was two days earlier."

The headmaster anxiously shuffled through our written statements. "Another lie! Your friends clearly state that the three of you went off together along the old railroad embankment toward Brentowo— unless," he said, looking up at Piotr and me, "you now deny saying that."

Piotr shook his head. "Oh, no, sir. We said that, but we didn't mean it was on the last day. It actually was two days before."

The headmaster loosened his tie so much it no longer looked anything like a tie; it resembled, rather, a narrow scarf twisted around his neck. The militiaman squinted at the statements and scowled, but this time, instead of raising his voice, he shot different questions at us, unexpected, cunning questions. He wanted to know where Weiser got his explosives. And what sort of dress Elka was wearing the last time we saw her. And if, before disappearing, Weiser had boasted that he'd "do something big." It all revolved around Weiser and Elka, but we knew they'd never get to the truth, because the trail they were following was false from the start.

After some time, M-ski suggested a new tack. Meanwhile I had the thought that Weiser and Elka, using a method known only to them, must be eavesdropping on us now, as we stood in the head-master's study answering the angry militiaman. Weiser was no doubt nodding with approval as he listened to the trouble we were giving the adults, and Elka was laughing out loud, showing her white squirrel's teeth. Piotr and Szymek must have been thinking the same thing, because neither protested when M-ski ordered us out into the main office, to wait there until we were called in one by one, to be questioned separately. This, he hoped, would produce better results.

In the main office we were allowed to sit down at last, and that was wonderful. In addition, our liberation from M-ski's stare and the militiaman's shouting was an unexpected blessing. We took it as a clear sign from Providence that the worst was over. The triumvirate in the headmaster's study was giving us a little time to appreciate the hopelessness of our situation and draw the appropriate conclu-sions. As for us, we didn't even need to confer on what we would say next, knowing that each of us would act on instinct, that that would give us the best chance of keeping up our resistance. First for the firing line was Szymek, who went in quietly and submissively, leaving Piotr and me alone, but not for long, because the janitor was sent for to keep an eye on us. We sat in a silence filled with the

6

ticking of the wall clock, the ticking interrupted only by the gong striking the hours.

How did we come to know Weiser? We'd seen him before, attending the same school, playing on the same playground, and going to the same shop, Cyrson's, to buy orangeade in those sticky bottles with the spring-top porcelain caps. But he never took part in our games; he'd stand to one side, aloof, obviously not wanting to be one of us. When we played soccer on the grass by the Prussian barracks, he was a silent spectator, and when we bumped into him on the beach at Jelitkowo, he'd say he couldn't swim and quickly disappear into the crowd of beachgoers, as if embarrassed. These encounters were brief and unmemorable, and his appearance, too, was nondescript. He was small, thin, and slightly stooped; his complexion was sickly pale, but his eyes, in striking contrast, were unnaturally large and dark. Perhaps that was why he always looked frightened, as if expecting to hear bad news. He lived with his grandfather in No. 11, and on the door of their apartment was a yellow plaque with the words A. WEISER, TAILOR. And this was all we knew about him, until that summer came along, heralded by mayflies and a warm wind from the south.

7

Corpus Christi came unusually late that year. It was in the dust and blazing heat of a June morning that we walked in procession, between us and Father Dudak a group of altar boys and children who'd just taken their first Communion. Singing along with the rest, "Glo-ory to Thee, Jesus, So-on of Mary, the One True God in the Ho-ost," we watched the swinging censer with great devotion. Because the censer was the main thing—not the Host, not the holy images of the Virgin Mary and God the Son of Man, not the wooden figures carried on special litters by the Rosarian lay brothers, not the standards and banners held in white-gloved hands— the censer, swinging left, right, up, down, releasing clouds of gray smoke, the golden censer on a thick golden chain, and the smell of its incense sharp in the nostrils yet also languorous and sweet. In the still air these clouds hung without changing shape, and we quickened our pace, stepping on the heels of the boys in front of us, to catch up with them before they dissolved into nothing.

And that was when we saw Weiser for the first time in his special role, the role he took upon himself and would later impose on the rest of us, though of course we had no inkling of this then. Before the altar set up each year near our apartment building, Father Dudak began to swing the censer mightily, producing a glorious cloud, just what we'd

8

been hoping for. We trembled with excitement. Then, as the gray smoke lifted, we saw Weiser standing on a small hill to the left of the altar, watching the proceedings with pride: the pride of a general reviewing his troops. He stood watching as if all the singing, the standards, images, guilds, and banners had been assembled for his benefit alone, as if these people had no other reason to go in procession through the streets of our district chanting plainsong. Today I know that Weiser had always been what he revealed to us then, for the first time, as the smoke lifted. The moment did not last long. When the final thread of incense faded away and Father Dudak's shrill intoning fell silent, the crowd began to move on toward the church, but Weiser had disappeared from his hill and did not escort us further. After all, what general follows his men when the review is over?

Soon you could count on the fingers of one hand the days left to the end of the school year. June was raging hot, and every morning we were wakened by a chorus of birds proclaiming the supremacy of summer. Weiser was the timid Weiser again, watching our boisterous games from a distance. But something had changed; now we felt, in his gaze, a presence that was cold, penetrating, able to see our every transgression. A gaze difficult to bear. On the day Sunday school diplomas were

9

handed out, we saw him again, just as on Corpus Christi. The rectory of the Community of the Resurrection Fathers was situated, like the rest of our district, on the edge of the forest. When Father Dudak finished his prayers and benedictions, he presented holy pictures to the most devout students. As soon as we had our diplomas, beautifully printed on glossy cards, a mad race to the forest began, because this was the real start of our vacation; yesterday was the last day of school, and now we had before us two whole months of heavenly freedom. We ran in a swarm, shrieking and elbowing one another out of the way. Nothing on earth could stop us—nothing, that is, but Weiser's icy stare. There he was, leaning against a larch as if he'd been waiting for us. Waiting only a few minutes, or waiting all his life? That we didn't know—not then and not later, in the headmaster's study and the adjoining main office, as we sat, each waiting his turn to be questioned. And not even now, as I write these words, when Szymek lives in another city, and Piotr has been dead since 1970, killed in the street, and Elka went to West Germany and never writes. Because Weiser could have been waiting all his life for us, and perhaps that's the most important thing in this story.

So there he was, standing and looking, just standing there and looking. Yet he stopped the surge of sweating bodies and screaming throats and for a brief moment made it recoil. But then the wild element, having recoiled, struck with redoubled force. "Da-vid Wei-ser doesn't go to chu-urch." The chant began from somewhere in the back, and was picked up in the front as "Da-vid Wei-ser is a Je-ew!" And as we said this, our old antipathy for him returned and grew into hatred, because he wasn't one of us, because he never joined us, and because of his big, bulging eyes, which said that we were different from him, not that he was different from us. Szymek came forward and stuck his face in Weiser's. "Hey, Weiser, how come you don't go to Sunday school?" The question hung in the air, demanding an answer. Weiser said nothing; he just smirked— an insolent smirk, we thought at the time. From the back arose a murmur to give him a couple of rolls. Rolls meant stretching the victim out on the ground and then kneeing and punching him in the back. Soon Weiser's white shoulders were bare, and his checked shirt was thrown into the air and passed from hand to hand. But suddenly Elka leaped into the circle of tormentors, her eyes flashing as she kicked left and right. "Leave him alone!" she cried. This had no effect, so she dug her nails into one of the assailants, carving long, red furrows across his cheek. We stepped back from Weiser, and someone even handed him his crumpled shirt. Without a word Weiser put it on, as if nothing had happened. We realized then that it wasn't he, but we, who had come out of this humiliated; he hadn't changed, he was the same old Weiser, he could look at us with the same look as on Corpus Christi, cold and aloof. But it's hard to swallow a thing like that, so when he'd gone only a short way along the overgrown churchyard fence, Szymek threw a stone, loudly singing, "Da-vid Wei-ser is a Je-ew!" The others followed suit, throwing more stones, but Weiser didn't turn, didn't even quicken his step; he preserved his pride and left us with a sense of helplessness and shame. When Elka ran after him, we stopped throwing stones. That was our first encounter with Weiser, his deathly pale shoulders, his crumpled checked shirt, and the unbearable gaze that we'd already felt upon us on Corpus Christi, when the smoke from Father Dudak's golden censer lifted.

Was this simply a coincidence? Or did Weiser stand near the rectory—as on Corpus Christi, when he stood on the hill overlooking the altar—by design? And if so, why did he choose to present himself to us in that particular way? For a long time these questions kept me awake at night, and they troubled me long after the investigation was over, for years, even when I became an adult. I still have no answers, and that is the reason I am filling these pages with my uncertainty. To the letters I send to Mannheim each year in the hope of clarifying some matters connected with what happened then, and with Weiser, there has been no reply. At first I thought that Elka, now that she was a German, didn't want any news from home, any reminders that might disturb her new, German equilibrium. Now, I'm not so sure. There was something between her and Weiser that we could never understand, something uncanny, which had nothing to do with puberty and the opposite sex or some such glib phrase from modern psychology. No, Elka's silence was more than a rejection of the country of her childhood.

On the day Weiser's shirt was thrown into the air and passed from hand to hand, we took the old broken-down No. 4 tram to the beach at Jelitkowo. Though it was early afternoon, the tram was crowded, and the strong sun and the heat filled it with the familiar smell of blistering varnish. Weiser and the morning's incident near the forest went completely out of our heads. As soon as the tram, with a monstrous screech, rolled into the loop by the wooden cross, we jumped off and ran to the beach, waving our towels, not watching out for the nets hung between the houses or the pyramids of crates that reeked of fish and tar. This was where the vacation really began, with diving for a handful of sand, with a swimming race to the red buoy, or running all the way to the Sopot pier, where the daredevils among us showed off with death-defying leaps. Without us, Jelitkowo couldn't exist, just as the town couldn't exist without the beach and the bay. We were all linked together, and although today everything has changed, the memory persists, vivid, indestructible. At the head of our riotous horde ran Piotr, eager to demonstrate his beach trick, which involved pulling off his shirt and shorts on the run and jumping, without stopping, into the water in a spray of white foam. His bare feet were already crunching over the beach, kicking up little fountains of sand behind them, when suddenly he stopped at the water's edge and cried out, as if something sharp had stabbed him in the foot: "Sticklebacks! Look! Millions!"

What we saw surpassed all preconceived notions of the criminal potential of nature. Millions of sticklebacks were bobbing, belly-up, to the lazy rhythm of the waves, a belt of corpses several meters wide. If you put your arm in the water, the scales clinging to your skin would glitter like chain mail, but it wasn't a pleasant feeling at all. Instead of a place to swim, we had fish soup, a sight so disgusting, you could throw up. But this, it turned out, was only the beginning. Over the next few days the soup thickened into a fetid glue. In the blaze of June the corpses rotted, swelling up like bladders, and you could smell the stink as far as the tram loop. The beaches emptied, the number of dead sticklebacks seemed to grow and grow, and our despair knew no bounds. Jelitkowo didn't want us. The coast changed color; it went from bright green to dark brown, and swarms of un- usually large flies appeared, to feed on the carrion and lay their eggs. Despite the great heat, the bay was unapproachable. It was all for nothing—the sun, the clear blue sky, the mockingly perfect wea- ther. The local authorities finally decided to close all the beaches from Stogi to Gdynia, which really was only an official acknowledgment of a state of affairs that already existed.

Nothing worse could possibly have happened to us, and when I thought about it as I sat in the school's main office waiting my turn to be questioned and wondering what I'd tell M-ski this time, I realized it was no accident. Because if it hadn't been for the fish soup, it never would have occurred to us to follow Weiser, to trail him across Bukowa Hill and the old firing range, and he never would have let us into his life. But I'm getting ahead of myself— this story, like any true story, should be told in its proper order.

The door opened a little, and I saw Szymek, M-ski's hand pushing him out. As Piotr's name was called, and the janitor escorted him to the door, I noticed that one of Szymek's ears was unnaturally red and pulled out of shape. I felt my stomach tighten and my heart jump, but I couldn't ask him what happened, because M-ski appeared in the doorway and as he pulled Piotr inside told the janitor that we weren't to exchange a single word. Szymek sat on a folding chair, bowed his head, and stared at his knees. Would they yank my ears, too? I wondered. One never knew what M-ski would do; there was no end to his arsenal of tricks.

Even now, today, M-ski's role in the story remains unclear to me. So how could I have been expected then, as I waited my turn for questioning, to figure out who and what exactly this man was? Also, I was too afraid of him to think about him clearly. But when the diamond-patterned leather-covered door closed noiselessly behind Piotr, I remembered something. Every year, our school, like all the other schools, marched in the May Day parade. M-ski always took the lead, holding a placard high and beaming at the men on the rostrum as his piping voice buoyed up our voices: "Fo-orward, youth of the wo-orld, our brotherly so-ong resounds to-oday!" And so we'd march along, in our white shirts and dark shorts, beaming and singing

16

like everybody else, but we knew that the very next day those who had failed to attend the festival of youth and enthusiasm would receive a home visit from M-ski. He would ask the parents what had happened—was it a serious illness? what could he do to help, so the student, next year at this time, would be fit as a fiddle? Last May Day, only one student from our school had not attended the parade: Weiser. Curiously enough, M-ski never called on the grandfather to ask why the grandson hadn't marched with us. We didn't attach much importance to this at the time, but now, as I sat waiting to be questioned, it seemed very important.

Yet what connection could there have been between M-ski and Weiser? None, surely. Why, then, didn't M-ski pay them a visit? Was it that he didn't like tailors? Or that he simply forgot? No, he definitely didn't forget; being a nature teacher and a lover of classification, he was the type who wrote everything down in a little notebook, which he always kept on his person. Unless M-ski knew something about Weiser that we didn't . . . But in that case the eccentric nature teacher would have been able to guess where our friend was now. M-ski was an eccentric, all right, the kind you find only in a book nowadays. Like us, he didn't go away for the summer vacation, and we often saw him in the meadow near Brentowo Forest, or down by the stream in Echo Valley chasing butterflies with his net. When he wasn't hunting things that fluttered, he'd walk along bent double, his eyes fixed on the ground, stopping now and then to pull up some weed and mutter to himself: "*Menyanthes trifoliata,*" or "*Viola tricolor.*" Then he'd place it in the cardboard folder he carried with him. M-ski was working on a book about the flora and fauna of the forest that went from the southern edge of town all the way up to Gdynia, a forest in which Frederick the Great himself once hunted. Perhaps that was the reason he pounced on and labeled everything that grew or moved within his field of vision. Fortunately he was nearsighted, so a good many plants and bugs and other minutiae of the forest were spared.

That hot summer, when Weiser let us in on his secrets, or at least some of them, we ran into M-ski many times on the firing range, on Bukowa Hill, at the Brentowo cemetery, and in Echo Valley. His fishlike eyes, interrupted in their examination of earth or air, would follow us, making us feel that we were specimens indispensable to his collection. I was afraid of that cold, blank stare; I was afraid of the man himself, not the "plucking of the goose," the "stretching of the elephant's trunk," or any of those other exquisitely painful corporal punishments he applied in the classroom. As I contemplated Szymek's reddened ear, I had the thought that perhaps M-ski, with his eyes, could change anyone he wanted into an insect, and I imagined myself growing steel-green chitinous armor, my hands twitching as they branched into a great number of small hairy legs. This was a hundred times worse than Szymek's reddened ear or the interrogation that awaited me.

In the first days of July the concentration of the fish soup seemed to reach its apogee. There was nothing to do at the beach, so we had to look elsewhere. And that's the first chapter of the book about Weiser, a book that none of us wrote or will ever write, because what I'm doing now is not writing a book but trying to fill in a hopeless blank. The first chapter, then, of the unwritten book about Weiser starts with the fish soup in the bay, and with our games in the Brentowo cemetery, which is where we went instead of to the beach, to engage in combat in the thickets of hazel and alder, among abandoned graves and fractured tombstones with German inscriptions. Szymek commanded an SS detachment, covering his jug ears with a rusty Wehrmacht helmet found in a ditch, while Piotr led a band of partisans, who were repeatedly hunted down, surrounded, and slaughtered to a man, but kept coming back to life to plan new ambushes. When Szymek and his men took us captive, we'd put our hands up just as in the movies, then march off with our hands clasped on the back of our heads, and just as in the movies, the documentaries about the real war shown at our local Tramway Theater, we'd fall, riddled by machine-gun fire, into an actual ditch at the edge of the cemetery where the pine forest began. Recalling with what expertise we tumbled into that ditch, and with what a thrill we awaited the moment when Szymek would give the command to fire, I realize how indebted we were to the Tramway, which was by the depot and not far from our school, because it was there that young citizens were so graphically acquainted with the history of their fatherland.

I don't remember what day it was, after which skirmish, battle, and capture, but we were standing with our hands up, looking down the SS's machine-gun barrels, and waiting for *Feuer!* to resound from Szymek's rusty helmet, when we caught sight of Weiser sitting in a pine tree. Perhaps he'd been watching our game all along. Actually, we didn't see him, we heard him first—a shout addressed to Szymek before Szymek could give the command—and only then did we see him in the tree. He was holding an old Schmeisser, pointing it beyond the belfry of the small brick church and looking at us in exactly the same way as on Corpus Christi when he'd appeared suddenly from behind the gray cloud of incense. At the foot of the tree stood Elka, leaning against its trunk. She said nothing, but it was clear that she was with him and not us. So this time we didn't hear the long *de-de-de-de-de* that meant we had to crumple to our knees and fall every which way, onto our sides, stomachs, backs, because Weiser jumped down from the tree and approached a stunned Szymek.

Today, just as on the day I sat next to Szymek in the main office, then next to Piotr, then next to Szymek again, waiting my turn, I'd give a lot to know what Weiser said at the cemetery, because those were the first words he ever spoke to us directly. When I asked Szymek in a letter, he didn't answer; he's busy in another city and doesn't like me to bring up the subject of Weiser. Elka, who would surely know, is a German now, in Mannheim, and doesn't reply to any of my questions. And Piotr went out into the street in 1970 to see what was going on and got hit with a bullet that was not pretend. But the unwritten book about Weiser should begin with those words, whatever they were. . . .

So Weiser jumped down from the tree, went up to Szymek, and said something like "This is how" or "Here, I'll show you." Except, it must have been different, because the next thing we knew, the rusty old Schmeisser was in Szymek's hands, and Weiser and Elka were walking off down the path toward the tumbledown cemetery gate, as if he'd only come to give us the gun and had more pressing matters to attend to. The execution was forgotten. We stood around Szymek, each eager to touch and hold the useless broken weapon, which we thought fabulous. We didn't think of Weiser then; we argued over which side should have the gun. I was in Piotr's band, so naturally I wanted the partisans to have it. After all, the Germans had the helmet. In the end we worked out a new and more interesting game. After each battle Piotr and Szymek would swap the gun and the helmet; when our commander put on the helmet, we'd be Germans, and the next time we'd be partisans and run in and out of the mossy tombstones with the gun.

I believe Weiser had planned from the start to involve us in his schemes, that all along he had been waiting for the right moment, such as on Corpus Christi or at the Brentowo cemetery, to catch us off guard. Initially, when we knew nothing about the cellar at the old brickworks or the explosives set off in the hollow behind the firing range or his collection of stamps from the Occupation, and while in our innocence we raced around the tombstones in the Brentowo cemetery, he'd appear and disappear, like a person in a dream whom we cannot forget, though all the details about him, his face and his words, are completely gone from our memory. Weiser thus introduced himself to us by imperceptible degrees, and after a few days, as we walked home along the dusty road on Bukowa Hill, beneath the red rays of the setting sun, we began to talk about him. The talk at first was incidental, nothing to do with the cloud of incense or the rusty gun; we'd ask out loud, jokingly, "What does he do if he doesn't play with us?" or "Why does that stupid Elka tag along after him like a dog, and look down on us as if we were just a bunch of brats?" or "What made him give us the gun?" Because who in his right mind would part with such a treasure? But this wasn't the preoccupation that came over us later, when the thought of Weiser kept us awake at night and we would spend hours spying on him and Elka. Meanwhile the reek of the fish soup in the bay grew steadily worse, and every other day one of us went to Jelitkowo to see how things stood.

I glanced at Szymek. His ear was no longer quite as red and even appeared to be returning to its original size. The janitor sat between us now, and through the open office window came the lazy sounds

of a September afternoon. The footsteps of passersby mingled with children's cries, and the sun
shone brightly on the red-tile roof of the building
across the street. All the houses in our part of
Wrzeszcz had the same red roof tiles, and on an
afternoon such as that one, at the end of the summer, when the sunlight has a special quality, a person would have a great view, I thought, from Bukowa
Hill, seeing the red rooftops and the airfield beyond
the railroad tracks and the white belt of sand along
the bay. Whenever we were on Bukowa Hill, our
town seemed to us completely different from the
one we lived in. Perhaps it was because from the
hill you didn't see the litter-strewn yards, the over-
flowing garbage cans, and all the dinginess of our
district—the symbol of which could have been
Cyrson's grimy, dusty shop, where we used to buy
orangeade in those sticky bottles with spring tops.

But it wasn't the panorama from Bukowa Hill
I had before me, it was the roof of the building
opposite, in the slanting sun, an attic window ajar,
the breeze gently puffing out a curtain. Then the
office clock struck five, and soon after that I heard
the familiar sound of the upright piano: the music
teacher was accompanying the chorus in afternoon
practice. First she played the introduction, then came
snatches, louder and louder, from "Song of the
Masses," or "Song of the Workers," or "Song of

the People"——I don't remember exactly what it was called. "We've you to thank, no-obles, lo-o-ords, and ma-agnates, for our ensla-aving cha-ains, we've you to thank, pri-inces, bishops, pre-elates, for our land to-orn and blo-odied." That was the refrain, repeated over and over, and the beginning was just as lofty: "Fo-orth went the na-ation in a-arms to battle, the no-obles on their re-e-ents confer-ring." I could never understand, not during school functions or in chorus, when we had to sing that song until we were sick to death of it, what chains had to do with bishops or what rents had to do with a nation going forth to battle. And why blame it on the nobles? There hadn't been any nobles for a long time now, and if there still were some in the nation, they weren't in our town. Thank God I don't have to worry about such things now; yet the tune has stayed with me, and whenever for some reason it runs through my head, I don't think of prelates, school functions, or the music teacher, but of the special light of a September afternoon as I sat in the main office waiting my turn to be questioned, of a curtain gently puffed by a breeze, of Weiser, and of the wall clock striking five, its gong reminiscent of Father Dudak's bell that was rung for the Elevation of the Host.

Szymek's ear had returned to normal by the time M-ski opened the door to eject Piotr and point to me. In the headmaster's study the smell of the polished floor, as cloying as eternity, mingled with the smells of tobacco and coffee, which all three interrogators were drinking. Only M-ski didn't smoke, picking instead at his shirtsleeve.

"So you maintain, Heller," the militiaman addressed me, because that was my name in those days, "that you saw Weiser and Elka for the last time on the twenty-eighth of August, in the hollow behind the old firing range. Is that right?"

"Yes, I guess so," I replied, gathering confidence.

"What do you mean, you guess so?"

"Well, after that we didn't see them again, not up close."

"What do you mean, not up close? You mean you saw them the next day in some other way?"

"No, the next day we didn't see them at all."

M-ski shifted in his seat. "Just tell us, exactly and in the right order, what happened that afternoon. And don't make things up, we'll know if you're making things up!"

Trying not to look M-ski in the eye, I spoke slowly and calmly, sure that they'd never find the scent, that they'd keep going in circles and finally give up and leave us in peace. "Weiser told us to wait, as usual, near the thicket of larches, and after he made sure we were there, he went to the other side of the hollow and signaled for us to lie flat. Then the ground shook, and we got showered with gravel and pieces of wood."

"And then?"

"Then we looked up, like after any explosion, and waited for him to give the next signal, to tell us if it was all right for us to go look at the spot, but this time there was no signal. Then we saw them walking, arm in arm like grown-ups, Weiser and Elka. They were walking, but not in our direction. They were up by the old oak tree and didn't turn around once, but kept walking up the slope, and reached the top, and disappeared. By that time we were at the place where the charge went off and found a huge crater, not an ordinary crater but one that could have been made by a bomb dropped from a plane. We stood there, amazed at what he'd done. Then we measured to see how deep the hole was and how wide, and the ground was full of ants going wild and cut-up earthworms. Then somebody pointed to the hill and shouted, "Look over there!" and we saw Weiser and Elka, we saw them at the very top of the hill, as they were disappearing behind the trees, but we didn't run after them.

"And that's how we saw them the very last time," I said. "It was from a distance, we were in the hollow behind the firing range, and the next day the militiamen came, and they found Weiser's arsenal in the cellar of the old brickworks, which even we didn't know about, because Weiser kept big secrets like that to himself. We didn't know about the TNT or the duds or the detonators or the ammunition, because we never asked him where he got the stuff for his mines, and if we had asked, would someone like him have told us? No, only Elka could have known about the arsenal, and if there was another arsenal, which we never heard about either, the only person Weiser would have trusted with the secret was Elka, so maybe that's why he took her with him."

They listened to my account with a careful show of indifference. The headmaster kept loosening and tightening his tie, the militiaman drank the rest of his coffee from a glass in a metal holder, and M-ski drummed his fingers on the shiny desktop, not looking at me at all, but at a point above my head.

"We know all this already," he suddenly shouted. "But why is one of you lying? Or all of you, together and separately?"

"Yes," said the headmaster. "One of your friends says you all played again the next day, by the Strzyża, at the blown-up bridge, which means they were out the whole night and you all knew it, and knew where to look for them."

"It's not a joke, boy," the militiaman added. "If

28

those children were killed by an unexploded shell, you'll be held responsible, and then it's reform school!"

"We played at the Strzyża the day before, not the day after," I said, pleased at how easily the lie came to my lips. "Whoever said after must have got confused."

Then they were all shouting, threatening, interrupting one another to ask questions, and swearing that we wouldn't leave until the matter was cleared up, that our parents had already been informed, that we'd get nothing to eat or drink, that we'd sit here until we told the truth, the whole truth, because they were prepared to question us till morning, longer if need be, and if anyone stumbled on a second arsenal and there was an accident, we'd have to answer for that, too, so it would be better all around if we confessed now. I knew that they would never understand the truth, so I stuck to my story. M-ski got up, marched toward me as if he were at the May Day parade, gripped my snub nose with thumb and finger, and asked if I re-al-ly had seen Weiser for the last time that day in the hollow. I said yes, and felt my nose gradually being flattened. This wasn't the usual stretching of the elephant's trunk he did in nature class. It was stretching the elephant's trunk with a special twist, because I found I had to stand on my toes, on the very tips of my toes, expecting that in another minute I'd be hanging in midair, and M-ski's arm shifted my center of gravity now to the left, now to the right, so that for a fraction of a second I'd have to put my whole foot on the floor, to keep up with the hand, and this made my nose hurt terribly, while he repeated his question slowly, stressing every syllable: Was it re-al-ly for the la-ast ti-ime? Finally he let go of me, and I reeled against the wall and had to wipe the blood off on my sleeve, because I've always had a delicate nose.

They called a break; so the three of us were sitting together again on the folding chairs in the main office, and I thought I could hear the rhyme about Weiser, the chant on the day we got our Sunday school diplomas, just before his checked shirt was thrown into the air and Elka came to his defense, when someone in the back shouted, "Da-vid Wei-ser doesn't go to chu-urch," and someone else made it, "Da-vid Wei-ser is a Je-ew!" And I realized that without Elka we'd never have got to know Weiser. We'd have given him a couple of rolls near the rectory of the Resurrection Fathers, and that would have been the end of it, an ordinary, uninteresting end. Weiser would have avoided us, would not have watched us at the Brentowo cemetery or given us the rust-eaten '43 Schmeisser, and that summer vacation would have been no different from any other summer vacation, past or future. So when Elka sprang to his defense with her claws bared, she must have had a premonition, I'm sure of it, because she never had anything to do with our fights and settling of scores, which were often very cruel. But on that day she threw herself into the thick of it, as if Weiser were her baby brother—and we let them go, because of our astonishment and not because we were afraid of her claws.

Did she love him? Yes, I thought as I sat in the main office with my swollen nose, while in the headmaster's study they were getting ready for the next bout of questioning, and I pictured her prematurely rounded breasts, her long blond hair, and the red dress she wore on blazing hot days. I know now that I was wrong; yet what, then, was their relationship from the moment they walked off together along the churchyard fence, after we dropped our stones? Elka, who had nothing but contempt for those who couldn't swim as far as the red buoy, jump headfirst from the pier, or kick the ball past the goalie when we played soccer on the grass by the Prussian barracks, suddenly saw someone very important in the skinny, round-shouldered figure of Weiser, so she sprang at us with her claws bared. Perhaps she felt what we were to feel a few weeks later, when we saw Weiser in the cellar at the old brickworks, which gave us goose bumps and sent an electric current up and down our bodies.

But I should present the facts in order. Because this is a book about Weiser, not about us a few decades ago or about our town as it was then or about our school or about M-ski and that era when he was second in importance only to the headmaster—none of this concerns me, and if I'm writing it all down, recalling the flavor of that summer when the bay was full of fish soup, it's only on account of Weiser. It was on account of Weiser that I went to Germany and am now recording everything from the beginning, leaving nothing out, not the smallest detail, since the smallest detail may turn out to be the key that opens the door. And so:

The first days of July went by, and in the sweltering heat the town, deprived of the bay, could hardly breathe, and the fish soup thickened and thickened, alarming the local authorities. At first they had hoped that this peculiar plague would pass of its own accord, so nothing was done. Then steps were taken: in the early morning, men with wooden rakes, the kind used for gathering hay, began to work on the beaches, making piles of carcasses, which were carried by truck to the town dump, doused with gasoline, and burned. But the number of dead sticklebacks swelling in the summer sun increased notwithstanding, and the papers reported mass deaths of cats and dogs in areas near the bay. It was also noted that for two whole months, since the beginning of May, not a drop of rain had fallen, which the old folks took pleasure in interpreting as a sign of divine retribution. We, in the meantime, ran through the Brentowo cemetery with the helmet and the gun that Weiser gave us, and took turns being Germans and partisans mowed down by bullets exactly as in the documentaries shown at the Tramway Theater. Once in a while we wondered why Elka didn't play with us, wondered what she saw in that skinny weakling Weiser, following him around for days in various parts of town. Someone had seen them in the Old Town by Neptune's Well; someone else crossed his heart and hoped to die if Weiser and Elka didn't sit for hours in the meadow by the airfield. Another time Piotr saw them going beyond Brentowo, to the blown-up bridge where the Strzyża ran through a tunnel in the railroad embankment, whose track not a single train had been on since the war. We paid little attention to this news. Each morning one of us would take the tram to Jelitkowo, to see how the fish soup was doing, and report back at the cemetery, saying that the stink was worse than ever and swarms of giant flies still hovered above the mess like locusts.

Life was more pleasant in the shade of the cemetery trees than in the courtyards or streets in town. One day, near the crypt with the gothic lettering, we saw a man in pajamas and a yellow hospital robe sitting on a tombstone, muttering under his breath, as if saying his prayers. Surrounded by us, he showed no sign of fear and with a wave of his hand indicated where he came from: the insane asylum, a reddish gray building on the hill on the other side of the highway leading out of town. Piotr suggested going to the asylum and telling them where the runaway was—no doubt they were looking for him—but none of us had ever seen a real madman before, and we wanted to find out if what Father Dudak said in his fire-and-brimstone sermons about the madmen who renounced God was true. Because Father Dudak, in our parish church of the Resurrection Fathers, which, like the Brentowo church and its cemetery, stood at the edge of the forest, said the same thing as the old folks, that the soup in the bay and the drought were signs from God.

"Repent while there is time," he'd thundered from the pulpit last Sunday. "Renounce not God, O ye of little faith, nor run to worship false prophets and idols, for He shall turn away from you. You are like the madmen who, trusting in their own strength, would build the world anew. But what sort of new world is it, I ask you, where there is no faith, where honor is not rendered unto Him,

34

the Creator and Redeemer? I ask you, I warn you, put not your trust in madmen, come to your senses while there is time. You can see for yourselves that God is full of wrath. . . ." Thus did Father Dudak alternately plead with and terrify his parishioners, and we concluded that it was because of some madmen that we couldn't go swimming at Jelitkowo that summer, and therefore we were curious to see what a madman looked like. Here was our opportunity; chance had sent the man in the hospital robe to the cemetery. So we didn't run to Srebrzysko to tell on him; we stood around him instead, staring at his wrinkled face and at the worn slippers in which he'd escaped. If he was a madman, he certainly didn't seem to be the kind Father Dudak ranted about from the pulpit. He said nothing. Szymek, the bravest of us, placed the rusty helmet on his head. At that, the man gestured, indicating he'd like to have a look at our gun, too, and with the Schmeisser in his hands he got up on a tombstone and addressed us in a beautiful, resonant voice:

"Brothers! The word of the Lord cometh into my ear, hark ye unto this thing to which I bear witness! Behold, the Lord maketh the earth empty, and maketh it waste, and turneth it upside down, and scattereth abroad the inhabitants thereof. The land shall be utterly emptied, and utterly spoiled:

for the Lord hath spoken this word. The earth mourneth and fadeth away, the world languisheth and fadeth away, withereth and crumbleth, and the nations sicken. The earth also is defiled under the inhabitants thereof, for they have transgressed the laws and ordinances and broken the everlasting covenant!"

We didn't understand the sense of these words, but they were so fine that we listened to the man in pajamas spellbound, completely forgetting that he had escaped from the Srebrzysko asylum. He held his arms high, waving our gun all the while, and stood on tiptoe, as if to make himself still taller, and the skirts of his dirty robe were like great yellow wings, on which he might fly up over Bukowa Hill or even farther, if only he wanted to.

"And man shall be humbled," Yellow Wings went on, "and his haughty eyes humbled and brought low. Therefore hath the curse devoured the earth, and they that dwell therein are desolate. Therefore they are burned, yea, and few live. Until the spirit be poured upon us from on high, and the desert become a fruitful field, and the fruitful field be counted for a forest!"

As I recall that clear, deep voice today, I have no doubt that Weiser was the only one of us who could have understood the words of the man with the yellow wings. But Weiser wasn't with us at the time; he was sitting with Elka in the cellar of the abandoned brickworks, or else they were walking in the dry meadow next to the airfield. In any case, we listened raptly. Then the man folded his wings, jumped from the tombstone, and, still speaking, led us down the moss-covered path toward the moldering belfry, which was still used by the parish priest at the Brentowo church on Sundays and feast days.

"Howl"—the man's voice took on redoubled force—"for the day of the Lord is at hand. The Almighty, He shall deal destruction in the midst of all the earth. And what will ye do on that day of visitation, in the desolation that cometh from afar? For lo, there shall be darkness and a great weight, yea, even the light shall be oppressed!"

We were standing by the belfry now. The man put the gun on a crossbeam, unfastened the ropes, and started to pull. With the first peals we heard words finer than any to be found in Father Dudak's sermons: "Therefore hath hell enlarged herself and opened her mouth without measure." Then, to the intoxicating, wonderful music of the Brentowo bells—because there were three bells there, not just one, as in our parish—the man in the hospital robe began to sing, "Woe, woe unto them that decree unrighteous decrees, woe, woe unto them that decree unrighteous decrees." As we stood around him, we started swaying to the rhythm of his song, though it wasn't a hymn—we'd never heard it in church—and it wasn't a song of the people, either, because in chorus we sang nothing but songs of the people, and this wasn't one of them. Perhaps in a few more minutes we'd have learned the words and the tune, and in that way it would have become a song of the people, or at least of a few people, but this was prevented by the lame sexton, who came hobbling toward us, shaking his fist. "Godless creatures!" he shouted. "No respect for hallowed ground! Off with you, or I'll—" He quickened his pace, and his white shirt gleamed bright against the thickets of hazel. Yellow Wings and we fled toward Bukowa Hill, but the sexton pursued us, right to the edge of the cemetery, which was marked by concrete bases for columns long since gone. "Juvenile delinquents!" he shouted. "Vandals!" he cried, shaking his fist and hobbling along. "Disturbing the sleep of the dead!"

We left the cemetery. Suddenly, as if springing out of the ground, there was M-ski among the pines, with his folder in one hand and a plant in the other. Distracted, he fixed his fishlike stare on us.

"What are you doing, boys? See this little plant? Pretty, isn't it? Now who knows," he said, turning to me, "what the family is? No one, eh?" He delighted in our ignorance, just as at school. "It's *Aggregatae*, subfamily *Liguliflorae*, the "tongued" flowers, literally. Yes, this is a genuine mountain tobacco plant, *Arnica montana*. It grows in highland pastures, and I find it here, in the north—unheard of in a morainal environment! Blossoms in June, July, and you see—"

M-ski's disquisition on his amazing discovery was interrupted by the sexton, who, knowing the nature teacher, didn't mince words.

"You have no business bringing your students here, Mister Darwin. This is holy ground," he said, puffing. "I'll write a letter to the education committee. Perhaps they can explain why the study of science calls for running around in cemeteries."

"I, er," M-ski faltered, "I'm here in a private capacity. These boys are not with me."

"Not with you?" the sexton flared. "What do you mean, not with you, when I saw you myself pulling on the bells with them like a hoodlum? Does the priest come and ring the bell at school during lessons? Certainly not! So I must ask you to keep away from the church."

This was the last straw. M-ski grew purple, and without stopping for breath expelled a torrent of remarks, in which the words "provocation," "the clergy," "Jesuits," "benighted," and "reactionary" were often repeated. He threw the *Arnica montana* into his folder and stalked off, telling us that if he saw us again anywhere near the cemetery, we would regret it all next year in school. The sexton stalked off, too, and only then did we notice that Yellow Wings was gone. He'd slipped away in the confusion, taking with him the Wehrmacht helmet and the rusty Schmeisser.

True, neither Elka nor Weiser was with us that day, so perhaps I did not need to record any of this, the madman in the pajamas and yellow robe, the three bells in the Brentowo belfry, the mountain tobacco plant with its bristly stem and splayed yellow flowers. Except that in this story—more, I think, than in other stories—it is only from a distance, in retrospect, that certain details take on significance, become connected, so connected that you can't separate them. Because had it not been for Yellow Wings and the Brentowo bells and M-ski's threat and the *Arnica montana,* our attention would never have focused on Weiser in the way he wanted. I believe Weiser was waiting all that time, waiting like a hunter for his quarry to be upwind of him, disoriented, vulnerable. He was waiting for the right moment.

So we didn't go to Brentowo the next day. Early in the morning a long line of thirsty customers formed outside Cyrson's. Sticky bottles of orange-ade were put into hands, the shopkeeper's wife weighed apples and cucumbers, and the strip of fly-paper hanging from the light dangled like a spider's

hairy leg. In our courtyard, Mrs. Korotek was pin-
ning up her wash. We knew that Mr. Korotek, who
worked in the shipyard, would come home roaring
drunk in the afternoon, because today was payday.
Just like our fathers, most of whom worked at the
shipyard, too, and came home drunk on payday.
And our mothers, just like Mrs. Korotek, would
wring their hands and shake their fists and unbur-
den their misfortune and grief before the image of
the Savior. But for the time being, the sun's heat
stifled all activity, and Mrs. Korotek, her basket
empty, surveyed the courtyard and said that such
weather boded no good. A cat with bald patches
was licking his wounds in the shade of the chestnut
tree, and over the whole district hung the sickly
smell of the butcher's that stood behind Cyrson's.
No more than once an hour did a car come rumbling over the cobblestones of our street, raising a
cloud of dust that slowly settled again. Suddenly we
saw Weiser and Elka emerge from the back door
of our building. They went through a mangy, sun-
scorched garden, between rows of yellowed bean
plants that hadn't even grown halfway up their poles
that summer. Weiser was telling Elka something,
and she was laughing. I elbowed Szymek in the side,
to suggest we follow them, but he said, "Wait,"
and ran upstairs for the French binoculars his
grandfather had captured at the Battle of Verdun

in the First World War. I don't know if Szymek still has them, but I remember that they were artillery binoculars, with calibration lines, and both eyepieces were adjustable. We regarded them with great desire and envy, which was why Szymek rarely took them outside, only on special occasions, like the year before, when from our roof we watched a fire on board a Chinese freighter tied up in the new port with a cargo of cotton.

Elka and Weiser crossed the tram tracks by the No. 12 loop and took Pilots Street toward the viaduct that connected Upper Wrzeszcz and Zaspa above the train station. They stopped on the viaduct and looked for a while in the direction of the airfield. So far, we didn't need the binoculars, which stayed in their leather case. From our hiding place behind the paper-factory fence, we saw Weiser pull something out of his pocket and show it to Elka, who took it in her hand and inspected it carefully. The fence and the leaves of the old trees concealed us, and if anything about that day was different from the way I have reconstructed it, those great maples are exactly right. They must have been growing there for ages. When the warehouses were put up on Pilots Street, the trees were not cut down; instead, holes were made for them in the roofs of the sheds. So there we were, concealed by branches that came straight out of the roof, and Szymek began to get impatient. "What are they doing?" he asked, and was about to reach for the binoculars, when Weiser and Elka started walking again. A blue-and-yellow train streaked by beneath us as we went up on the viaduct, following them. They were heading for a hole in the fence around the airfield.

"They're not afraid of the guard," Szymek said with approval, taking the binoculars from their case. "Now let's see what they're up to." He put the dark-brown barrels to his eyes. Elka and Weiser disappeared in the thick broom that grew near the runway, more precisely, at the southernmost end of the field, where the runway began its northerly course perpendicular to the bay.

"Where did they go?" growled Szymek. "Oh, screw," he said (we said *screw* a lot in those days). "I bet they're playing doctor."

"Playing what?" I asked in disbelief.

"Doctor," said Szymek. "He'll get her panties off and see everything. But where are they?" Leaning against the viaduct's iron railing, he turned the rings, focusing on the clump of bushes.

To our right was a clear view of old Wrzeszcz, the dark, red-brick houses and church towers; to our left, farther off, the dim outlines of Oliwa. Directly before us was the airfield, the small passenger terminal, hangars, a striped wind sock drooping in still air. Where the runway ended, we could see the white thread of the beach, the bay, and ships at anchor.

"Where can they be?" demanded Szymek. "They haven't come out of the bushes." He handed me the binoculars, reluctantly, because he never liked to part with them. When the black lines of the cross hair appeared against the clumps of broom, I felt like the French artillery officer killed at Verdun. No sooner did I start to focus than from the hills behind us came the heavy drone of a plane. The bushes nearest the concrete runway moved, and then I saw the two of them, lying side by side, holding hands, impatiently lifting their heads as they waited for the approaching Ilyushin. But they weren't playing doctor; they were on their backs, legs braced, the fingers of their free hands clutching the roots of the broom, which were thick and tangled in that spot.

The plane, losing altitude, passed Bukowa Hill and came in almost at the height of the viaduct and the railroad tracks. I kept the binoculars on Elka's red dress and bare knees, sharpening the focus. What I saw in the next few seconds, as the huge gleaming hull of the plane practically brushed the bushes with its belly, I saw with perfect clarity.

The plane is ten, maybe fifteen meters above the ground, only a feeble stone's throw from the broom and the start of the runway. Elka raises her knees; her face is contorted; she looks as if she's screaming in terror, her mouth wide open. Weiser's mouth is open, too, but not in a scream, and he hasn't got his knees up. The bushes, as if mown, are flattened by the blast of air. Without losing contact with the ground, Elka lifts her knees higher, her hips, too, and her red dress is whipped upward by the powerful gust, revealing a dark place between her legs. But that isn't panties, that isn't underwear, it's slightly raised, strangely soft, tender, and undulating at the o mark in the artillery binoculars from the Battle of Verdun. Then the triangular phenomenon vanishes back in the folds of the red dress, which falls back over Elka's hips and knees as the wheels of the great Ilyushin 14 touch the runway ten or fifteen meters beyond her and Weiser. And that's all, because they both get up and run for the fence before the guard can come after them with his rifle. Szymek tears the binoculars away from me and, putting them to his eyes, shouts, "See, they *were* playing doctor, and the plane scared them off!" But I knew that their game was not the one Szymek wanted. Throughout the time of the plane's approach, Weiser's hand had stayed where it was; it was not his hand that lifted Elka's red dress. No, Elka's game with Weiser and the airplane was stranger and more exciting. I don't know what surprised me more, the fact that the silver Ilyushin 14 had pulled up Elka's red dress, or the fact that between her legs was the same dark, triangular phenomenon my mother had, and Piotr's older sister had, which was not hard to know, since our building had only one bathroom on each floor.

In the afternoon, the heat let up a little, and through the open windows wafted sounds of domestic discord. The last of the drunks were coming home; on their way they'd dropped in at the Lilliput Bar, opposite the Protestant chapel, which was going to be converted into a new movie theater. The Protestant community in our part of town had active members, but their number was shrinking from year to year, so much that they couldn't keep their church going. They were mostly old Gdańskers, whom the new population called Germans, which wasn't always strictly true. Mrs. Korotek was shouting at her husband, "You good-for-nothing bastard!" while the radio played a lively folk dance. By now all the boys knew from Szymek that Weiser had gone to the airfield with Elka to feel her up, though not all of them knew exactly what that meant. When Elka crossed the courtyard, someone called out to her that she should let us feel her up, too, and not just that Jew-boy from the second floor. Elka came up to the bench where we were sitting, her eyes shooting fire.

"You're stupid," she said through clenched teeth.

"Stupid asshole brats. All you can do is kick a ball around and knock each other's teeth in, that's all you can do."

"So?" was the sullen reply.

"So nothing," she said. "*He* can do anything, do you understand, you moron brats? Anything he wants. Even animals obey him."

"Hoo hoo," Szymek jeered at her. "I suppose he can stop a moving car or a plane in the air?"

This cut Elka to the quick. She jumped at Szymek with her claws, and we'd have had another fight for sure if it hadn't been for the voice from the second floor. At his window, Weiser was watching the whole scene, and just as Elka's nails were about to sink into Szymek's face and hair, we heard: "All right, tell them to be at the zoo at ten tomorrow, at the main entrance." Weiser said this to her; I remember it clearly. "Tell them," he said, although he had us all there as if on the palm of his hand and could just as well have told us himself, "to be at the entrance to the zoo at ten tomorrow." And it was that way later, too, whenever he invited us to his explosions in the hollow behind the firing range.

"You heard," Elka repeated. "You're to be at the zoo gate at ten. Then you'll see." She didn't say what we'd see, she just walked off. Now we could hear Mr. Korotek beating his wife with his belt.

47

She was calling on all the saints for help, but apparently without sufficient faith, because the vigorous smacks and cries of pain coming through the open window did not abate. In the evening the old people lay on the benches and gazed at the sky, looking for a promised comet, and we played soccer on the parched grass by the Prussian barracks. Piotr, who'd been to Jelitkowo that day, reported that the fish soup was a violet color and stank worse than ever; admission to the beach was forbidden by large notices signed by the authorities of all three towns along the bay.

"Why weren't these boys at a summer camp or work project or training center? Why didn't anyone think of giving them something to do, so they wouldn't run loose in the woods finding unexploded shells and ammunition? You, too, are in part responsible," said the public prosecutor in a high voice. The headmaster was no longer loosening his tie; by now it was completely undone. "Why didn't these boys go away for the summer? You know as well as I do," he went on, "that in such surroundings"—emphasis on *such*—"parents, having neither the time nor the pedagogical skill, lose all influence over their offspring, and that's precisely where you must step in, the school, the collective. Surely you don't need me to tell you your job. We've had a number of similar incidents in Poland this year, and I'm convinced that most of them would not have happened if there had been proper supervision during the summer vacation, too!" Emphasis on *too*.

We held our breath, listening to the prosecutor, then to the headmaster and M-ski. Not every word could be heard through the half-open door to the study, but we could tell that they were still on the wrong trail. M-ski, the headmaster, the militiaman, and the prosecutor, who had come at seven o'clock, all believed that Weiser and Elka had been blown into a thousand tiny pieces by the explosion in the hollow behind the firing range. The only problem was that during the search not a shred of clothing or of body had been found, so they were furious with us, shouting and threatening, as if this were our fault. They didn't believe we saw Weiser and Elka walking up the hill on the other side of the hollow. And they had no suspicion that our last meeting had actually taken place the following day, at the Strzyża, by the blown-up bridge, where the river flows into a narrow tunnel under the railroad embankment. They thought that in a panic we had hidden the pieces of body somewhere and now were desperately lying. It never occurred to them that if that had been the case, eventually we would have told them where a scrap of Weiser's shirt or a shred of Elka's dress was buried.

"The Germans left behind more than one cache of ammunition," the prosecutor went on, "and that is by far the most tragic harvest of the war." Emphasis on *by far*. "Yet at your school not one lesson was devoted to this problem." Emphasis on *your school*. "Tell me, Headmaster, what did you do to alert the young people to this danger? You know how much was discovered at the brickworks? Enough to blow not only this building sky-high but every house in the vicinity as well."

The headmaster went into an involved explanation, and then M-ski spoke of the growing lack of enthusiasm for group activities, a decline in vigilance, and so on, and finally concluded with the politics of the Vatican and the intransigence of the clergy, with whom he himself had had occasion to lock horns. And he told the prosecutor about our encounter near the Brentowo cemetery.

"It's the facts I'm interested in, not generalities," said the prosecutor. "I want a full account of what took place on that critical day. Sergeant"— here he must have turned to the militiaman— "you're preparing your report, and I don't have to instruct you how to go about it. Proceed as you like, but see that it is ready Monday morning, with not a thing in it unclear! A year ago," he said in conclusion, "these boys would have been behind bars on Okopowa Street as a band of saboteurs, and the Mother of God herself wouldn't have been able to help them. Yes," he said, emerging from the study, "times have changed." He passed through the main office and left a strong, sweet smell of eau de cologne behind him.

"Well, we have a problem," said M-ski after a short pause, probably pointing a stubby finger at the papers scattered on the headmaster's desk, "because these statements are unclear from start to finish."

"The boys are all lying," said the militiaman. "They're afraid, but they're still lying."

"They're lying because they're afraid, I think," the headmaster observed, and they batted *lying* and *afraid* back and forth for a while, and I wondered why Weiser's old grandfather, who was a tailor and rarely left the house, had died the moment the investigation began. When no one answered the door, it was pried open, and it turned out that Mr. Weiser had died of a heart attack. They found him sitting in his chair, his head propped against his old Singer sewing machine, over an unfinished piece of work, a vest for a suit ordered by a captain's widow. What a widow wanted with a suit, I don't know. Remembering Mr. Weiser, I felt a shiver of fear. His death, so sudden, couldn't have been an accident. I saw that clearly now. Weiser's silent grandfather was the only person we could have told how Elka and Weiser left us that sunny day—left us in a way that we ourselves did not completely understand.

Because to understand it completely, we would have had to do more or less what I am doing now, more than twenty years later: recall all the important details, put them in order, and examine them together, as one examines a million-year-old fly trapped in a piece of golden amber. But at the time, none of us was able to do that, not Szymek, not Piotr, not I. None of us would have seen the connection between the fish soup and the cloud of incense produced by Father Dudak on Corpus Christi as we sang "Hail to Thee, the Living Host." None of us would have dreamed that the drought that year was anything other than an ordinary drought. Or that Weiser's explosions in the hollow behind the firing range and what he did in the cellar at the abandoned brickworks had anything to do with the gleaming fuselage of the Ilyushin 14 that lifted Elka's dress, and her body with it, among the clumps of broom. And even had we described exactly what we saw that final day by the Strzyża, at the blown-up bridge, neither M-ski nor the headmaster nor the militiaman nor anyone else in the world would have taken it seriously. "That's impossible," they would have said, wiping their glasses, swallowing their coffee, or picking at their cuffs. "You're lying again," they would have said. And the inquiry would have continued revolving around that big explosion, which in their opinion concluded everything. We were bound by a promise, too, an oath sworn to Weiser. But I am determined not to get ahead of myself. So there I was, sitting in the main office between Szymek and Piotr, my left leg still aching. Through the open window wafted a hint of elegant bouquet from the prosecutor's eau de cologne. He had left the school at exactly half past seven. "Wojtal," Piotr's name, was called in the doorway, "you're next," and Piotr went inside as the clock's gong struck the hour.

Why had the prosecutor mentioned Okopowa Street? He said that a year ago the three of us would have been behind bars there as a band of saboteurs. Today I know perfectly well what he meant, but then, as Piotr disappeared behind the door and the third round of questioning began, the word *Okopowa* gave me no peace. I remembered how one afternoon, a couple of years before, a putrid-green car had stopped in front of our building and two men in overcoats got out. They made their way to Mrs. Korotek's and led out her husband, Mr. Korotek, who was dead drunk even though it wasn't payday. The adults all whispered, off to the side, that Mr. Korotek was being taken to Okopowa Street because someone had informed on him for listening to the BBC. Mr. Korotek came back, three weeks later, with a black eye like an overripe plum, and when the next payday came, he stood in the middle of the courtyard and took off his shirt, letting everyone see his back, which was like a zebra with red and yellow stripes. He shouted terrible curses, bemoaning his fate and saying that the world was run by whores, thieves, and bastards. I was standing by the gate and saw the women closing their windows so as not to hear his terrible words, and Mr. Korotek, until his wife ran downstairs and dragged him up to their apartment, shook his fist at the Lord for looking down on all this and doing nothing about it, just sitting in his office with his arms folded like a boss and not a worker. So when Piotr disappeared behind the door to the study, and Szymek and I sat listening to the lazy ticking of the clock, I thought of Okopowa Street and realized with a shudder that no stretching of the elephant's trunk or plucking of the goose or any other of M-ski's tortures could compare with those livid furrows on Mr. Korotek's back, like the grooves in a pine tree that ooze resin.

It was growing darker and darker outside when the janitor, summoned by the headmaster, went into the study, leaving the door ajar. I whispered to Szymek, suggesting we change our statement: How could we hurt Weiser or Elka, after all, by telling what happened at the river the day after the explosion in the hollow? If they were somewhere nearby but well hidden, it didn't matter, and if they were somewhere else entirely, then they were even safer. But Szymek was firm. He was always firm, all through school, and for the investigation he'd made up his mind to be even firmer. He clenched his teeth—I distinctly saw him do it—and shook his head. He gave me that same shake of the head when I visited him in a distant city and questioned him one more time about the summer when fish soup filled the bay and Weiser and Elka went to the airfield together. He had no desire to go back to his school days; he was no help. He didn't remember—or didn't want to remember—the gray cloud from Father Dudak's golden censer, and on the subject of Weiser only made a few banal remarks. This was his new, adult toughness, which I don't hold against him, because Szymek is the only one of us who has amounted to anything in life. Meanwhile the janitor came out of the study with a china coffeepot and told me to run to the lavatory for water. As I went down the empty corridor, I thought that there was nothing sadder than a deserted school building, where only a few hours ago hundreds of kids, big and little, had been racing around. A shame I didn't have any fast-acting poison with me. But I spat into the coffeepot as M-ski's face and fishlike stare appeared in my mind, and stirred the white froth with my finger to make the spit dissolve. When I returned to the main office, Szymek was in the headmaster's study and Piotr was sitting, just as before, on the folding chair to my left. The janitor took an electric coil from a cupboard and began to heat the water then and there, so as not to let us out of his sight. The water hissed lazily, the clock ticked softly, and I felt warm and drowsy.

The next day, Weiser met us, as arranged, at the entrance to the Oliwa zoo. Was this planned, or did it result from the moment when Elka came within an inch of sinking her talons into Szymek's face? I'm really not sure. But the word *arranged* is wrong. He had told us to come as a feudal lord gives orders to his vassals, through a herald. Sitting in the main office on a folding chair while the coffeepot bubbled and the wall clock ticked, I began to have a vague sense that Weiser was our feudal lord and that nothing could change this fact. And now I see that the first chapter of the unwritten book about him should start with the words "All right, tell them to be at the zoo at ten tomorrow, at the main entrance," which he spoke from his second-floor window over the familiar whir of his grandfather's sewing machine. And if I said this before and am repeating certain things and not erasing them, as I would for school composition, it's because this thing I'm doing is not the writing of a book. Possibly Elka, Szymek, Piotr, and I together could have written such a book, but Szymek doesn't want to remember, Elka doesn't reply to my letters, not even after I visited her in Germany, and Piotr was killed in the street in December 1970 and now lies in the fifth row in the Srebrzysko cemetery.

M-ski often stated, in his nature classes, that no European city would be ashamed to have a zoo like the one at Oliwa. Did he mean that we didn't live in Europe? Or that, apart from the zoo, we had something to be ashamed of? But the zoo really was beautiful, set away from the town in the deep valley of the Oliwa River, which flowed from seven wooded hills covered with pine and beech. Roe deer lived there in sunlit glades, and the elk had dark and murky fens, and the wolves had dens dug in the hill, and the kangaroos gamboled in fields of sorrel and clover. Only the predators brought in from tropical countries were imprisoned by iron bars, confined to a few dozen square meters of space.

Today's tourists or people from the town can

reach the zoo by bus from the tram loop at Oliwa. But back then, one had to walk. We passed the Cistercian abbey, then the shaded slopes of Mount Pachołek, where right after the war an obelisk stood with an inscription in German, and we continued on past the ponds of an old farm, now marshy and choked with weeds. The heat and dust were mixed with the scent of the blossoming limes that bordered the road. At last, tired, we caught sight of the hills at the head of Echo Valley and, to the right of them, the zoo. And there was Weiser, leaning against the gate, dressed in green trousers and a light-blue Cossack shirt that looked unnatural, funny on him, like a hand-me-down from a big brother. The three of us approached him first; then came Janek Lipski, the railroad man's son from Lida who'd been born in a railroad car; then Krzysiek Barski, whose father fought in the Warsaw Uprising and whose mother was a shopkeeper from Gdańsk; then Leszek Żwirełło, who always wore clean shirts and, unlike us, said please and thank you, probably because his father was of the nobility. Bringing up the rear that day was Basia Szewczyk, meek as a mouse; her father had given up mining after the war and come here to find happiness and a stepmother for his daughter. We formed a circle around Weiser.

"Well?" asked Szymek. "What do you have to show us?"

Weiser led us to a small side gate, where we entered the zoo without tickets. We passed a succession of pens, stopping whenever he stopped. He'd lean against the fence and spend a long time gazing at a sleepy llama, or pause at the seals, even though in heat like this there was no chance they would come out of the water. Elka was waiting by the birdcages. She was admiring, I remember, the huge Argentine vultures. Their black wings shimmered dark blue in the sun; they nodded slowly, as if dozing. We came to the reptile house, but Weiser didn't go in, so we followed him toward the baboon and chimpanzee cages, around which a large crowd had gathered, shouting and laughing. Every now and then an imbecilic chimpanzee would throw a handful of sand at the crowd, and the people would whistle, stamp their feet, and retaliate by throwing pieces of apple at the bars. Then the animal would crane his neck and ruffle the fur on the crown of his head, exactly like M-ski when he forgot something important. But the ape was only pretending to be puzzled—a cunning piece of chimpanzee deceit—because in the next moment he'd lower his head below his navel, piss into his mouth, look up, purse his lips, and suddenly the spectators would be sprayed as if from a fire extinguisher. Each time, the chimpanzee was faster than the people, and those closest to the cage had to wipe the stinking yellow liquid from their faces and arms. We loved this game, and for a while forgot about Weiser, who wasn't at all amused by the shenanigans. The ape finally hid in the depths of the cage, and the crowd moved on. We looked expectantly at Weiser. If this was all he had to show us, he was wasting our time. But Weiser was only testing us. He stood a while longer, then proceeded to the beasts of prey. Even today, as I write this, those cages have a smell all their own, a smell unlike that of the other animals, both horned and hornless, a sickly sweet, repulsive smell hanging in the clammy air of July, the fetor of the moldy lairs of the African lions, of the Bengal tiger, and of the black panther, who lay on a dead and naked bough.

Weiser stopped before the panther. Elka put a finger to her lips and signaled to us to stand back and give him room. He stood motionless for several minutes, until there were no other people near the cage besides us. Then we saw the panther, who had been taking his afternoon nap, slowly raise his head. His muzzle, with long, needlelike whiskers, puffed out slightly, as if he had burped, but that was only the beginning. His upper lip quivered, lifted, and from under the black velvet a row of white fangs appeared. We heard a soft sound, which turned into a deep, rumbling growl. Slowly, softly, the panther slid from the bough and approached the bars, his fur bristling, his tail twitching, then rhythmically lashing his sleek flanks, left, right, like the pendulum of a clock. Now the animal had his muzzle against the iron bars opposite Weiser, and the sound that came from his throat suddenly was a drumroll combined with the rush of a swollen river, or an autumn gale filled with Resurrection bells. The panther grew frantic, pawed the cement floor, lowered and raised his head. Finally he lifted his great body high and leaned against the bars, and we saw his large, thick, curved claws. But that wasn't all. Weiser climbed over the barrier that separated him from the cage, now stood so close to the bars that with another step he could have touched the great cat's claws with his forehead. The panther stood rooted to the spot. The roar became a rumbling growl again, and the growl returned to the soft sound he had begun with. Fur still bristling, tail still lashing his sides, he backed away, his eyes fixed on Weiser. It was incredible. The panther slunk backward into the depths of the cage, slowly sliding his belly on the floor, and his narrowed eyes gleamed like two small mirrors aimed at Weiser all the while. When his tail touched the back wall, he sat, crouched in the corner, and finally lowered his eyes. His entire body, every muscle, trembled, as if from cold, and the great cat resembled Mrs. Korotek's little cat, who would retreat to the corner of the courtyard at the mere stamp of a foot. We were silent as Weiser came up to us and Elka gave him a handkerchief; he wiped beads of sweat from his forehead, as if after strenuous labor. But that was not the end of our day spent with Weiser, just as this is not the end of the story of that summer when fish soup cooked in the bay and people in church prayed for rain.

Weiser showed us a different way home from the zoo. We didn't go by the tram loop and didn't take the rickety No. 2, which in those days ran between the Coal Market in town and Oliwa, passing the depot, our school, and our apartment house along the way. Instead, we took a road that went uphill from Echo Valley, past the old smithy that belonged to the Cistercian abbey, and along a tributary of the Oliwa River. From a high field, where the grass came up to our knees, we could see the bay, just as from Bukowa Hill. In the shade of the beeches there were gullies and crevices, and a narrow, sandy trail cut through the ancient pines dotted here and there with copses of birch and thickets of hazel. When Weiser showed us a place by the spring where Frederick the Great used to rest while hunting, and when startled roe deer pattered through a sun-dappled clearing, and when we gathered whole handfuls of sweet raspberries, we felt we were in paradise, a paradise far from town and as somber and cool as a cathedral on a blazing summer day. Weiser, in the lead, spoke as if to Elka, but really to us: "Here is where wild boar come in winter"; "There, that's the way to Matemblew"; "Look, a red ants' nest in a rabbit's skull." With particular satisfaction he showed us where trenches had been cut in the last war, and pointed out, "There's a crater from a mortar shell," and, "Here's a dugout for an armored car," and we listened with bated breath. Finally he led us across the hollow behind the firing range and to the edge of the moraine, from where we could see the belfry of the brick church at Brentowo and the familiar outline of the cemetery. I've been up and down that road many times since then, in both directions, alone and in company, walking or cycling in summer and on skis in winter, and I call that six-and-a-half-kilometer route Weiser's Way—in the guidebook it's a blue stripe, described as a natural trail—but I can't remember whether Weiser, guiding us home, pointed everything out by hand or used a gnarled hiking stick, like Moses leading his people.

That evening we sat on a bench under the chestnut tree, and Piotr wondered what would have happened if the black panther hadn't been separated from Weiser by iron bars. "It would have been like the circus," Szymek said. "Wild animals obey the man there. They even eat from his hand." "But Weiser isn't a lion tamer," I argued. "He doesn't have tall shiny boots or a whip, or a white shirt with a bow tie, and he doesn't train black panthers every day." We agreed on that point. Then we thought about how to test Weiser again, on a different animal, perhaps, and perhaps not at the zoo. We didn't realize that for the next few days Weiser would go his own way again, and that for a person like him our doubts were of no importance. Elka's mother came out the door and stopped for a moment. "What are you doing here, boys?" she asked in a reproving voice. "You should be in church. Father Dudak's saying Mass today." But before she went off down the cobbled street to the church of the Resurrection Fathers, she added that yesterday a huge comet had been seen above the bay and we were in for nothing but trouble.

In the meantime the janitor had brewed the coffee and taken the pot into the headmaster's study. The telephone rang, and I heard the tired voice of M-ski. I froze. "Yes, Mr. Heller," he was saying. "Your son is here with us. Just a moment, I'll put the headmaster on." Then it was the headmaster who spoke, or, rather, who replied to my father's questions. "Not at all," he said in an ingratiating voice. "He isn't being accused of anything. We're merely gathering information, on the prosecutor's orders. . . . No, no, certainly not, it's clear your son was not responsible for the accident, it was the Weiser boy. . . . You see, of course, we must learn all the circumstances of the tragedy, all the circumstances." My father apparently was not satisfied, because the headmaster continued, louder. "Why are you so upset? I see no reason to register a complaint, no reason whatever. . . . No, this is not unlawful detention, Mr. Heller. You might do better to ask yourself what your child was doing there. . . . He was, after all, in great danger, and you, as his father, did nothing to . . ." The headmaster was unable to continue, and I suspected that my father was giving him an earful. My father was usually a quiet person, but when he lost his temper, nothing and no one was sacred. A shame he wasn't here with us now, I thought, and I saw M-ski flying out the window, the headmaster hanging from the ceiling by his tie, and the militiaman flattened against the door. But my father still wasn't finished, because the headmaster kept clearing his throat, and was probably squirming in his chair and straightening the knot of his tie with his free hand. At last he interrupted sharply: "No, impossible, the school is closed until we've finished our work." Then he said, as in a movie or a book, "Good-bye, Mr. Heller" and slammed the receiver down on its hook.

It was dark outside. The street lamps shone into the main office, and we sat in pale-yellow gloom, like old widows in church long after the service is over, until the janitor switched on the lights. I wondered why Weiser had no parents and lived only with his grandfather. I never found out what his father had been, or his mother. And perhaps the tailor in No. 11 was not really his grandfather, not even a relative. Years later, with a little cunning, I managed to look through the school records in the municipal archives. The old registers had been discarded by then, but the transcripts were left, and on one of them was written, in faded ink: "Weiser, David. Born September 10, 1945." The space for place of birth, divided into town and district, was not filled in, and below it someone had simply written "Brody" and, in brackets, "USSR." In the spaces for father and mother the same hand had put dashes, but later someone else wrote "orphan" in blacker ink. Farther on was the information, "Legal guardian: A. Weiser, of . . ." and then our address with the number of Weiser's apartment. Today, as I pick all this out of my memory like fragments of amber from the bottom of a murky bay, I see Weiser's parents as two straight dashes, in black ink, on a transcript. Two dashes, nothing more. At the census-files window of the archives, which looked like the window of a ticket office in a dingy train station, the clerk handed me a small card: "Abraham Weiser. Nationality: Jewish. Citizenship: Polish. Place of birth: Krivoy Rog (USSR). Date of birth: 1879. Repatriated to Gdańsk in 1946. No mention of any child accompanying him on that journey. In 1948, Abraham Weiser registers a boy in his care, of Polish nationality and Polish citizenship, born in Brody, September 10, 1945. No information about the boy's parents, no copy of the birth certificate. The tailor claims the child is his grandson. Questions forever unanswered. Just as those surrounding the disappearance of twelve-year-old David Weiser, who presumably was blown to pieces by an unexploded shell in Brentowo Forest in August 1957. But there is no uncertainty about the death of Abraham Weiser; there is a certificate signed by the physician on duty then. "Do you wish to see a copy of the certificate?" asked the woman clerk, since I still stood at the window, while people silently passed by in the dismal corridor. But I had no more questions, at least none for her or for any of these people who carried files under their arms, forms, applications, affidavits, duplicates, requisitions, appeals, writs, and all the other paperwork with which our life is cluttered, even after death. I had no more questions—that is, I had the same question, the one I began with: Who was David Weiser? Because if he wasn't Abraham Weiser's grandson, why did he have the same name? Unless it wasn't his real name. Why, in registering the boy as his grandson, had Abraham Weiser said nothing about the parents? Because if David really was his grandson, bone of his bones and flesh of his flesh, then David's father must have been either Abraham Weiser's son or son-in-law, and his mother must have been the tailor's daughter or daughter-in-law, and even if both father and mother were in the earth, having frozen to death or died of typhoid, the old man must have known this. Unless he didn't want to tell. Or else he didn't know; in which case David Weiser wasn't David at all, wasn't a Jew, and wasn't born in Brody and not necessarily even in 1945. Because at that time, just after the war, when thousands of people were moving from east to west, south to north, and west to east, papers were lost and a person could say all sorts of things and there was no way to check. Disappearances and miraculous reappearances were the order of the day for registry officials then, so Abraham Weiser's statement that the boy was his grandson and had the same last name as himself would go unchallenged. As for the Polish nationality, perhaps that was because the other race had by then completely ceased to exist. When Abraham Weiser filled out the form, his people had vanished from Europe, so he said the boy was Polish. Citizenship must have been unimportant to a man like him, who originally came from the southeast, where he'd lived among Ukrainians, Germans, Russians, Poles, Jews, Armenians, and others. Leaving the dark building, I saw again the two dashes on Weiser's transcript, two dashes in ink that each year faded a little more. And as I write now, perhaps the ink has faded completely, and the spaces for father and mother look as if nothing had ever been there.

In the main office, after my father's phone call, in which he vented his wrath on the headmaster in particular and all schools in general, I guessed that Mr. Weiser's sudden death, from a heart attack, was David Weiser's doing. If Weiser could tame wild beasts, and make our hair stand on end in the abandoned brickworks (of which, more later), why couldn't he suddenly stop his grandfather's heart, I thought, releasing the old man from his sewing machine, from the needles, chalks, patterns, linings, and buttons over which he toiled, bent double, for days on end? That way, no one would be able to ask the old man questions. The removal of a witness. And I have to admit that when Piotr died in 1970 in the street and Elka left for Germany, I had the same thought: Weiser is removing them. And

Szymek's departure for a distant city, too, was a way of getting him out of the way. Out of the way of what, I didn't know, but Weiser surely knew. Even in the main office I was frightened: perhaps this whole interrogation was a test and Weiser was watching us, and if we did anything wrong, he would stop our hearts, just as he stopped his grandfather's heart. Meanwhile Szymek had been in the headmaster's study awfully long, and I began to think of the time I didn't go to play soccer on the grass by the Prussian barracks, and how, because of that, Weiser and Elka took me with them on an outing, which was no ordinary outing.

It was the day after our visit to the zoo. The first thing in the morning, my mother sent me to Cyrson's for greens. I liked going there. Inside, it was cool and smelled of vegetables; there were boxes crammed with the first green apples of the season; and from glass jars gumdrops and candy mice beckoned, twenty-five groszy apiece. The owner's wife, who served the customers from behind a wooden counter, had breasts as large and round as mixing bowls; she was very cheerful, and when she bustled around, getting things, giving things, her breasts bounced beneath her cotton dress and dirty apron like melons on springs. If there was a zloty's change left over from the shopping, I could use it to buy a handful of gumdrops, or four candy mice, each mouse a different color, or drink orangeade from a bottle with a spring-top porcelain cap. Opening these bottles as you sat on the concrete step at the entrance was an important ritual. If the seal was good and no tiny bubbles were escaping, you'd shake the bottle first, and the cap, gently prized up, would fly off by itself with a loud pop, and an aromatic wisp would rise in the air as all the customers turned to look at you. You'd throw your head back and tip the bottle just the way my father or Mr. Korotek tipped his bottle of beer at the Lilliput Bar. But opening your orangeade was a double lottery, because in addition to the surprise of the exploding cap there was the surprise of the color. In those days orangeade came in two different colors; usually it was yellow, but sometimes it was red, an especially pretty red, and even now I'd swear on a stack of Bibles that the red variety had a stronger bouquet and was more carbonated.

So there I was, sitting on the concrete step of Cyrson's studying the bottle's dark-green glass and trying to guess which kind of orangeade it would be, yellow or red, when through the haze of dust in the road I saw the boys on their way to the Prussian barracks. At their head marched Piotr, a real soccer ball under his arm, and I remembered that we were going to try out that ball, which Piotr had got the day before from a rich uncle. A leather ball was really special; until now we'd played with a rubber ball, which never lasted more than a month, but now, thanks to Piotr's uncle, we could feel like professionals. As they approached, I could hear them shouting "Red!" "Yellow!" "It'll be red!" "No it won't, it'll be yellow!" and when I prized up the porcelain cap with my thumb, and suddenly it flew from its rubber seal, they all cried, "Red! It's red!" and we drank the red orangeade, a small gulp each, as we always did when one of us managed to sell some bottles or had change left from shopping money. They went off toward the field, but I had to take home my mother's greens. I ran back downstairs and from the bottom of the stairwell saw Weiser and Elka walking in the direction of Oliwa. Something struck me, just as it had on the day Szymek and I observed them through the French binoculars from the viaduct by the airfield, and although I had neither Szymek nor his binoculars with me, I decided to follow them.

Our street ran in a long arc parallel to the tram line about two hundred meters away, then turned sharply left when it reached the wall of the depot. In my thoughts I passed the ball to Szymek on the left, he charged forward, dodging defenders left and right; but I kept Weiser and Elka in sight until they disappeared behind a broken pillar at the exact moment for passing to the center and shooting. I quickened my pace, in case a sprint to the goal was needed, and also not to lose those two, but when I reached the corner, Weiser and Elka were waiting for me just behind the pillar. "There's no need to spy on us," said Elka, looking at me, then at Weiser. "You can come with us if you like. He says it's okay." With a nod to him again. I nodded, too, though Szymek was surely scoring at that very moment, but I pictured Weiser face-to-face with a wild jaguar with no bars between them, or all three of us beneath the shining fuselage of an Ilyushin 14 at the edge of the runway, and a wonderful tremor ran through me.

But Weiser never repeated himself, or at least not when one of us was present. It may have been different with Elka—it probably was, because he was with her all the time. That day he chose—I don't know why—to have me join him and Elka, although this time there were no wild beasts or roaring planes. It was an ordinary walk to various places, and even a little boring at first, because not everything that Weiser said, and he really spoke only to Elka, made sense to me. On Polanka Street he stopped in front of one of those old houses in which rich Germans were said to have lived. The conversation between him and Elka went as follows:

"Schopenhauer lived here. In the autumn he took walks under these chestnut trees."

"And who was Schopenhauer?" asked Elka.

"A great German philosopher, very famous."

"No kidding. But what exactly does a philosopher do? I mean, to become famous."

"They don't all become famous," answered Weiser.

"But what does a philosopher do?" Elka asked impatiently. "Famous or not."

"He knows everything about life. Knows what kind of life it is, whether it's good or bad. And why the stars don't fall to Earth, and what makes the rivers run. If he wants to, he writes books about this, and people can read them."

"He knows everything?" Elka was doubtful.

"Everything," said Weiser. "About death, too, philosophers know a lot."

"About death?"

"Death, dying," said Weiser. "A philosopher has to think about that even when he's taking a walk under chestnut trees."

The next house looked a little like a country mansion, set back thirty meters from the street, near the forest. As we passed the alley of lime trees leading up to it and a tumbledown gate, Elka asked another question:

"And you're a philosopher, too, aren't you?"

74

"No," said Weiser. "Why should I be a philosopher?"

"Then how do you know all this?" she added quickly.

"From my grandfather. He's a philosopher, the greatest in the world, but he doesn't write books."

That was that, it seemed, and I don't believe I've left anything out of Weiser's answer. Yet whenever I recall it, I feel the same shiver down my spine I felt when the Ilyushin lifted Elka's red dress in the broom, and when Weiser tamed the black panther, and when in the cellar at the old brickworks he did something that made our hair stand on end. Because I very much doubted that Weiser's grandfather knew anything besides his sewing, and certainly not philosophy.

In the Oliwa cathedral, Weiser showed us the Gothic vaults and the great organ, and explained why the angels needed those brass horns, which were like sabers, long and curved. Then we stood on the little bridge in the park, near the old granary, and looked at the reflection of the cathedral towers in the water that flowed beneath our feet. Elka asked if the perch that was darting among the waterweeds could talk. A stupid question, typical of Elka, because how could fish talk? Didn't M-ski tell us, in almost every nature lesson, to sit as quietly as fish, and even if that perch, its scales gleaming in the sun, could talk, who was it going to talk to, us or its cousins underwater? That's what I was thinking, but Weiser answered seriously. He told about his grandfather, the greatest philosopher in the world, who before the war wasn't a tailor at all but went from village to village as an itinerant glazier, and when he made enough money, he went into the mountains and there spoke with everything that God created: birds, stones, water, fish, clouds, trees, and flowers. That's what Weiser said, and I stood leaning against the bridge's knobby railing, my mouth hanging open, and looked now at him and now at the slopes of Mount Pachołek rising beyond the cathedral towers, because I had never been in the real mountains, and here Weiser was telling us that his grandfather sometimes spent a whole six months there. I could see Mr. Weiser among the beech trees on that mountaintop, his ear pressed to the ground or a stream, without his wire glasses and without the tape measure around his neck. Today, I'm not sure of anything. Perhaps Weiser made up the story of his grandfather, was lying from start to finish for some reason known only to himself. But the picture of Mr. Weiser with his ear pressed to the ground on Mount Pachołek is one of the finest life has granted me.

After that, the three of us took the tram to Wrzeszcz, where Weiser got off especially to show

Elka yet another house, not the house of a philosopher this time, but of Schichau, the man who owned the shipyard when this part of town was called Langfuhr, before the war, and who must have had an awful lot of money, because the house was huge, with several entrances and round turrets. Elka loved the turrets. "This is like a fairy tale," she said with a laugh, pointing to a window. "That's where I'd like to live, guarded by dragons, and you'd come and save me from Merlin, the wicked wizard, or, better, you'd be Merlin and torture me cruelly. You'd change me into a frog or toad, or a spider, and I'd cry but no one would come save me." Elka prattled on, but Weiser said nothing, and I wondered why this Schichau and other rich men like him had built such strange houses. Why did they need these useless turrets, these fancy gables and crests and balconies and spires? Then I thought that they must have done it out of boredom, because in our nature lessons, when M-ski talked about exploitation and the class struggle, he always said the rich did the dreadful things they did out of boredom, like shooting at the workers and taking away their wives and daughters. The rich were immoral and degenerate because they had nothing else to do. I imagined Schichau sitting in his study, fat and greasy, bathed in sweat, smoking a cigar, while outside the window, down Beanstalk Valley, as the street with

77

the turreted houses is named, our fathers came marching and singing "When the nation took up arms and went forth to battle." Mr. Schichau picked up the receiver of his solid-gold phone, held it in fingers thick as frankfurters, and called the police, telling them that he, Mr. Schichau, had had enough of this noise outside his window and it was time to restore order. Our fathers actually never marched down Beanstalk Valley in front of Mr. Schichau's house singing "When the nation took up arms," but in 1970 they did march past the Party Committee building singing "Arise, ye slaves who know starvation!" And Piotr went out into the street to see what was happening and got a bullet in his head.

From Schichau's house we returned to the tram stop, and Weiser took us to Gdańsk. To this day I wonder if they had planned that route, or altered it on account of my presence. Unless there was no route at all, no plan, only Weiser showing things to Elka as a way of killing time. But I doubt that. And where did Weiser get all his information? His knowledge seemed to me, especially then, awesome. When he showed us the post office, I couldn't get over my amazement at how he knew so much about the siege. "Here stood a German armored car," he said, pointing. "And here the soldiers attacked with flamethrowers, and over there were the machine guns, and there, at that spot, a German soldier fell from the roof when a post office worker got him in the head. And they led them away there." He said all this very naturally, as if he'd been there himself and seen with his own eyes the armored car, the flamethrowers, and the machine guns. At Long Market he told us exactly where the Nazi Gauleiter, Albert Forster, had stood as he publicly announced the annexation of the city to the Third Reich. Weiser surely couldn't have learned that from his grandfather, or from any history textbook, because even the most meticulous historians don't bother with such details. And no historian tells you exactly where Frederick the Great stopped to rest while hunting in Oliwa Forest. By the time I was sitting in the school's main office, I knew that Weiser took particular pleasure in finding traces of the German presence, but for what reason, that I never learned, not then, not now, or the reason behind his stamp collection, his hoard of weapons at the old brickworks, and his explosions in the hollow behind the firing range. The rusty Schmeisser he gave us in the Brentowo cemetery when Szymek was on the point of starting the execution, which we tragically lost with the flight of Yellow Wings, was a pitiful specimen compared to the others in his possession, as we discovered later, when we tracked down Weiser and Elka at their hideout.

Anyway, from Long Market we went back to the rattling tram, and as it carried us away toward Wrzeszcz, I started thinking again about Piotr's new ball, about Szymek's passing, and whether or not we'd be playing that afternoon on the grass by the Prussian barracks.

In fact, we did play that afternoon, but it was no ordinary match. If it had been ordinary and like all the rest, and had nothing to do with Weiser, I wouldn't be writing about it now. So then. While I was with Weiser and Elka, the boys had been playing on the grass by the Prussian barracks, savoring the joy of kicking a genuine leather ball. It was the ball that caused the misfortune of that day. After about an hour, the army boys showed up on the field. They weren't soldiers in uniform, of course, just boys whose fathers were in the army and who lived in the new buildings near the barracks. They acted important, being a little older than us and better dressed—better dressed, because their mothers had washing machines and their own bathrooms, which ours didn't, since at our place, as I've mentioned, there was only one bathroom to a floor, and only Leszek Żwirełło's mother had a washing machine. So they acted important, but they didn't have a ball like ours, and their eyes lit up with envy. At first they stood on the side and watched us kick the ball, and now and then they got in our way, threw pebbles, or laughed, as if to ask why we needed a ball like that when we didn't know how to play. "You should have a rag ball," they shouted, "instead of wasting a good one." Szymek, stung, went up to their leader and said, "Have a game with us, and we'll see who can play." But they were cunning. "All right," they said, "but if you lose, the ball's ours." We agreed, and Piotr, too, because it wasn't just the ball at stake but our honor, as in war.

Teams of six plus a goalie were chosen, and it was agreed that the match would be a real one, that is, in two halves, one then, before lunch, and the second in the afternoon, when it cooled off a little. Although Szymek played as if he were two or three people and Piotr outdid himself, and Staś Ostapiuk passed to Krzysiek Barski bang on target as never before, the army boys won the first half, four goals to one. As I was going home, passing the concrete bill post, on which the same old tattered posters had been fading and graying for months, I saw my friends trudging along miserably, having no hope of victory in the second half. Szymek told me what had happened. After lunch we went back to the field, where a cow was grazing on tufts of withered grass. The other team appeared a little later, confident, as if the ball were already theirs. We began to play. Piotr sent the ball in a sweeping pass to

Leszek, our left wing. Leszek dodged two of the army boys and was getting near their penalty area when a defender got the ball away from him and fired it back into our half, where there were only Krzysiek and our goalie against four of the enemy. They dodged Krzysiek and went straight for our goal, and a second later the score was five to one. Szymek said nothing, and Piotr had tears in his eyes, because, quite apart from our honor, it was clear that he'd lost the ball, his present from his rich uncle. Then something unexpected and extraordinary happened. Coming toward us down a small hill was Weiser. Only now did we notice him. He said we would win the match if he played with us and we did everything he told us to do. Szymek was the captain, and for a moment he hesitated, but there was no time to argue, because the army boys were starting to press us.

And a wonderful show began. Although we didn't have a hundred thousand fans or even identical shirts, and although Krzysiek and I were playing barefoot, any coach would have been in seventh heaven. This was not ordinary soccer, not your usual shooting, crossing, tackling, and passing; it was an epic poem with six heroes and an omniscient narrator, as Weiser turned out to be. First, he put us in positions, so we wouldn't run after the ball in a pack. Szymek was left forward, I was right forward,

Weiser was center forward, and not far behind him, a couple of meters, stood Piotr as center halfback. Krzysiek and Leszek, as right and left fullbacks, played defense, and the goalie, as before, was Janek Lipski, in his father's too-long railroader's vest. Staś spent the first couple of minutes scowling on the touch-line, because this meant he had to give up his place to Weiser, but he sulked only a few minutes, until our first goal, which was made by Szymek after I'd passed to Weiser from the right. Weiser dodged two army boys, but instead of going straight for their goalie, he fooled him by sending the ball backward with his heel, and Szymek understood at once and slammed it home. The score was now five to two. But that was just the beginning, be-cause, to our astonishment, Weiser played bril-liantly. Whenever he went into the enemy half, first he'd hang back, slow down, wait for them to sur-round him, lure them to him by looking helpless. Then he'd flip up the ball with the side of his foot and head it left or right, shouting to me or to Szy-mek, "Now! Now!" And we would ram the ball in for a goal. I made the third; Piotr the fourth, after the play went from Weiser to Szymek, back to Weiser, who drove for the goal again, then flicked the ball backward to Piotr, who didn't let the op-portunity go to waste. The fifth, tying, goal came off a free kick, and here Weiser showed what he

83

could do, because the ball sailed literally a centimeter over the wall of army boys and flew between the wooden posts right under the nose of their goalie. Elka went wild, shouting and waving her arms, and Staś did a crazy dance beside her, giving us the thumbs-up. There were only five minutes left to the end of the match, but Weiser calmed us with a gesture. He was clearly waiting for the right moment, and the right moment came. Although he played with us only that one time, we talked about his feat long afterward. Piotr, unexpectedly finding himself on the left beside Szymek, dug the ball out from under the feet of an enemy and passed to center, but passed a little too hard, and Weiser, no matter how fast he sprinted, couldn't reach the spinning ball; he was a good half meter short of it. So he curled up, sprang, and did a somersault in midrun. When his body reached the vertical—that is, his hands practically touching the grass and his legs straight up in the air like beanpoles—at that moment he let one beanpole fly and gave the ball a mighty kick, then gently fell to the grass, and that was our sixth, victory, goal. Elka bellowed from her place, and the army boys, to the end of the match, were completely demoralized.

When time was up, and nothing could save them, the biggest and brawniest one came up to us and said, "You're still a bunch of stupid little shits."

But we were looking for Weiser, to carry him on our shoulders. He was no longer interested in us, however; it was as if he'd never really cared about the match. He'd put his trousers back on and was walking away with Elka. The leader of the army boys meanwhile grabbed Piotr's treasure, ran to the bushes with it, where they'd left their clothes, and quick as lightning took a knife from his knapsack, stabbed a hole in the ball, and threw it back at us, shouting, "Here, you can have your shit." His cronies laughed at that and kept repeating the word *shit,* as if they couldn't come up with anything else. We couldn't do anything, because all together they were twice as many, and it was plain, besides, that they ate better than we did. I looked toward the spot where Weiser ought to be, and the others all turned their heads that way, too, because suddenly we realized that the only person who could help us was skinny, round-shouldered Weiser, who never played soccer with us or swam with us at Jelitkowo. But he'd already disappeared behind the barracks. And what did our petty problems matter to him, anyway? He'd finished his performance and, like a true artist, left the stage, despising the roar of the crowd—leaving us with the bitter crumbs of his glory. That's how I see him today: he hadn't played because of Piotr's ball or on account of our honor, but only to show us that he could play better than we could, that he was better in every respect.

As I sat on a folding chair in the main office, while Szymek was in the headmaster's study, now for a really long time, I began to wonder why Weiser, all those years, preferred to appear a weakling in our eyes rather than play soccer even once or go for a swim with us at Jelitkowo as far as the red buoy. We were going home from the field by the Prussian barracks with Piotr's punctured ball, very happy in spite of that, but then a sort of anxiety came over us. Because if Weiser had been hiding his ability from us, not showing us how he could dodge three opponents at once or flick the ball up off the ground with the toe of his shoe, balance it on the side of his foot, knee it higher, and head it right or left, if he sat instead on the edge of the field and watched us all play far worse than he did, he must have had a reason. And a reason, too, for deciding to play with us, for revealing his ability on that particular occasion. Szymek said, echoing Elka, that Weiser could do anything, and no one laughed at that now, remembering yesterday's zoo and black panther. I, moreover, knew that Weiser and Elka hadn't been playing doctor at the edge of the runway, though I didn't really understand why they went there. It was only when the clock struck nine that a very simple thought came to me, namely, that Weiser lifted Elka's red dress by means of the gleaming airplane because he didn't want to do it himself. That would have been for him too simple and perhaps too common. As the headmaster's study door opened and they finally let Szymek out, I saw once more the great silver fuselage of the Ilyushin 14 coming in over the bushes, Elka's lifted knees, the rising and falling of her hips, and that soft, dark triangle undulating between them, and I saw her face, her mouth wide open as if to outscream the terrible roar of the machine. I haven't yet said, I don't think, that Elka turned up again afterward and continued to live among us for a long time, until she went to Germany for good. But neither then nor later, when I wrote letters to her and even went to Germany with the sole purpose of seeing her, did she say one word on the subject of Weiser, or tell me what happened on that final day by the Strzyża. The doctors attributed her stubborn silence to psychological shock, partial amnesia, and so on, but I knew, and still know, that that wasn't the truth. Elka alone knows who and what Weiser was, if not still is. Her silence, to this day, as I again start writing letters to Mannheim despite what happened between us during my visit, is eloquent proof of that. Yes, and when I summon the image of Weiser when we were in the cellar of the abandoned brickworks, my hair stands on end even now. We were there only once, but Elka must have been there, assisting him, many times. And all those explosions in the hollow behind the firing range must have been for her, too. But I'm not writing a book about Weiser, a book that could begin with the scene at the abandoned brickworks. No, I'm only putting down all the facts and circumstances, and that's why Szymek is sitting on a folding chair beside me now and I'm hearing my name, "Heller!" I get up slowly, my legs aching, and walk toward the diamond-patterned leather-covered door, afraid of M-ski and the tortures he'll apply in this next round of questioning.

The militiaman had undone the top two buttons of his blue tunic, and I could see that he wore a mesh undershirt, through which jutted thick black hairs. I thought of the chimpanzee at the Oliwa zoo, which had the same kind of chest, and I imagined how funny it would be to see the sergeant there in his place, throwing sand at the public, jumping up and down, and occasionally spitting piss on the first few rows of laughing spectators. So I smiled at him, and he thought I meant it and smiled back; he pointed to a chair and said, "Please have a seat." M-ski gave me a suspicious look, and the headmaster fiddled with his tie, which resembled not a Jacobin jabot now or even a scarf but a wet rag not completely wrung out.

"We want to know everything about the explosions behind the firing range," M-ski began. "How many and on what days. Where did your friend get the gunpowder? From cartridges? Shells? Or was it TNT? And tell us again about that final explosion, when Weiser and the girl perished. There's nothing to be afraid of, just tell the truth. Didn't you find a piece of shirt, a piece of flesh? Nearby or on one of the trees?"

He asked these questions quickly, one after the other, like themes in an overture. The real interrogation hadn't begun yet.

"All right, then," sighed the militiaman. "Tell us about the first explosion. When was that?"

"Around the beginning of August, sir," I answered.

"Can't you be more precise?" the headmaster said.

"It was definitely the beginning of August, because that was when the parish priest started saying the Masses."

"Now it's Masses!" M-ski jumped up as if he had been burned. "Headmaster, will they never stop? All right, what Masses are you talking about?" he said, turning to me again.

"The Masses for the farmers and fishermen, sir,"

I answered politely. "For rain, I mean, to clean the bay and because there was such a bad drought, which Father Dudak said was God's punishment."

"Punishment for what?" asked the militiaman.

"Well, our sins," I said, not entirely sure. "The priest said people had turned away from God and the Catholic faith, so God sent the drought as a sign to tell us to mend our ways or else."

"Or else what?" the headmaster prompted, twisting his tie even more.

"Or else God would do the same to us as He did at Sodom and Gomorrah, burning up the cities and the people and . . ."

"That's enough!" M-ski shouted. "Do you hear that, Sergeant? Worse than the Middle Ages, and we're supposed to work in such conditions! A pity the prosecutor didn't hear this—it might just come under some paragraph of the law!"

The militiaman cut him short with a wave of his hand. "Let's keep to the facts, Comrade M-ski. Emotions can impair our judgment." He turned to me again. "So you're telling us, my boy, that it was at the beginning of August?"

"Yes, sir," I said.

"Good. And how did you learn that Weiser was going to do this?"

"He told us himself."

"How did that happen?"

"We were playing at Brentowo, and he came and said that if we wanted to see something great we should follow him, and he led us to the hollow behind the firing range."

"And what about Wiśniewska?" he said, meaning Elka. "Was she with him then?"

"Yes. She was always with him, everywhere."

"Everywhere? Then other places, too."

"Well, yes, they were always together."

The militiaman undid the next button on his tunic, and even more hairs jutted through the mesh of his undershirt.

"So naturally you followed him," he continued. "Or, rather, them, since Wiśniewska was with Weiser. Then what happened?"

"When we got there, Weiser told us there would be an explosion and we had to do everything he said, in case anything went wrong. He told us to lie down in a trench, then did something with the wires from the . . . the . . ."

"Magneto," said the militiaman.

"Yes, the magneto. Then he said, 'Watch out!' and turned the crank, and there was a boom and sand and grass rained down on our heads."

"That's all?"

"Yes, because after that he hid the magneto somewhere and told us we could go home."

"Just a minute. From what you're saying, Weiser

had no explosive charge with him when he led you to the hollow. Is that correct?"

"Yes, sir. Every time we went to watch an explosion, he had the charge already in the ground, and all he did was connect the wires to the magneto."

"So he set the charge and the wires when you weren't there. I see. How long was the charge in the ground before it was detonated? An hour, two hours, an entire day?"

"I don't know, sir," I said. "None of us knew that. Weiser didn't explain those things, and he always took us to the explosion at the last moment."

The militiaman scratched his head and glanced at the headmaster, then at M-ski.

"Well, but weren't you ever tempted to go there without him and see if the next charge was ready?"

As he said this, he leaned toward me, and I could smell garlic coming from his mouth, as if from a jar of pickles, although that summer there hadn't been many cucumbers in the garden next to our building, or much dill or garlic.

"No, sir. Weiser forbade us to go there without him. He told us that the whole hollow was mined."

"And you believed him?"

"He never lied. Besides, each explosion was in a different spot, so we were afraid of stepping in the wrong place."

The headmaster, instead of loosening his tie more, suddenly tightened the knot.

"Do you recognize this?" said the militiaman, showing me a photograph of a black box with a crank and a plunger that looked like the badly attached handle of a corkscrew.

"Yes, that's the magneto Weiser always hid after an explosion."

"Where did he get it?" M-ski asked sharply.

"I don't know. Maybe he found it with all that stuff at the brickworks."

"And what did he have there at the brickworks? What did he show you when you went there?"

"We went there only once, sir."

"Tell us about that," said the militiaman.

"Sometime after the second or third explosion, Elka came and said that if we wanted a real gun to play with, an automatic, we should follow her. She didn't say where we were going, but took us to the old brickworks, where Weiser was waiting, and he gave us a rusty gun and a German helmet, because we played partisans a lot, and he said they were ours. That was all he showed us."

"What part of the brickworks were you in?"

"Near the kilns, sir, where all those carts and rails are."

"And you didn't know about the cellar, the arsenal he had there?"

"No, sir. It was only when the investigation began and the militia found the walled-off cellar that we heard about that."

"But didn't you suspect something? Didn't you wonder where he got the magneto and the gunpowder? Didn't you ever ask him?"

"We did, but he said the helmet and the gun were for keeping our mouths shut and that once he was sure of us—that's exactly what he said— once he was sure of us, we'd get something even better. So we didn't ask."

"All right," said the militiaman, clearly disappointed. "And Weiser didn't play partisans with you?"

"No, sir. There was nowhere to go swimming, so we went to the cemetery at Brentowo, and sometimes he came along, but he never played war with us."

"He was waging his own war," said M-ski, and the headmaster nodded slowly.

"Didn't it occur to you that you ought to tell an adult about all this?" the militiaman went on. "Didn't you realize that it could end badly, for all of you?"

How was I to answer such a question? What could I say to this man who wore a mesh undershirt and was as hairy as Tarzan? Eventually I got out the words he wanted to hear:

"Yes, I think now we should have told someone."

"Yes, only now," sneered M-ski, but the militiaman cut him short:

"What on earth possessed you to give that gun and helmet to an escaped mental patient? He ran around the neighborhood terrifying people. Whose idea was that?"

"It wasn't like that, sir. Whenever it was time to go home, we hid the gun and the helmet in an empty crypt in a corner of the cemetery. Until one day we went there and they were gone. And later someone told us there was a crazy man running around Brentowo with our gun and helmet, but we never actually saw him."

"If that were the only problem," sighed the headmaster, loosening his tie, which now looked like Mrs. Korotek's colored scarf. "My God, what am I to do with you boys?" He didn't go on, because M-ski stopped him with a fierce look. Then the militiaman asked:

"Now tell us how many of those explosions there were, and if they were different."

"There were six in all," I said, counting in my head. "They were alike except for the last one, which was very big, bigger than all the rest."

"Now then, my boy, tell us again exactly what happened in the hollow that last time."

So I told them again, just as before, when M-ski had done the stretching of the elephant's trunk on me. I spoke slowly, in order not to change anything, and they listened carefully, as if the words coming out of my mouth were little bugs that had to be examined under a magnifying glass from every angle. When I came to the part where Weiser and Elka vanished at the top of the hill, which was the truth, M-ski couldn't contain himself any longer and roared at me:

"How could you have seen them? They were dead! Are you trying to tell us you saw two spirits ascending to heaven?"

And he loomed over me dangerously, but the militiaman restrained him and told me to come up to the desk, where he spread out an army map, on which the hollow was marked by black contour lines.

"You were standing here, by the crater, is that right?"

"Yes, sir," I said.

"And the hill you're talking about is here, is that right?"

"Yes," I said and nodded.

"Well, that means you were exactly one hundred meters from the foot of the slope, so how can you be so certain that it was Weiser and Wiśniewska you saw? Perhaps you only thought you saw them. Perhaps you were afraid they'd been blown to pieces, and someone, Korolewski, said, 'Look, there they go up the hill,' and you saw them out of fear, because you didn't want not to see them. It was that way, wasn't it? Admit it."

I said nothing, disconcerted by the map and its accuracy. It must have seemed that I was admitting he was right, because he continued:

"You've said you don't know exactly where Weiser and the girl were when the charge went off. In your words, 'Weiser told us to wait near the thicket of larches, and after he made sure we were there, he went to the other side of the hollow and signaled for us to lie flat. Then the ground shook, and we got showered with sand.' That's what you said, isn't it?"

I nodded. The smell of garlic was stronger now, and my mouth watered to bite into a pickle.

"Well then, look here," said the militiaman, tapping the map with a pencil. "Follow me carefully. First, you're standing near the larch, here. Weiser is about twenty meters away, here. He walks toward the charge, because he's crossing the hollow, as you said. You can't see Wiśniewska at this moment, because she's over here, behind the hazel bushes. Now pay attention, this is the important part. Weiser waves, gives you the signal, here, and

97

you lie flat, and your heads are down, so you can't see at that moment that the girl goes up to him. What happens then? Immediately after the signal, the explosion. Where was Weiser? This red circle marks the place of the explosion, where the crater is. He waved to you from that spot. Here's what happened. Once you were lying facedown, he leaned over the charge to check the wires. Then he turned to go with Wiśniewska to the magneto—the magneto was here, this was where we found it—but this time the charge exploded by itself, without the turning of the crank or the pushing of the plunger. It was probably an unexploded shell, not the charge set by your friend. With the explosions before— so you've told us—roughly two minutes passed between Weiser's signal and the moment of detonation. That's about how long it would take him to retreat to a safe place, where the magneto was hidden. Because Weiser, though the charge was put in a different spot each time, always did the same thing. First he gave you the signal to lie down, here, here, or here, then he checked the wires connecting the charge to the detonator, then he retreated to the magneto, here, here, or here, and turned the crank and pressed the plunger. But this time he checked the wires—fifteen seconds at most passed since he gave the signal—and turned to go to the magneto, which was here, but never got there, because the

98

charge went off by itself. He was blown up, with Wiśniewska. You desperately wanted to see them, so you saw them, in your minds, going up the hill, a hundred meters from the crater where you were standing. That's what happened, isn't it?"

I stood by the desk, amazed at how well everything in his story fit together—though it wasn't true. But I said nothing. The militiaman didn't know that we'd all met again, the next day, at the Strzyża, that that was really our last meeting. And he didn't know about the black panther, or about our soccer match with the army boys on the grass by the Prussian barracks. He didn't see Weiser in the cellar of the old brickworks, and his hair didn't stand on end, or, at least if it ever did, not for that reason. He sighed, and again I caught a wave of garlic. Then M-ski said:

"It makes sense, yes, and I bet you don't know who testified that, the day before, you were all at the Strzyża." I was silent, and M-ski went on: "It was the sexton from Brentowo who saw you." For the first time that day, he smiled in triumph, and it was my turn to sigh—with relief. Obviously, the sexton, when they questioned him, got the days mixed up. Good, I thought, if they were putting the puzzle together that way. But the interrogation wasn't over. The militiaman sat down, and M-ski approached me.

"There's one thing we have to clear up. Where did you hide the bodies of Weiser and Wiśniewska? Speak!"

I said nothing.

"It's a criminal offense," the headmaster put in. "Not reporting the accident, and this ghastly burial . . ." His voice grew ominous. "How could you have done such a thing? It's worse than cannibalism! Don't you have any conscience? What do they teach you in Sunday school?"

"Come, tell us what happened to . . . the remains," the militiaman joined in. "You must have found some scraps of flesh and clothing."

My head down, I imagined myself holding one of Weiser's eyeballs in the palm of my hand, and Szymek holding a shred of a dress. Solemnly we laid them in the hole we'd dug, while Piotr intoned, "Beloved Christ, grant them eternal rest." Then we filled the hole and stamped down the earth with our heels, but Weiser's eye still winked at us from under the ground, and it will go on winking to the end of time, holding us in its power like the panther at the Oliwa zoo. Awful. My whole body trembled. M-ski grabbed me by the hair at my temples and tugged upward, but the hair, short there, slipped out of his fingers. He grabbed again, a little higher up, and began the plucking of the goose.

"Whe-ere did you bu-ury them?" he chanted,

pulling up harder with each syllable, until at last I was standing on tiptoe and swaying like a penguin. He pulled even harder, actually pulling out my hair. "Whe-ere did you bu-ury them? Te-ell me or I'll pu-ull your he-ead off, so he-elp me."

Another moment of that, and I'd have screamed, and in that scream might even have told them what really happened. But the telephone on the head-master's desk rang. M-ski let go of me and looked the other way. The headmaster, who picked up the receiver, said to the militiaman: "It's for you."

There was a moment of silence, and I felt as if my head were on fire, because a goose-plucking made your whole head ache, not just your cheeks and temples. The militiaman nodded, said, "Yes. Yes. Of course. Yes. All right. Fine. Yes. Good." To this day I don't know who was talking to the militia-man around nine o'clock that night, but whoever it was, I feel enormously grateful to him, my deliv-erer, because it turned out, after the militiaman hung up, that they had things to discuss, so I was sent back to the main office and the folding chair, whose wooden slats, after a while, hurt your behind.

So there we sat, the three of us together again, under the watchful eye of the janitor. I looked at the wall clock, and it seemed to me that the bronze disk at the end of the pendulum was exactly the color of Father Dudak's golden censer, from which clouds of pale gray smoke had poured on Corpus Christi as we sang in chorus "Glo-ory to Thee, the living Ho-ost."

It was the same kind of clock, with a bronze disk at the end of its pendulum, that I saw in Elka's apartment in Mannheim when I went to Germany to see her many years later. Of course, I never told her the real reason for my visit. When she heard my voice on the phone, and my name, she said nothing. Maybe she saw before her all the letters I'd sent to Mannheim that she'd dropped in the wastebasket. After a long silence I heard the cogent question:

"Where are you?"

"At the station," I shouted into the receiver. "I'd like to see you!"

Again a pause.

"All right. I'm home all day," she said, as if we'd last seen each other only yesterday. "Do you know how to get here?"

Of course I knew how to get there; I had planned all this in advance, every detail, the sequence of questions, the topics of conversation, the photograph of Piotr's grave, all leading up cunningly, inexorably, to the subject of Weiser. The taxi I took through the city was driven by a mustached Turk. He was burning to talk when he realized I wasn't a German, but in my thoughts I was already with Elka. I remembered the September morning in 1975 when I saw her off at the port in Gdynia. She was taking a ship to Hamburg.

"Elka," I had asked her for the last time, "you really don't remember anything of what happened that day? Weiser was leading you by the hand. You're hiding something, you've been hiding something all along. Please tell me now, since you're going away for good, what happened that day at the Strzyża." I was practically shouting as Elka drew nearer to the customs barrier, until finally she said:

"Keep your voice down. People are looking."

Those were her parting words. Not "Good-bye" or "Stay well," but "Keep your voice down." And then she never answered my letters. As I rode now in the taxi through Mannheim, I resolved not to make the same mistake twice. I would take an altogether different tack; I would circle, skirt, wait patiently for the right moment, then pin her to the wall at last and force her to confess.

For the first year and a half, Elka's life here hadn't been easy. She worked as a maid for a distant aunt, a spiteful old woman who called her a Communist and humiliated her at every opportunity. But Elka bore it, because the aunt was rich and had her in her will. At the reading of the will it turned out that the aunt hadn't left her a penny. Elka sank to even worse drudgery. She worked two jobs, cleaning private apartments in the mornings and in the evenings washing floors in a restaurant owned by a friend of the aunt's. That's where she got to know Horst. Horst had lost his wife in a car crash in Hesse and now, instead of keeping an eye on his business, would drink there late into the night, until closing time. When he proposed, she didn't hesitate long. He was not old, not ugly, raised horses, had his own business, therefore she wouldn't need to wash floors. Horst was often away, leaving Elka alone for days on end, because he had no family and she didn't like to go visiting or receive guests herself. Sometimes they went away together, if Horst had time to spare, south, to the mountains. All this I learned about fifteen minutes later, after the taxi left the center of town and the mustached Turk and I had gone down several side streets, and I found myself sitting opposite Elka and drinking coffee. She showed me a picture of Horst from their most recent vacation in Bavaria. On the walls of the large sitting room hung watercolors of horses and riders, and in the center of one wall was the clock, the same kind as in the main office at our school, a bronze disk at the end of a long pendulum. But Elka wouldn't remember that. I showed her the photograph of Piotr's grave. Elka had been there several times, but the stone was put up after she left. I told her about the trouble we'd had with it, because no one was willing to carve "murdered," so in the end it said "perished tragically." All Piotr's friends made contributions; it was really our collective monument to him, though he hadn't taken part in the demonstration or the fighting; he'd just gone out into the street to see what was going on. But I told her this later, over toasted sandwiches she made—wonderful sandwiches, with lettuce, spring onions, sliced tomato, caraway seed, pepper, paprika, ketchup, and I don't know what else, served hot, straight from the oven. I still remember them. Then unexpectedly Elka said:

"I didn't answer your letters, or anybody else's. Once you're here, you see, you can't be here and back there at the same time."

I wanted to make some casual remark that would prompt her to say more, but she changed the subject and cleverly got me to talk about myself, about my present life, that is, which had nothing interesting or fine in it. A dull, dreary story, but Elka now and then interrupted to ask about some person or thing—probably out of politeness. Finally I told her what I was doing in Germany, and she asked if I had to go back that day to Munich, where I was staying for a couple of weeks with my uncle, who had never returned to Poland from the POW camp, because in his opinion it wasn't Poland any-more, just a stage set, the cheap kind you see in second-rate theaters. But I didn't go into that; I said no, I didn't have to go back that day, which was true, and anyway we hadn't got around to Weiser yet.

"Wonderful," she said, pleased. "You're wel-come to stay here a few days. Horst will be glad, when he gets back, because right now he's away." I didn't see why her husband should be glad, but I agreed to stay until the next day. Fortunately, I had a little money, and when we went into town I didn't need to count my marks. While Elka was getting the car out of the garage, I looked at the house. Like all the houses in that neighborhood, it had a small garden; there were three rooms upstairs, a kitchen, dining room, and sitting room on the ground floor, and I thought to myself, Not bad for two years of cleaning floors. But perhaps, for a lifetime, it was bad. The front lawn was like a carpet, and the furniture, wallpaper, and paneling were good quality.

So when exactly did the game begin between Elka and me, the game for Weiser, the sneaking up on each other, holding our breath, always down-wind, never upwind? A game that in a sense is still going on. I know now that Elka was playing from the start, from the moment I called from the station. She must have realized what I wanted, and then and there devised her plan. But that day, in Mannheim, I let myself be taken in by appearances; I didn't even stop to wonder why she had invited me to stay. I thought to weave a subtle net of hints, questions, seemingly innocent remarks, but fell into a net that was more subtle. When I'd finished my inspection of the house, Elka said, "Wait a minute. For an occasion like this, I must put on something special." And a moment later, I saw her in a red dress, not the red dress she wore back then, of course. It was well cut, expensive, but I couldn't help remembering the one she wore that day at the Strzyża, where the river flows through a narrow tunnel under an embankment that carries railroad tracks that haven't been used since the war. Yes, as she got into the car, Elka knew what I was thinking, and as we passed the Daimler-Benz factory she suggested we take a walk along the Rhine, because she felt like watching the water. We stood on one of the concrete parapets by the dam, and she threw twigs into the water while I wondered if the amnesia the doctors had diagnosed was Weiser's idea to begin with, or whether she came up with it herself. For lunch she took me to a restaurant. Through the windows we could see the walls of Friedrichsburg, and by the time dessert was served she had told me the history of the city, from a guidebook she had once read. Over ice cream, the conversation somehow turned to animals.

"There's one thing I hate," she said, licking her spoon. "In the zoos here there's a practice they call feeding the lions. In every town that has a zoo, people come at a particular hour to watch bloody chunks of meat being thrown to the animals, and it's considered great fun when the lions fight over the pieces." And she added, "They don't do that in Poland, do they?"

"No, they don't," I said. "Do you remember our trip to the zoo at Oliwa?"

Elka nodded.

"Yes, of course. The zoo's in the forest, and that day we went back through the forest."

"Do you remember the panther?" I asked, not giving up.

"Yes," she said quickly. "It was in a bad mood, I remember that, and the keeper told us to move away from the cage."

"There was no keeper," I said, putting down my spoon. "It wasn't that way at all. It was Weiser—Weiser, the one all that trouble was about. . . ."

She interrupted me:

"You're always bringing him up. It's so boring! Let's not argue over details, all right?"

"It isn't a detail," I said, "that you turned up again, and he . . . ?"

Elka made a sad smile.

"I fell from the embankment and cracked my head. If you remember everything so well, then you know I was in the hospital two months."

"You were, but you didn't fall from the embankment," I said, growing feverish.

At this, Elka called the waiter, and said to me, as if explaining:

"Well, apparently you're one of those people who always know better, so what can I say?"

It went on that way until evening. When I mentioned the airfield, Elka said, sure, she flew kites there, maybe with Weiser, if I insisted, but with other boys, too. When I brought up the match with the army boys, she said we were always playing soccer, like all the boys in the world, so how was she supposed to remember one particular match. But she said nothing when I spoke of the old brickworks, except to agree that the explosions were first-rate. Weiser, according to Elka, must have been blown up, and she fell from the embankment the next day, while we were playing at the Strzyża. All this was said later, not in the restaurant, but back at her house, after we had fixed supper together and were drinking the second bottle of wine. The first was red, the second, white vermouth, and I could feel the anger building inside me, because I knew she was playing blindman's buff with me and that my trip to Mannheim was as pointless as the letters I had stubbornly kept sending. I went upstairs, where Elka had prepared a room for me, and lay down on blue sheets.

Then I heard her calling me from downstairs, apologizing; she had forgotten something. Looking down from the top of the stairs, I froze. What a cruel trick to play on me. The sofa that stood under the dining-room window was now in the sitting room, as if it were an extension of the stairs. And she herself was lying on that sofa, with two pillows, one under her head, one under her hips. Her legs were slightly apart, and the red dress rippled against them to the rhythm of her body. Nothing, no force could have kept me from stepping forward—or, rather, downward, since I was at the top of the stairs. And that was Elka's diabolical plan, because with every step my legs met with less resistance, as if they had lost contact with the ground, and half-way down, my body was floating, no longer my body but the fuselage, gleaming in the sun, of an airplane. My arms were no longer arms but silver wings, and the sofa was the start of the runway. I came in over the hills at the southern edge of town, flew low over the red roofs of the houses, across the railroad tracks under the viaduct, and now saw only Elka's open thighs, her dress riding up, and, in a gust of wind, that soft, dark, naked triangle, which I approached with thunder and quaking. But this time the silver fuselage didn't set down on the concrete runway; with all its mass and momentum and a whistle of air, it landed in the broom, entered her perfect softness, and she received the cold metal with a cry that was lost in the crash of machine and air. But one plane crash wasn't enough for Elka. Bent on mad destruction, she forced me, as I was on my way back upstairs, to become a gleaming fuselage again, and repeat the landing over and over, until at last the bird of steel, no longer able to endure the constant rising and falling between heaven and earth, lay broken in the clumps of broom, which smelled of almonds. Elka dug her fingers into my hair, and I thought I could hear the voice of Yellow Wings saying that the Earth would be burned, and the inhabitants thereof; then there was Father Dudak's sour breath from behind the grille of the confessional, refusing to grant me absolution. But no, the only voice was Elka's, whispering a name not mine, and the only smell was the smell of her body, a blend of wind, salt, and essence of almond. The game for Weiser was over, and I had emerged from it neither spotless nor victorious.

The next day, I went to Munich, where I also

played a game, this time with my uncle. After I'd washed his car and cut his front lawn, he sat opposite me and said, "How can you go on living there?" And I replied, "Pinch my ear, Uncle." Amused, he pinched my ear. Then I said, "So you see, you're wrong." "How so?" he asked, and I replied that if I really existed, as he'd proved to himself just now by pinching me, then I couldn't be only a stage set, a piece of scenery. And if I was part of a whole, then that whole was real, too; therefore Poland was no stage set, and even though all the world was a stage, or, better, a brothel, my uncle was wrong. Yes, dear Uncle, you're in your grave now and don't know that your nephew went to the Germans that time not to make Western money for a car or some other consumer marvel, like thousands of Turks, Yugoslavs, and Poles, but only to see Elka and ask her about Weiser.

What happened then? M-ski came out of the headmaster's study holding large sheets of official paper. He handed us each a sheet folded in two and told us that now we must put down everything we'd said, in simple words and full detail. We were to describe all Weiser's explosions in proper order, including the last one, leaving nothing out and adding nothing. The janitor switched on an extra light, and we were made to sit away from each other, just as if we were taking an exam in class. I was only sorry Miss Pawłowska wasn't going to read our essays; in all the school, she was the one teacher we loved. Miss Pawłowska taught us Polish, and she never talked about the exploitation of the masses or shouted at us; instead, she read us poetry so beautifully that we held our breath, listening to the story of Lieutenant Ordon, who blew up the redoubt, himself, and all the storming Muscovites, or how General Sowiński died with his sword drawn against the foes of the Fatherland. Miss Pawłowska didn't concern herself too much with the curriculum, and today I'm grateful to her for that. But that's another story. In the main office, I wasn't entirely sure what I was supposed to write. A couple of times I started a sentence, then crossed it out with a feeling of despair. Anyone who's been through an interrogation once in his life will understand. It's one thing to give evidence orally, quite another to write it down. How do you write and say nothing? Or write and say only what is permitted? You have to watch every word, every comma and period, because they'll put it under a magnifying glass and read each sentence two or three times.

If, in reply to M-ski's question, I said, "I saw Weiser," I could add at once, "but not clearly." And if he frowned, I could instantly correct myself.

"No, that was another time I didn't see him clearly. On the day you're asking about, yes, I saw him as clearly as I see you now." But a sheet of official paper is an entirely different matter. What to admit, what to keep secret? There wasn't much to tell. Not much at all—because how could I describe to them the mastery of those explosions, each different from the one before? Or explain to them the way Weiser bewitched us with his ideas? And even if I could, were they worthy of this?

I touched my swollen nose, my temples. They ached. I decided that even if I didn't tell what happened at the Strzyża on that final day, I had to tell them something, I had to write something on this huge sheet of paper to avoid rousing their wrath. I remember my first sentence: "David didn't play war with us, because his grandfather didn't let him." Perhaps that should be the sentence that begins the book about Weiser. Because the first explosion we saw in the hollow behind the firing range was no war game. To this day I don't know why Weiser set off those explosions, why he needed them, but the moment I saw a blue fountain of dust shoot into the sky, I knew it had nothing to do with war. Weiser added colored material to each charge, and the first, as it ripped open the ground, was sky blue. After the last pieces of gravel and wood fell to the ground, a blue mist still hovered in the air, an azure cloud swirling above our heads, slowly rising higher, changing shape, until at last it disappeared. We were enthralled, but Weiser shook his head, as if something hadn't gone right. Perhaps he was experimenting, and we were like a group of uninitiated laymen admitted to an alchemist's workshop full of crucibles, retorts, and flaming burners. Before we had time to recover from our first excitement, he told us to wait in the same place, laid a new charge, connected the wires to the black box, and again the air was torn by the roar of an explosion.

This one was even more impressive. The cloud that now hung in the air was in two colors; its lower half, in the sunlight, went through every shade of violet, while the crown of the swirling column was a bright red pom-pom. Weiser seemed satisfied. The cloud hovered over the hollow for maybe three minutes, turned into a brownish green sphere, then dissolved into nothingness. This was better than the gray smoke emitted by Father Dudak's golden censer. But that was all. Weiser hid the black magneto somewhere and told us we could go home. Today I know there's nothing very complicated about such tricks—the Tatars used colored clouds against the Christian knights, which filled both men and horses with terror—but at the time we thought Weiser was a magician. And after our visit to the abandoned brickworks, which we found by following Elka, nothing could shake our belief that Weiser could do anything. But of what we saw in that dank cellar, later. For that I must prepare myself better than for Easter confession, when, fearing the wrath of God, not to mention Father Dudak's, I would write down my sins and learn them by heart, as an actor does before a rehearsal.

The next explosion—or Weiser's next performance—took place about a week later and was completely different. A pillar of glittering spangles rose in the air, then fell slowly to the ground. This time, the beauty was in the falling; the cloud didn't dissolve as it did before, but drifted down and settled on the grass and ferns that grew densely in the hollow and covered them with a gray powder. I couldn't understand why the tiny fragments had sparkled so in the air, whereas now they resembled the usual grimy dust of July, which coated everything that summer.

Weiser didn't care for simplicity and each time tried for more complex effects, though this observation occurs to me only now, many years later. When the earth shook again, we saw something that surpassed our wildest expectations. What was it? If I said it was the French flag, that wouldn't be a lie, but it wouldn't be the truth, either. If I said it was three pillars side by side, each a different color, that, too, would not give the real nature of the thing. Can one ever give the real nature of a thing? I do not think so, and perhaps that is why I am not writing the book that should have been written long ago. Just as there should be a book about Piotr and the December when helicopters flew over the city, or a book about our fathers, who got drunk on payday and, like Mr. Korotek, reviled the Lord God for allowing to happen all that happened. In the hollow, Szymek nudged me in the ribs and said, "Jesus, how beautiful!" and added, "How does that Jew do it?" Which was meant not as an insult but a compliment, like saying, "How does that son of a bitch do it?" I stared up at the three swirling pillars of smoke, one white as a sheet, one dark blue, and one as red as a matador's cape used to lure an enraged beast straight to the fatal point of the sword. The colors didn't merge this time, but simply floated higher and higher, until they vanished beyond the tops of the pines.

That day, on our way back along the gully toward Brentowo, as Szymek quarreled with Piotr over whether it was the French flag or ribbons on a hat, we encountered M-ski. First the familiar butterfly net came into view near the mouth of the gully; then we saw the nature teacher hurrying horizontally along a steep slope, clutching the staghorn moss as he went. The butterfly M-ski pursued was fluttering near the ground, so the teacher had to crane his neck as far forward as possible, almost putting his nose in the moss. When he was halfway up, the butterfly changed its mind, performed a shaky somersault over his head, and flew downhill, flashing its colorful wings. M-ski went after it, but as he rushed down the precipitous slope, he couldn't stop himself and fell at our feet with a crash, and with a crack, which was the handle of the net breaking. But M-ski took no notice of us or of the broken handle, because there in the net was the huge butterfly, quivering.

"Gently does it, my little one," whispered M-ski and, still prone, took a small bottle from his knapsack and with a skillful motion caught the butterfly in it. "At last I have you," he addressed it lovingly. "You'll get my prettiest pin, little beauty." Getting up from his knees, he finally saw us, but wasn't at all embarrassed. He smiled triumphantly. "Well, boys," he said, "do you know what this is? It is not, unfortunately, *Parnassius Mnemosyne*—that would be next to a miracle—but it is still quite a find. You can't guess? This, my dear boys, is a *Parnassius Apollo,* yes, a *Parnassius Apollo* here in the north, in a postglacial moraine! Totally disappeared from the Sudetic Mountains, it lives in the Pieninys and the Tatras, yes, and no scientist would dream the *Apollo* could turn up here, too! But I have found one. And will write about it in *The Universe.* Its caterpillars feed on stonecrop. Do you know at least the Latin name for stonecrop? It belongs to the Succulentae. It's *Sedum acre,* remember that, class, *Sedum acre,* which translates to sharp houseleek!"

We stood, our mouths open and our eyes fixed on the bottle, which was a tiny cylinder, and we could see the butterfly trying to flap its wings, but there wasn't enough room in its glass prison. It fretted like a fish in a tank, not understanding its situation. M-ski, who immediately went on his way, had nothing to do, of course, with Weiser's three-color explosion. But as I wrote, slowly and thoughtfully, the next sentence of my statement on the sheet of official paper, I thought that Weiser was a little like that butterfly, especially when something didn't go right, because he would cover his confusion with a lot of arm waving. The fourth explosion didn't go right, that was clear; after the blast, an ordinary gray cloud of dust appeared, soon fell, and that was that. Weiser ran to the spot where he'd laid the charge, flapped like *Parnassius Apollo,* then turned to us, frowning. "We'll try again," he said to Elka, and again we heard the crank churn and the plunger click, but this time there was no explosion at all. "The wires might not be connected," Piotr suggested timidly, but Weiser waved his arms even more. "Impossible," he said, looking at the sky. "We'll try again." And again he ran to the charge and flapped. This time there was an explosion, but apart from a small yellow cloud that lifted briefly after a spray of sand, nothing. Weiser walked home with us and, I remember, said not a word, not even to Elka.

As the office clock struck ten and I wrote down the last line of my first page, I thought the comparison of Weiser and the butterfly a good one, but today my older, poorer imagination is not up to such metaphors and images. I kept the butterfly and the three-color cloud to myself, and so did Szymek and Piotr. Not a word did I write about Weiser's experiments, or what the final explosion really was. I wrote ordinary things, things those three behind the diamond-patterned leather-covered door could understand. I wrote that, each time, Weiser went to the magneto on the other side of the hollow, and that we kept our heads down during the explosions, to the ground, and that there was no difference between the explosions except that some were stronger than others. When the janitor stepped out for a moment, Szymek looked up from his paper and whispered, "I'm going to write"—and Piotr and I knew what he was going to say before he said it—"that we found a piece of red dress and threw it in the trash. Or else," he quickly added, "we burned it." Yes, that would satisfy them, confirming their picture of what happened. The janitor came back from the lavatory, and I wondered how one could describe the final explosion the day before what happened at the Strzyża, an explosion that I'm convinced must have had special meaning for Weiser. It wasn't for the color; it had to do with something far cleverer.

What was it like? If I'd had to describe it at the time, I might have said it was like the funnel my mother used for pouring raspberry juice into bottles. The cloud of dust was completely black, narrow at the bottom, broadening toward the top, and it turned, rotated. But it wasn't really a funnel, unless you think of it as a tornado, a spinning column of tiny black particles. It appeared immediately after the blast and circled above the hollow for a good minute before it dispersed in the air. Only years later was I struck by the similarity of Weiser's funnel to the Archangel Michael fighting the dragon. The angel's flowing robes, unfurled wings, and the host of heavenly warriors, all were contained in the swirling black cloud, though of course Weiser might never have actually seen the woodcut. "A funnel like that," said Szymek, "can suck up anything, even a whole man." Elka, who always tended to exaggerate, said, "A man, pooh. It could suck up an entire house and carry it off." When I finished the last sentence of my written statement,

I fell to thinking that Weiser could suddenly send a tornado like that to whisk away our school building and carry it over Bukowa Hill, to a spot near the old cemetery or, better still, to the hollow behind the firing range, and then M-ski, the headmaster, and the militiaman would realize that they were dealing with something more than an ordinary accident with an unexploded shell. But wherever he was, Weiser didn't rush to our aid, so I put a period on my last page and waited to see what would happen next.

The janitor collected our papers. I thought again of Miss Pawłowska, who taught us Polish and read poetry so beautifully. Especially the poem about the evil woman who murdered her husband, because whenever Miss Pawłowska got to the part where the two brothers fight and the ghost appears in armor in the church and cries out in a voice as if from the grave, no one talked, no one spilled ink, and the classroom became more solemn than during the Elevation of the Host, when Father Dudak lifted the blessed wafer as round as the sun and sang in Latin. If Miss Pawłowska had told us to write an essay about Weiser, it would have been completely different from the one I was giving now to the janitor. Maybe I wouldn't have written everything, but certainly the panther would have been in it, and the wonderful soccer match, and over the fish soup in the bay a mighty tornado would come and suck up all that filth so we could go swimming the next day, as in any other summer.

Meanwhile we sat there on the folding chairs with wooden slats that hurt our behinds, and the janitor, not closing the door behind him, vanished into the depths of the headmaster's study. Then he came out and said, "You must wait. Once they make sure everything's in order, you'll sign your statements and go home. But you're still not allowed to talk," he added, glowering at Piotr, who had leaned over in my direction. So we didn't talk, just as we hadn't talked in all those hours since they brought us here, and I could hear Szymek's stomach, mine, and Piotr's, too, rumbling, because they hadn't given us anything to eat. The janitor switched on the radio, and from the wooden box came the sound of folk music. "There'll be news in a minute," he said to himself, and set about wolfing down his next sandwich. The music in fact stopped, and an announcer said that now we would hear portions of a speech made by Władysław Gomułka, whose bald head had recently been put up in all the classrooms. A funny, squeaky voice said something about our common home and keeping order. Why did the grown-ups speak this man's name with such reverence, when what he said was even more boring than Father Dudak's sermon at High Mass on

Sundays? But then, who can fathom the mysteries of politics? Today I understand why people went into raptures over Władysław Gomułka, and I remember how those same grown-ups exulted over the words of his successor, especially at the shipyard, when Piotr was not yet cold in his grave. He, too, spoke of our common home and keeping order. But enough of this; it's not what I wanted to talk about. My theme is Weiser. Only Weiser. And there's much more to tell. The game is not yet over. The game? I don't know how else to put it. I think that Weiser was playing with us then, when the three of us sat waiting to sign our statements and for the investigation to end, and that he is playing with me now, in the same way, watching what I do, watching with his dark eyes.

What happened after the match with the army boys? The main thing was the weather. The mad sun blazed down on the city and the bay, the leaves on the trees turned yellow, as if it were autumn, and the birds, tormented by the heat pouring from the sky, stopped singing. One day, we went to Jelitkowo to check the condition of the fish soup, and what we saw surpassed our blackest fears. Because now, besides the sticklebacks, hundreds of eels lay in the stagnant water, and flounder, and herring, and other fish whose names I don't know to this day. A terrible stench, and convulsive twitching. The eels, the toughest fish of all, took the longest to die, and I can still see their writhing bodies, a symbol of that summer. The fishermen waited in front of their shacks, sitting on benches day after day, puffing their cigarettes and cursing their fate. One of them spoke to us as we made our way around the empty crates.

"What are you doing here, kids?" he grumbled. "There's nothing for you here." Then, without being asked, he elaborated. "It's the mustard gas, that's what it is, kids, that filthy work of the Prussian devil." Seeing our blank faces, he explained: "Mustard gas from the German U-boat. You didn't know that? It sank off Hel right at the end of the war, and it was packed with mustard gas, loaded to the gills with the stuff, and now we have a cesspool, not a bay!"

"Come on, Ignacy," we heard from a window, "don't tell the kids stories. Everyone knows it wasn't the U-boat, it was the Russian maneuvers they had here on Saint John's Day. They put something in the water, and it'll poison us all like the fish!"

The fisherman lost his temper. "You're jabbering, old woman," he growled at his wife and, turning to us again, said, "It was the U-boat, and the canisters rusted through and let out that filth, damn those Hitler sons of bitches! As if they haven't done us enough harm!"

So we divided into two camps, and argued in loud voices as we waited for the tram by the stone cross at the loop, the U-boat versus the Russian maneuvers. I looked up at the white-hot sky and the ball of the sun, and knew that neither the U-boat nor the Russian maneuvers in the bay had caused all this. But if someone had asked me then what *had* caused the fish soup, I wouldn't have been able to give a clear answer; nor could I now. It certainly wasn't the sins of the people or the wrath of God, as Father Dudak thought and many who lived in our building also thought. In the evening they'd gather in the courtyard and talk in lowered voices, as if afraid of even greater misfortunes. Stranger and stranger things could be heard in their conversations. The fishermen at Hel had seen an orange sphere that looked like ball lightning move across the water of the bay. The Virgin Mary of Matemblew had appeared to a woman who was walking through Brentowo Forest. Sailors had seen a sailboat without a crew passing at night among the anchored ships. And a comet in the shape of a horse's head had been sighted, circling above the town, and some swore it would return after orbiting the earth and fall with tremendous force.

Meanwhile each day seemed hotter than the one before. We couldn't even play soccer by the Prussian barracks, because of the heat and the clouds of acrid dust that rose from the scorched grass. What was there to do? Despite M-ski's threat, we continued going to the Brentowo cemetery. In the shade of the old beeches, it was cooler. Except we no longer had the helmet or the rusty Schmeisser, and Yellow Wings had disappeared without a trace. We guessed he'd been caught somewhere in the neighborhood, and that our weapon had been confiscated. The game of Germans and partisans, without the helmet and the gun, lost its charm, and our hearts grew heavy with boredom. Ah, if only Weiser would come, just as he had that day, and bring us something interesting, something that would make war fun again. But Weiser didn't come. His feat at the soccer match was the last sign he would give us; he was now waiting for us to come to him. This idea ripened in us very slowly, however. One day, Piotr, lying in the shade of a hazel bush, said, "The beach is closed, the soccer field useless, so what is there for us to do around here?" It wasn't clear what he meant by *here* — the cemetery or the whole town, which was gasping its last beneath the blazing sun — but it was from this remark, addressed to no one in particular, thrown simply into the air, that our adventure with Weiser really began. After a moment of silence, Szymek spat out some chewed grass, as he always did, and said, "Weiser could come up with something." And we agreed. Yes, Weiser could come up with something for sure, because he was a genius; we were convinced of that now. But how to approach him without looking like fools unable to do anything for themselves? Maybe he would share an idea with us—not a game of tag or catch, of course, nothing ordinary or everyday, because the heat had increased our natural contempt for the ordinary and the everyday. We needed novelty. Who knows, perhaps this was an unconscious desire for risk, which can be seen in any young boy who gazes at a map or reads *The Count of Monte Cristo.* The yearning for novelty filled our stifled souls. And we realized suddenly that only Weiser could provide us with that novelty. "We'll have to start following them," Szymek decided. Piotr informed us that Elka and Weiser were no longer going to the airfield, but to Brentowo, or beyond, where they'd disappear for hours on end. So it was settled that first thing the next morning we'd hide behind the corner of our building and find out exactly what they were up to, where they went, and why they were avoiding us.

It wasn't as easy as we'd thought. From the start, we had problems. Szymek left his French binoculars at home and had to go back for them at the very moment Weiser emerged from the stair-well with Elka. Then those two, as if on purpose, changed their plans that day, and instead of going straight down the street toward Bukowa Hill, as we thought they would, they turned into a lane between garden plots and headed for the airfield. Also, it is difficult to follow someone without being noticed when you're in a large group, and that day there were five or six of us. Every few minutes we had to stop and tell someone to be quiet, and each time we'd lose sight of them. At the No. 12 loop, Szymek caught up with us. "Didn't I tell you?" he said triumphantly. "They're going to the airfield." No one bothered to point out to him that he had said nothing of the kind. I trembled with the hope of seeing the airplane game again, but Elka and Weiser went down the steps to the platform for the electric-train line that in those days bore the sign GDANSK AIRPORT. Before we knew it, they were on a blue-and-yellow train bound for Sopot, and that was that. "They made us look like jerks," sighed Piotr. "We might as well go home." We stood on the viaduct, waiting for an idea, but no idea came. Instead, we saw a plane taking off, its hoarse engine rattling.

"A biplane!" said Piotr.

"That's not a biplane, it's a crop duster," Szymek corrected him, and took his French binoculars from their case. "Let's have a look."

We lined up for the binoculars along the iron railing. The plane, gaining altitude, was leaving us, making for the bay. Szymek reluctantly shared his binoculars. Then the biplane, high enough, turned back toward the field, gliding, its engine off and its propeller sputtering *trak-trak trak-trak*. As the sickly green fuselage passed over the Zaspa cemetery— all we could see of the cemetery was a clump of trees—from a door came the opening puffball of a parachute. One, then another a few seconds later, then another after that, and two more, until five paratroopers were floating down toward the airfield. The plane passed over our heads, turned, straightened, then landed by the hangars. There was nothing unusual about this; every spring and summer, once or twice a week, paratroopers practiced here, and I remember the *trak-trak* of the biplane over our district in those days, like the refrain in an old movie. But we had nothing better to do just then, and it was fun watching the parachutes, so we stayed on the viaduct, and the biplane continued to take off and land, and the white puffballs opened in the sky, while every six minutes a blue-and-yellow train went past behind us, its cars inherited by our town from the Berlin metro.

Did our staying on the viaduct to watch the parachutes have any connection with Weiser? Yes and no. I mention this scene from that broiling summer because it came up once when I was talking to Piotr. Every year on All Souls' Day, I visit him at the cemetery, and when everyone is gone, all the grown-ups who believe in God but not in ghosts, when they've left their flowers, wreaths, black flags, and burning candles on the graves, I sit on his stone, and Piotr and I talk. Sometimes we even get into an argument over some unimportant detail, just as if we were back at school in Upper Wrzeszcz. One year, as I took a seat on the corner of the stone and was brushing away the dead leaves, Piotr suddenly asked me:

"What's new in town?"

"Nothing, really," I told him. "Just some fuss about the transportation system."

"What sort of fuss?"

"Not that it affects you—you're not going anywhere," I said, "but they're replacing the railroad."

"Replacing it?"

"The old trains, the ones from the Berlin metro, are being scrapped, and we'll have new ones, just like everywhere else in Poland, like Warsaw, Łódź, and Kraków. It's electric, too, but runs on three thousand volts, not nine hundred, like the old trains."

"Nine hundred?" said Piotr. "Our railroad ran on eight hundred volts."

"No, Piotr," I said. "You don't remember. It wasn't eight hundred volts, it was nine hundred."

"It was eight hundred," Piotr insisted.

"Nine hundred," I said.

"Eight hundred," he said.

"They're replacing all the third rails," I said, "so we can connect directly with Bydgoszcz."

"That's no argument. They would have to do that anyway. I'm telling you, the old railroad ran on eight hundred."

And so we argued, like two good friends. Meanwhile the last of the old trains continue to run, at odd intervals, between Gdańsk and Wejherowo, because the work is still in progress. And when I made my way down the winding cemetery path into an ever larger sea of candles, I remembered that day when we stood leaning against the iron railing on the viaduct watching the paratroopers and not thinking about Weiser, as the blue-and-yellow cars inherited from the Berlin metro went flashing past behind us. Piotr's memory, it turned out, was better than mine: the old railroad actually ran on eight hundred volts.

The biplane made its final landing on the grass, the paratroopers vanished into the depths of a hangar, and the binoculars from the Battle of Verdun were taken out of Piotr's hands and put back into their leather case. Szymek sent a gob of spit over the railing. "There's nothing for us here," he said. "Let's go home." And the conversation again turned to Weiser. I don't remember exactly what we said, but there was a heated debate about how to approach him, how to surprise him, how to get him to do something with us.

Two more days went by, excruciatingly boring, empty days. Weiser kept giving us the slip. He would disappear somewhere near the church of the Resurrection Fathers, or we would lose sight of him at the top of Bukowa Hill. We decided to lie in wait for him by the old embankment, because if it was true that he and Elka were going to Brentowo and beyond, they would have to come that way. From early morning we sat in the cemetery, at the corner beside the dead railroad line. Now, as I try to piece together the events of that day, many blanks remain, but that whole line, though it was no longer in operation, emerges from the mist with the clarity of a map. It ran in a southeasterly arc. Branching off from the main artery at the Gdańsk Airport stop, it crossed Grunwald Avenue, Wit Stwosz Street, and Polanka Street on the abutments of three blown-up bridges, then went along the edge of the forest by the church of the Resurrection Fathers, through a gorge cut deep in the hills, past the Brentowo cemetery, and over another set of broken arches it jumped the Rembiechowo highway and entered, less than half a kilometer farther on, at the height of the insane asylum, an even deeper gorge, just beyond the place where the Strzyża flows under the embankment into a narrow tunnel. The line, after that, went into unknown territory; all we knew was that there, too, it was accompanied by blown-up bridges all the way, with the stubbornness of an incomprehensible logic. Why, of all these blown-up bridges, were the only survivors the ones that served absolutely no purpose, such as the bridge between Father Dudak's church and the Brentowo cemetery, fantastically high, joining two slopes filled with broom and wild raspberry bushes?

We settled down to wait for Weiser in an empty crypt overgrown with nettles and ferns, which made an excellent hiding place. Szymek was glued to the binoculars, and the rest of us lay on our stomachs and chewed blades of grass, and occasionally someone would say a lazy word or two over the hum of wasps and bees. Gradually the heat worked its way into the crypt, and the odor of damp, cool cement was replaced with the stifling smell of flowers. The sun was high, and around noon Szymek put down the binoculars and said, "God knows why we're lying here. If Weiser hasn't turned up by now, he won't be turning up at all." He'd probably gone someplace else, or skirted this spot, going by way of the quarry and the hill that we called a volcano because of its conical shape and sunken top. Or perhaps Weiser was now sitting in the bushes at the airfield with Elka, waiting for a plane to land. Anything was possible, with him. I began thinking that in a moment we might hear the clatter of iron wheels coming around the bend, a long whistle, the screech of metal, and see hissing clouds of steam as a locomotive appeared with Weiser, in an engineer's cap, at the controls. He'd stop, climb down the rungs of a narrow iron ladder, and wave for us to get on board quickly, because the train was leaving. The pistons would start thumping faster, steam would roar through the valves, and we'd be on our way, past the Strzyża and the last blown-up red-brick bridge, to where there would be, finally, real tracks and real switches. In those days I believed that the embankment led to such a place, and I imagined us riding with Weiser, chugging through abandoned little stations and by rusted semaphores and linemen's huts covered with rank weeds. Weiser, like the captain of a ship, would send me up to watch ahead for junctions hidden under clumps of grass, because treacherous dead-end tracks might branch off from them. All this I said out loud, I really don't know why—and no one laughed or thought it silly. What were blown-up bridges and missing rails to someone like Weiser? *His* locomotive could reach us here, in puffs of steam, and take us on a journey into the unknown. But Weiser didn't come, and time slowed to a painful crawl.

We sent someone—I no longer remember who—to Cyrson's for orangeade, and someone else for rolls or anything to eat he could smuggle out of his house. I can't remember how many bottles of orangeade we had, or if they were all opened properly. Everyone liked my idea about Weiser and the locomotive, and I had to tell the whole thing over again, with each of my listeners adding something of his own, and that's how our story of the phantom locomotive got started. While the few remaining drops of orangeade were drying in the sticky green bottles and red ants were dragging away crumbs of bread as we watched, we invented more and more details for the story, touches of genius, we thought. The locomotive and its engineer appeared only at the full moon. Headlights blazing, and in a shower of sparks, the locomotive came slowly from the direction of Wrzeszcz, crossing the broken bridges in light, easy leaps. At the small bridge near the church of the Resurrection Fathers, it stopped for a moment, and a tiny man in a frock coat scuttled out of the sacristy. He approached the panting train and handed the engineer a purse full of clinking coins. The locomotive continued on, saluting the midget with a short toot, and he trotted off into the dark pines on the other side of the embankment. For what did he pay the engineer? The reason will be revealed. . . . The locomotive, now entering the deep gorge, picked up speed, shot beneath a stone arch, and came to a sudden screeching halt at the edge of the cemetery, exactly where we were sitting and making all this up. Weiser pulled a lever and gave three piercing blasts on the whistle. In the light of the moon, the crypts all opened, the cracked tombstones moved aside, and the dead, bones clicking, climbed out of their graves and made for the train. When they were assembled, the engineer let them in the coal car and continued on over the next blown-up bridges and grass-covered junctions and missing switches. And this happened every month at the full moon, no matter what time of year. The engineer would return just before daybreak, the weary passengers would go back to their crypts, and the locomotive would vanish near the airport, where the old embankment met the real railroad. Some people living in the more distant suburbs had seen these things and, scared out of their wits, confided in a few trusted friends. And there were, of course, a few brave souls who wanted to solve the mystery. But you pay a high price for curiosity. One night, the sexton's brother jumped into the coal car and went off with the dead in the direction of the Strzyża. But he could not tell what he saw, because when the train came back and stopped at the cemetery, the skeletons grabbed his arms and took him with them into one of the crypts. From that time on, you could hear, on windless nights, the sexton's half-dead brother crying, "Let me out! Let me out!" But no one knew where the skeletons hid him, and anyway the cry was so dreadful that no one had the courage to go looking for him.

I may not have all the details right, but now, as in the main office, where we were waiting for the verdict on our written statements, I think this story is no worse than the one Miss Pawłowska used to read to us in our Polish class. That story takes place at night, too, and the dead man rises from his grave and speaks to the living. We weren't afraid of the cemetery, and it was the middle of the day, but after we'd imagined everything, spun it out, and told it in a chorus of mingled and alternating voices, and after the finished tale filled our crypt with silence, we had an eerie feeling, as if it were true that when something is said, contrary to all common sense, it will come to pass.

Meanwhile, no Weiser. Opposite the cemetery, on the other side of the embankment, a Brentowo farmer was mowing the grass with a scythe. A horse, unharnessed from the cart, was nipping at the clover, and once in a while the man would stop, straighten his back, and with a whetstone from his pocket hone the blade. The metallic sound traveled lethargically through the summer air. There were fewer of us now, because every minute someone lost faith and went home, by way of Bukowa Hill, abandoning hope and his place in the crypt.

"Ask, and it shall be given you," said Szymek weightily, the way Father Dudak did.

"Do you think," said Piotr with surprise, "God cares about such things?"

"What things?" I asked.

"Well, like having Weiser come, if we asked really hard," explained Piotr, but Szymek quickly put his mind at ease.

"Ridiculous! The Lord has more important matters to worry about. Anyway, Weiser's a Jew."

"Jesus was a Jew, too," said Piotr, not giving up, "and that means the Lord God, His Father, is also a Jew, doesn't it? Just as your father's Polish"—he turned to Szymek—"so you were born Polish. But if he was German, you would have been born German. Isn't that right?"

"If my aunt was a man, she'd be my uncle," Szymek snapped, and the subject was dropped.

In the distance, beyond the Niedźwiednik hills, a plane started droning. We sat in silence, just the three of us now. I thought, and they probably did, too, that Weiser wouldn't be coming this way today, and we could go home, and if we hurried, we could return the orangeade bottles to Cyrson's before it closed. The sun stood lower in the sky, and the pines threw long shadows across the embankment, like planks across a brook. The trunks, lit from behind, were an unnatural red, as in a sidewalk artist's painting. The farmer had finished raking the cut grass into small piles, and now harnessed the horse and rode off toward some buildings. The smell of hay and animal sweat. The air was still, as it had been through all those days, from the time the fish soup filled the bay. "We could come here at night," said Piotr, breaking the silence. "What for?" asked Szymek. To see if it was true, Piotr said, that the dead left their graves at midnight, or at least talked to each other. People said they did, and maybe they knew, but maybe they were simply afraid and had never seen for themselves. We could find out the truth. "All right," agreed Szymek, "but who's going? Because only one can go to the cemetery at night. The dead can tell if there's more than one, just like animals, and then it won't work." We decided to draw lots; we'd all three go together, of course, but at the edge of the cemetery the one who won would cross himself and continue alone. He'd wait at least fifteen minutes at the very center, near the stone angels with the broken wings. But the lot-drawing didn't take place.

"Look," whispered Szymek, crawling out of the crypt. "They're coming. There!"

Indeed, Weiser was walking along the embankment, and right behind him, holding a package, Elka skipped like a little girl. We scrambled out of the crypt and hid behind a hawthorn bush, which was no more than five meters from the embankment. They passed us and turned down a path that led to the firing range. As soon as they vanished into a gully, we set off after them. This was the same gully in which, much later, we ran into M-ski pursuing the *Parnassius Apollo* with his net. We were like hunting hounds let off the leash at long last, catching the scent, rushing forward in order not to lose it. Where the gully ended, the path went uphill. We clung to the slope and watched as Weiser and Elka reached the flat top of the ridge. In strict observance of the rules of war, we snuck up on them, which wasn't easy, considering the advantage of height they had over us. From behind a spreading broom, prone, we observed their every move. They were completely relaxed. They sat facing the bay, discussing something, probably of little importance, judging by Elka's face. We concluded that they were waiting for some signal, something important that would release both them and us from this inaction, but today I know that they were simply waiting for the sun to set. Because what happened afterward could not have happened in the presence of the sun.

The orange sphere finally disappeared behind the trees, the sky glowed deep red, and, against this red, black dots of insects darted at dizzying speed. Weiser got up, gave Elka his hand, and they went on toward the firing range. We trailed them like ghosts—swiftly and silently—through a grove of old trees, around the hollow behind the firing range, uphill on a narrow path between mournful beeches and hazels, then across the Rembiechowo highway and into endless forest, in an unfamiliar direction, away from the farm buildings of Brentowo. The air was heavy with the scent of resin and dried bark, and there was not the slightest breeze. In the dark of the moonless night, with only the stars looking down on us in silence, the old brickworks suddenly towered before us, a colossus, its chimney like a spire, its windows like yawning pits, and its exposed rafters like the ribs of a great beast.

We stood, uncertain, at the edge of the trees, until the booming sound of Weiser's voice returned us to reality. He was talking to Elka, and she was answering in short phrases. Their words came from below, amplified by the echoes of empty rooms. It was clear that they were in a cellar. We tiptoed past wheelbarrows and the mouth of a kiln. The part of the building where the voices came from had a wooden floor, and the wood was rotten. Taking our shoes off and carrying them, to be as quiet as possible, we crept up to an open trapdoor and saw steps leading down. A match suddenly flared below us, and a candle shone, which Elka put by the wall. We pressed our faces to the floorboards, and luckily the cracks in them were wide enough for us to see everything. Elka sat down cross-legged, near the candle. Sitting on the dirt floor in the middle of the cellar was Weiser, bent over, as if he were saying his prayers. They fell silent, and I swallowed hard, feeling that something terrible was about to happen. I could hear my own blood coursing like Niagara Falls in every vein.

Elka unwrapped the package. By the flickering light of the candle I saw in her hands a peculiar musical instrument, a panpipe, which she put to her lips, waiting for a sign from Weiser. At last, when he raised his head, we heard the first notes, strangely distant, as if someone were playing on a mountaintop, playing a slow, plaintive melody. The instrument had a soft and rippling tone. Weiser stood up. He raised his arms, and held that position for a while. The melody grew more animated; passages followed fast on one another, but kept returning to the same theme. And Weiser, the Weiser we beheld on Corpus Christi through a cloud of incense, the Weiser of the airfield and the Oliwa zoo, the Weiser who won the soccer match against the army boys, now danced in the candlelight, to a tune played on a ridiculous panpipe. He danced in the cellar of the abandoned brickworks, and kicked up a cloud of dust, threw his arms here, there, and turned his head in every possible direction. He danced faster, in a frenzy, as if the melody, accelerating, held him in its power, and he leaped and twitched, his eyes half-closed, like a drunken guest at a wedding, or a madman, or one possessed, for whom limits and fatigue do not exist. On and on he danced, and our eyes grew wider and wider, for this was no longer Weiser; it was a total stranger. Gone was our schoolmate who lived in No. 11, on the second floor, the grandson of Abraham Weiser the tailor. In his place—a frighteningly alien presence that under these special circumstances had assumed human form, which clearly hampered its movements, and the presence struggled against the shackles of Weiser's body.

The music stopped. The effect was even more uncanny than if the sounds of an organ or hunting horns had come from Elka's pipes. Weiser fell to the floor. Red dust hung above him, and in the candlelight I saw whirling red motes. Then, in that ominous silence, Weiser opened his mouth, as if to gasp for air, and we heard a deep voice, a man's voice, speaking fitfully in an unknown tongue. I felt a hand on my back, but it wasn't a hand, I know, it was my terror, because of the voice, stern and strange, that came from Weiser's throat without his knowledge. His eyes were shut. His fists clenched and loosened with each word. He looked exhausted, as though he was pushing out syllables in pain, against his will. Only when he stopped—and he looked like a corpse now—did I glance at Elka. She sat against the wall, motionless, not Elka anymore, a wooden doll, and her eyes, fixed on Weiser, were like the glass eyes of a puppet. They didn't move, didn't blink, when finally he got to his knees and moved the candle more to the center. And then it happened. Weiser stood, stretched out his arms as if for flight, and stared at the candle flame. I don't know how much time passed, but the next thing I noticed was that his feet were not touching the ground. At first I thought I was seeing things, but no, his feet were clearly floating above the dirt floor. He hung in the air some thirty or forty centimeters from the ground and was slowly rising higher. "Christ!" I heard Szymek whisper. "Christ, what's he doing?" Weiser was levitating, that's what he was doing, and his body began to lose its stiffness. Piotr gripped my shoulder.

But what had actually happened? The thing we

saw in the cellar of the abandoned brickworks, was it only an illusion, our imagination, a trick of the flickering candlelight? Twenty-three years later, I asked Szymek this very question. We were sitting opposite each other in his sunny apartment, in a different city—and in a different era. Outside, below, people were marching with signs that said: WE DEMAND REGISTRATION, THE PRESS LIES! and LONG LIVE GDAŃSK! I also saw, in the middle of the throng, a large portrait of the Pope carried by a young girl. Szymek, of course, was not the same old Szymek with the French binoculars from the Battle of Verdun. Still, I hadn't expected such a change; it was more than a matter of twenty-three years or the kilometers that lay between our two cities. He was interested in current events and asked me for many particulars about what was happening in Gdańsk. I explained what things were like, describing the scenes at the shipyard gate and the wooden cross to which people had attached pictures of the Black Madonna, and all the flowers laid around it.

"This time they didn't shoot," he said with the pleasure of a child. "But what happens next?"

That I didn't know, nor was anyone from the Tatras to the beach at Jelitkowo able to predict what would come next. But it annoyed me that my questions about Weiser went unanswered, just as did the great political questions that commentators around the world were racking their brains over.

"Is it really so important," said Szymek, "after all these years, what happened then, particularly now, when such things are in the news?"

I could find no words to tell him that, yes, to me it was more important than anything.

"But what actually happened?" I asked, not giving up. "Did Weiser levitate, or did we suffer some kind of mass hallucination?"

Szymek opened a bottle of beer—the beer is better in the south—and cocked his head skeptically. His voice, as always, was even.

"If you read in a book that God appeared to the author in a pillar of fire and a noise of wings, you don't know whether it really happened or the author only thought it did. Assuming," he added, tilting his glass, "the author isn't trying to put one over on you."

"But that time in the cellar," I said, "did Weiser float in the air or didn't he?"

Szymek lit a cigarette.

"I don't know," he answered after a while. "But mass hallucination is more common than levitation, don't you think?"

And that's the way it was throughout my stay at his house, the only visit I paid him in all those years. Szymek would not commit himself about Weiser, and answered all my questions with "Maybe yes, maybe no," "It happened so long ago," and "Our memory plays tricks on us, doesn't it?" When he heard I'd gone to see Elka in Mannheim three years before, he asked what kind of car she had and how she was doing. He didn't ask—wasn't interested—if she had had anything to say on the subject of Weiser. There was one thing Szymek remembered well, and that was the instrument Elka played in the cellar of the abandoned brickworks. "A panpipe, an unusual sound, eerie," he said, smiling. "I wonder where she got a panpipe."

I knew where, having looked into that the year I went through Weiser's school records. I even saw our indefatigable music teacher, who said that, yes, the panpipe had been taken from the glass case that held the school's collection of folk instruments, a wonderful collection, though why that had been taken and not the xylophone, ukulele, balalaika, or Scandinavian violin, for example, was beyond her. "Who would need a panpipe?" she exclaimed, spreading her arms, which were bent from years of waving at chorus practice. "Who would know how to play it?" But I didn't tell Szymek this. As we drank the last of the beer, with the hum of traffic and the chirping of birds coming through the open window, Szymek's wife brought in a tray of sand-

wiches, a tray big as a tablecloth, and I finally asked
him what he thought about that day by the Strzyża,
when Weiser spoke to us for the last time, and
why Elka showed up a week later, and Weiser didn't.
And what he thought about her amnesia, which
remained permanent wherever Weiser was con-
cerned. First Szymek changed the glasses, because
in place of the beer a bottle of homemade wine
now stood on the table.

Yes, he, too, had puzzled over that, privately,
many years later. Everything indicated that Weiser
possessed hypnotic powers of some kind. That trick
with the panther, for example. He must have used
it on people, too. Why did he need Elka? Obviously
he was using her for experiments, to test his ability,
which was still developing then, unfolding, being
discovered. There, in the cellar of the abandoned
brickworks, Weiser experimented with Elka, and
even we, as spectators, fell under his extraordinary
power of suggestion. He didn't levitate, he only
pretended that he was levitating, and made Elka
and us believe it. Psychology knows of such cases
of suggestion. The mechanism is relatively simple.
The explosions? That, too, can be explained. Weiser,
after all, was raised by a solitary, eccentric old man,
and could have had all kinds of persecution com-
plexes. He was a pyromaniac, that much is clear.
And those visual effects? Simple, no mystery, he

read a couple of books. Why did he and Elka lie down at the end of the runway? That was to train her to resist fear, because anyone who has lain beneath the belly of a landing plane won't be afraid of hypnosis or being put into a trance. At the Strzyża, on the last day of our vacation, Elka was simply swept away by the current, which we failed to notice, and Weiser, realizing what had happened, hid and waited for us to leave, then started searching for her himself. Except that he overestimated his strength and, while diving for her body in the pond nearby, through which the Strzyża flows, drowned in the most ordinary way, and the water carried his body into the sewer that goes under the town. That's the only possible explanation. But Elka, by some miracle, didn't drown; the current carried her into rushes on the riverbank, and there she lay until the militiamen and the dogs found her. It was foolish of Weiser. He probably couldn't even swim. Remember, he never went with us to Jelitkowo.

How did Elka survive for three days in the rushes? You'd probably have to know a lot of biology to answer that one. Such cases have been documented. Anyway, if he hadn't been brought up by that crazy tailor, which was no upbringing at all, Weiser would have gone on the stage or into the circus, where his talent would have won him applause and renown. So in a sense he was a victim of the war, suffering the psychological damage of orphanhood. Did he ever think about his parents? He must have. And who knows what old Weiser told the boy about them? That miserable old face reproaching people for no other reason than that they were alive—an unhealthy face. The child was clearly obsessed with things German; the arsenal he collected at the brickworks is the best proof of that. He wanted to kill them, and what he did with weapons was in preparation. Consider whom he used for a target when we went to the brickworks later on. Those effigies leave no room for doubt. An overheated imagination, an uncommon cleverness, a child's naïveté combined with a hypnotic ability that must have frightened him far more than it did Elka. All this made David Weiser what he was.

Over the third glass of wine, Szymek stopped his monologue. There were things I wanted to ask him. For example, why was he so sure Weiser couldn't swim? Weiser might have been as good a swimmer as he was a soccer player. And why did Szymek think the current carried Elka away, without our noticing? Weiser and Elka disappeared at the same time, after all. What Szymek said didn't make sense. And even if Weiser drowned, his body couldn't have got into the sewer, because the entrance to the sewer, at the end of the pond, was covered with an iron grate. But at that point Szymek and his wife asked me about Gdańsk, and especially about the monument that was being built at the shipyard gate, in the very place where the shots were fired. They asked if Piotr's name would be on it. A difficult question, after what his parents had gone through: the night burial, armed grave-diggers, and Piotr's body in a plastic bag dropped into a hole in the ground. I doubted that the monument, big and magnificent as it would be, could pay them for that winter. "That's not the point," said Szymek, losing patience. "You're right, it isn't," I replied, and remembered Piotr's mother telling me that he couldn't stand the sight of the helicopters circling the town that day, and had set off for Gdańsk on foot—the trams had already stopped running—to see what was going on. "They killed him from a helicopter," she insisted, even though eyewitnesses told her that he had got between the crowd and the soldiers, and by accident a bullet hit him in the head, from the left. She waved her hand and said it wasn't true; he was shot from a helicopter. And she became even more annoyed at the mention of soldiers. In her opinion, they were only militiamen dressed as soldiers. So I told about the monument, and Szymek and his wife listened attentively.

And Weiser? He left our conversation, evaporated, as if he'd never been, and when I was sitting in the train, swaying to the steady rhythm of the wheels over switches and ties, it seemed to me that I was riding that nonexistent line across the ten blown-up bridges and past the Brentowo cemetery with the small brick church hidden behind trees, and that Weiser was the engineer, wearing an engineer's cap, in a cloud of incense that smelled of eternity.

Meanwhile, the janitor was called into the headmaster's study. "Intolerable," I heard M-ski's voice say, "that these brats keep lying! I told you that stiff measures were needed from the start. I know the little villains inside out. And you," he said to the janitor, "will have to stay. This will take a little longer." The janitor muttered something under his breath, and other mumbling came from the depths of the study, including M-ski's familiar phrase, "We'll do what we have to do." Piotr was summoned. A contradiction in our written statements, I thought; that had to be the reason M-ski was so angry. Yes, of course, it was the dress, or the scrap of Elka's dress, red, that Szymek had mentioned to satisfy them, saying that we burned it after the last explosion. It wasn't in my statement or in Piotr's, so now they were going to ask about that dress, that scrap. Who found it, where, and when. We'd blundered, we should have settled on the details while the janitor was out of the room; then each of us could say the same thing now, and that would be the end of the interrogation, with their believing it happened exactly the way they thought. But the janitor made himself comfortable in his chair and clearly wasn't going to leave us alone again. On the radio Władysław Gomułka's speech was just over, and there were cheers and deafening applause. Next, operetta music, a painfully thin, woman's voice wailing, "Oh, oh, I lo-o-ove you so!" while my leg went numb and the pain in my left foot wouldn't stop twinging. I owed that pain to Weiser, and in a sense still do. Whenever rain clouds gather in the sky, I look at the small scar below my ankle and know I'll be limping soon. But I mustn't get ahead of myself. Let me return to the abandoned brick-works, because not everything has been explained.

"Christ," whispered Szymek, "what's he doing?" Piotr gripped my shoulder, and the next moment we heard a loud cracking of wood. Down we went, splin-tered boards and all, with a great crash, on top of Weiser and Elka. The candle went out, but I knew they were among us, very near. They were waiting for us to speak. Finally, Piotr, who was the first to dig himself out of the pile of broken boards, said timidly:

"Elka, don't be angry, we only . . ." But his words stuck in his throat, because something moved a little among the boards.

"Anyone have a light?" came Weiser's voice, betraying no anger or impatience. "If you do, use it!"

Szymek took a lighter from his pocket—he had stolen it from his older brother at the very beginning of the vacation—and a feeble flame lit up the cellar. The steps were smashed in the middle. To get out, we had to put together something that would serve as a ladder and set it against a wall. Weiser directed this task, and when we were all upstairs, he looked at us and asked:

"Do you know how to keep your mouths shut?"

We answered not in words but by nodding.

"All right, then," he said after a pause. "Be here tomorrow at six, but only the three of you."

So, unexpectedly, we had achieved our goal: Weiser was inviting us to join him. Curiously, as we went back the way we'd come, toward Brentowo, none of us wanted to talk about what we had seen at the abandoned brickworks. Today I know the reason: it was simply fear. Forget the cloud of incense, the fish soup, the jet landing, the panther, the soccer match, and that excursion, when for the first time I heard of Schopenhauer and saw where the German armored car stood during the siege of the Gdańsk post office. Forget all that—and in any case we didn't connect these things, at the time, in a chain that led to Weiser—it was enough to have seen him floating above the cellar floor. Suddenly Weiser, first the taunted Jew and then the animal charmer and soccer wizard, was a totally different person. It is hard to describe what we felt. Because it wasn't simply fear, as I wrote a moment ago. No. Sometimes, if I drink too much, I have this peculiar dream. I'm in the kitchen of my mother's apartment. I'm standing by the window, and behind me Piotr is putting a blackened kettle on the stove to heat water. I turn around and see not Piotr but a complete stranger. I go up to him, demand an explanation, but the unknown man, instead of speaking, smiles. The worst thing is that there is something of Piotr in that smile, the same curl of the upper lip, and I don't know what this means. That's similar to what we felt then. The Weiser we had known all those years at school, then more and more differently after we encountered him on Corpus Christi, the day our Sunday school diplomas were handed out, was now a stranger. He was Weiser, and he wasn't Weiser. But what had he become, at the moment he ceased to be himself? Or perhaps there was no particular moment of change, perhaps he had been pretending all along to be an ordinary boy. But how were we to know that then if even today I cannot answer the question?

We walked on in silence, and the fear that he would suddenly appear before us in the starlight, against the black wall of the forest—appear as he had done in the cellar, a meter or more above the ground—that fear kept our lips closed. Down from the ridge of the moraine, we entered the gully. It was even darker there. We could see, at the far end, the blacker silhouette of the Brentowo church, and, against it, tiny glittering golden specks.

"Christ!" said Szymek. "Falling stars!" But it wasn't stars. A swarm of fireflies hung in the air above us like golden rain, and the night was so still, we could hear ourselves breathing. "I thought," said Szymek, "they only shine in June."

It really was odd. Never before or since have I seen such a great cloud of fireflies on a July night in our district.

"Those are the souls of the dead," whispered Piotr, perfectly serious.

"The souls of the dead in fireflies?" snorted Szymek. "Who told you that?"

But Piotr was reluctant to speak. Only after we reached the railroad embankment near the church did he tell us that when a penitent soul enters the body of an insect, it begins to shine. Fireflies ordinarily don't endure this long before they die, and that's why you see them for so short a time, at the beginning of summer. "These must be the souls of great sinners," Piotr said, "to be still shining."

Szymek was indignant, as if the argument involved his binoculars or the rules of soccer.

"That's stupid," he said. "You can't see a soul, souls are invisible! Father Dudak told us that in Sunday school."

"He said souls were immortal," Piotr retorted, "not that you couldn't see one."

"He said they were immortal *and* invisible. Didn't he say that?" Szymek turned to me for corroboration. I wasn't sure what the truth of the matter was—nor am I sure today. Can you see a soul? If so, it ought to be visible when a person dies, when it leaves the body, which in a day or two will be put in the earth. But what form does the soul assume? A white puff of vapor? A soft shaft of light that moves upward without attenuating? I don't know. And they wanted *me* to settle their dispute, as if I were a theologian or the Pope.

"Father Dudak doesn't really know," I said. "He only says what he says because . . ."

"Because what? Why? Tell us!" they pressed me, challenged me.

"Because that's what he was taught at the seminary," I explained, "and that's what the bishop tells him to say, and a priest has to do what a bishop tells him, just as in the army."

"Are you trying to tell us that a priest doesn't know about souls?"

"No one does," I said confidently. "You only find out when you die."

We looked over at the cemetery. The broken statues and tombstones looked like people bent in prayer.

"That's awful," Szymek sighed. "To have to die to find out something." We nodded.

At that moment the Brentowo bells began to ring, and a powerful voice resounded through the forest, through the night, like a siren. "Christ!" it said, and it was Szymek yelling Christ, the third time now. "There's someone in the cemetery!" My first thought was that Weiser was playing a trick on us, or testing us, to see if we would run home, over Bukowa Hill. He could have taken a shortcut and got here a quarter of an hour before us. Then another idea came to me. It wasn't Weiser's style, this sudden alarm tearing the warm night among the quiet pines, this racket beneath the starry dome of heaven. And in fact it wasn't Weiser who had pulled the ropes under the moldering beam of the belfry: it was Yellow Wings. As soon as we recognized him from our hiding place behind a hazel bush, the suggestion was made that we go home. "He got us into trouble before," Szymek reminded us. "Someone's sure to come running from the rectory, and we'll be blamed." But I didn't think so. "Now, in the middle of the night?" Piotr pointed at the building beside the church. "Look!" There among the branches a light went on in one window, then in another. Meanwhile Yellow Wings was jumping up and down, sitting on his haunches, swaying, all in time with the clamoring bells. He looked like a marionette dangling on strings, a little ridiculous and a little sinister. He no longer wore his hospital robe, but was dressed in a denim shirt and trousers, no doubt stolen. We couldn't take our eyes off him. With each pull on the ropes, he said something to himself, but his words were lost in three-part clangor. Perhaps it was those bells that kept us rooted to the spot, rooted even when we saw two men coming quickly from the rectory— the sexton and the local priest, who was not at all like our Father Dudak. Yellow Wings, it seemed, had wanted to lure them out of the house, because he waited until they were very close before he let go of the ropes, leaped into a nearby hedge, and fled toward Brentowo. "Reverend Father," puffed the sexton, "you go back and call the militia, and I'll run after him!" The two men separated; the sexton, panting, gave chase to the runaway, while the priest trotted back to the rectory. We couldn't leave now, that was clear. What happened to Yellow Wings didn't really concern us, but we had to see how this episode would end.

We followed the sexton down a barely distinguishable path that lost its way among nettles and ferns. Yellow Wings had a thirty-meter lead and better knowledge of the terrain. He jumped from bush to bush, hid among the tombstones, and whenever we lost him, he would suddenly spring up, as if out of the earth itself, and run on. He was playing with the sexton. At last he reached the edge of the cemetery, stood on a split stone, and screamed in defiance: "Eeeee—eeee—eehee—eeeee!" The sexton quickened his pace, but Yellow Wings was already far away, running toward the first of the Brentowo houses, where people were peering out of their windows to see what the disturbance was. "Stop him! Stop him!" cried the sexton. "He's mad!" And more and more windows lighted up, as if there were a fire or a war had started.

Yellow Wings ran to the first house and scrambled up the lightning rod onto the steep roof. At the very top of it he spread his arms, as if to greet the crowd that was beginning to form below. Men in pajamas and slippers, or barefoot and in underpants, were pointing him out to each other. "People," the sexton said, running up, "that's the one who's been frightening your wives and children in the cemetery! He escaped from the asylum! We have to catch him! The militia's coming, someone get a ladder, quick, or he'll escape again! People, what are you waiting for?" But no one was eager to grapple with a madman, on a roof. The men stood undecided, shifting from foot to foot and looking at one another. A few of the wives came nearer. The whispering and giggling grew in volume, until suddenly Yellow Wings spoke.

It was more music than speech; whole sentences were sung, rising and falling one after the other, with short pauses in between. "Woe unto ye, inhabitants of the coast of the sea! Woe! The word of the Lord entereth my ear, and my lips will speak. The day of the Lord is near, it is at hand, and maketh haste, and, yea, the man of power shall weep bitterly!" Saying this, Yellow Wings stood on tiptoe, lifted his arms, and his long curly hair was like the beard of Moses, which I remembered well from the picture Father Dudak showed us at Sunday school of the crossing of the Red Sea. "He'll fall," "No, he won't," "He will," went the whispers below, but Yellow Wings' next harangue silenced everyone. "And I will visit terror upon men, that they walk like the blind, and their blood will be dust, and their innards mud! Neither silver nor gold will save you in the day of the Lord's wrath, for

His fire will consume the land utterly, and all the inhabitants thereof will be destroyed!"

As the word *destroyed* resounded especially long and loud, I saw some of the women cross themselves, and the men looked up, as if they were watching a comet in the sky. "And I caused a drought upon the land, and upon the mountains, and upon all that the earth brings forth and the labor of thy hands. . . ." His voice grew even more powerful, and rang like all three Brentowo bells at once. "Woe unto ye, inhabitants of the coast of the sea! Therefore doth the heaven above withhold its dew, and the earth her fruit." The sexton stood there with his arms folded like Pontius Pilate, until finally, white with helpless rage, when the next phrase of the chant concluded, he burst out: "People! Christians! Don't listen to him. He's an Antichrist, a heretic, a madman, and it's a mortal sin to listen to such things. Catch him! Come! Now!" But no one moved. Yellow Wings had won.

"Do you think to dwell," he bellowed to the crowd below, "in tiled houses while the house of the Lord lies in ruins? You thought to build much, but lo, it was as nothing, for I did blow upon it, and it withered. So saith the Lord of Hosts: because of my house that lies in ruins while you build, each of you, every man, his own house!"

From the direction of town we heard the wail

of a siren, and a minute later headlights appeared on the Rembiechowo highway. "The militia!" exclaimed the sexton with joy. "Surround the house so he can't escape!" But even now, no one rushed forward. Yellow Wings stretched out a hand toward the approaching car. "Woe unto him," he thundered, "who increaseth that which is not his! The heart sinks, the knees tremble, the loins are seized with pain, the face doth blacken." Four militiamen jumped from the car, armed with clubs and pistols. The officer in charge, a dark-haired lieutenant, shouted, "Disperse! Out of the way, citizens!" But Yellow Wings, who still had a chance to escape, given the darkness and his familiarity with the area, addressed the lieutenant instead, in a singsong howl: "Woe unto him who builds with blood, and establishes the city in iniquity! In the day of the Lord's sacrifice I will visit punishment upon all who clothe themselves in foreign garb! Woe, woe unto the city of blood! In it, all is deception and theft!"

The militiamen formed a huddle around the lieutenant, who gave them orders. He looked up at the roof, where Yellow Wings was hurling imprecations down on the men in uniform. "Your whelps they will perish by the sword! I will cease your plunder in the land, silence your emissaries! The worst of the nations will possess your gates! Thus will I humble your pride and power! Bitterness will be your portion, and you will seek peace, but there will be no peace! I will do unto you as you have done, and judge you by your own laws!"

"Down from there!" the sharp voice of the lieutenant broke in. "At once, or I'll have to use force!" "Thy minions are as the locust!" was Yellow Wings' melodious reply. "Because thou hast spoiled nations, nations shall make spoil of thee, on account of the blood that flowed and the violence done to the land!" We saw that two militiamen were going around to the back of the house, while the lieutenant drew his pistol from its holster. "Down from there," he repeated, "or I'll shoot!" "And I shall cast abomination upon thee," came Yellow Wings' answer, "and make thee vile and a fright, that whoever sees thee will flee from thee. And fire will eat thee, and the sword cut thee, and the locust consume thee!"

A shot rang out—the lieutenant had fired into the air, as a warning. The people gathered at the gate of the neighboring house, and all the faces in the windows flinched and drew back. Meanwhile, the two militiamen who had gone to the back of the house climbed onto the roof. Yellow Wings' moments of freedom seemed numbered. Again he lifted his arms high, as if calling on the stars as witness to his innocence, and, with a cry of "The Lord is my strength," turned to face the militiamen, who now were on the roof. Their white clubs, raised to strike, stood out against the black sky. But Yellow Wings did not have the spirit of Christ within him, for instead of submitting meekly to blows, he pushed both militiamen off the roof. Angry shouts and the sound of falling tiles accompanied Yellow Wings' new song. "The Lord is my strength! For he maketh my legs as the legs of the hind, and leadeth me over high places." With these words, he jumped from the roof onto the soft ground of the garden and quickly made for the cemetery. The two militiamen, somewhat the worse for wear, ran after him. "Stop!" cried the lieutenant. "Stop, or I'll shoot!" But Yellow Wings had no intention of stopping. A volley of shots rent the air, but they were fired upward, like the first one, as a warning.

And that would have been the end of it, if it weren't for the fact that the madman and his pursuers now came straight at us. We ran as fast as we could, but Yellow Wings was faster, and in no time we felt his breath on our necks. He said nothing, but seeing that we, too, were trying to escape, gestured that we should separate. But that was not possible, because from Bukowa Hill, at the opposite end of the cemetery, figures in flapping white coats were running toward us. To this day I don't know who called the asylum people, and particularly why they appeared from that direction, cutting off our retreat. Perhaps, after phoning the militia, the priest had also phoned the asylum. So we had after us not only the militia and the madman but also the men in white, who looked like ghosts among the tombstones. For the first time I knew what it was to be a cornered hunted animal, and frantically tried to think what sort of explanation we could give. Would they arrest us? Would we be treated as Yellow Wings' accomplices? The hunters closed in, and it seemed that nothing could save us now, when suddenly Piotr gripped my arm. "The crypt! They'll never find us there!" It was a brilliant idea. We rushed toward the embankment, to our hiding place, Yellow Wings right behind us. The entrance was ajar as usual, and we had no trouble crawling inside.

What else happened that evening, or, rather, that night? After all these years my memory tells me that when the hunt was over and I emerged from the crypt with Szymek and Piotr, leaving Yellow Wings there, and went over Bukowa Hill and up Kmieca Street, which leads from the forest to our building, and knocked on the door of my apartment, my father opened it in his pajamas, with belt in hand. Without a word he put me across his knee, and the number of blows that fell on my backside was astronomical. When his arm got tired, he rested and said, "This isn't because you came home late, it's because your mother's spent the last four hours crying her eyes out over you, you little bastard!" And that must have been the most affectionate thing my father ever said to me, because it stuck in my memory the best. But at the time, all I could think of was that we now had Weiser in the palm of our hand, or maybe he had us, though I didn't know how brief that would be. Why have I written about Yellow Wings? Why didn't I stop with the collapse of the rotten floor or with the fireflies? As if it had some connection with Weiser. But perhaps it did, because the next day, when the three of us met and it turned out that I wasn't the only one to have red welts on his behind, Piotr suggested we go to the crypt to see if Yellow Wings was there, and Szymek said we should tell Weiser what happened and ask him what he thought about madmen and this one in particular.

Curiously, when Weiser came out of the gate, not one of us went up to him, as if the meeting with him at the brickworks at six was a line we shouldn't cross. We didn't follow Elka either, when she ran out after him. Yesterday's events had woven the threads of an understanding between us, though it was a one-sided understanding. It was Weiser, after all, who'd told us to come, not we him. And that had to be respected. As soon as Elka had vanished beyond the bill post, Janek Lipski came up to us. He had been at the zoo with us and played in the celebrated match against the army boys.

"Well, did you finally see them?" Not counting us three, Janek had been the last to leave the crypt during the wait for Weiser.

"Oh, yeah," said Szymek. A silence followed, with looks of suspicion on both sides.

"So what were they up to?"

"Nothing much. It wasn't worth the wait. They went fishing in the clay pits."

"You're lying."

"Oh? Then you go follow them. We don't feel like it right now."

This argument prevailed. We didn't notice how Szymek's lie united us in secrecy on the subject of Weiser. But for the moment we had another matter to see to.

We found Yellow Wings in the crypt; he hadn't left his hiding place since the day before. That was evident from the way he bolted down the roll Piotr gave him. The hero of last night was shaking with fear. We couldn't understand how this extraordinary man, who'd spoken so beautifully and thrown the militiamen off the roof, had changed so much in less than twelve hours. When he saw our faces over him, he cringed and threw up an arm, as if expecting to be hit. He communicated with us in grunts and syllables—"eeh," "aan," "uhm"—and if it hadn't been for his performance yesterday and the time before that, when we ran into M-ski and his *Arnica montana,* if it hadn't been for those sublime, fervent, full-throated sentences, one would have thought that this unshaven man in tattered denim was a deaf-and-dumb tramp who had taken shelter in our crypt. Today I have an idea about the reason for this: I think Yellow Wings could speak only in poetry that threatened vengeance, death, and doom. This was his illness and his greatness both.

Piotr asked him if he wanted to stay there. He nodded. Szymek proposed we get some food. A smile, and instead of words of thanks, a click of approval deep in his throat. We divided the tasks. Piotr would take care of food supplies; Szymek would get some clothing; and I would bring cigarettes, because Yellow Wings indicated that need by urgent gesturing. We went back over Bukowa Hill to our respective homes, and it never crossed our minds that we were doing something against the law, something punishable. I don't mean to suggest that we defied the law in the name of the Christian spirit, about which Father Dudak so often reminded us. No, that wasn't true. On the other hand, I have to admit that had we stopped for a moment to think and realized we were assisting not only a dangerous lunatic but one who had assaulted militiamen, Piotr still would have stolen a loaf of bread, a yellow cheese, and some pork fat from the larder; Szymek still would have brought a pair of patched trousers and a checked flannel shirt; and I still would have contrived to get hold of a pack of Grunwald cigarettes, the kind my father smoked, sending me to Cyrson's to buy them for him, because in those days there were no newspaper-and-tobacco kiosks in our district. Yellow Wings beamed at us when we returned to the crypt with our arms full. He ate and smoked as if there were no tomorrow. And when Piotr pulled out of his canvas bag a bottle of orangeade for each of us, and two for Yellow Wings, and we drank that bubbly ambrosia, our friendship with this strange person seemed sealed. I remember that only my bottle had red orangeade, and I also remember that I didn't ask Piotr where he obtained the money for this. Five orangeades — that was five zlotys, and five zlotys was not so small a sum. But I never asked Piotr that question, not when we were in school together, nor later, when our paths parted, nor even when I visited his grave to chat about this and that. When someone's on the other side, it's not good manners to bother him about such things. So we drank the sugary, tangy liquid slowly, prolonged the fizz of it in our mouths, and Yellow Wings smacked his lips in contentment and smiled at us, as if we were his best friends.

What time was it? How many hours, now, of interrogation? With Piotr still in the headmaster's study, and as I recalled the wonderful orangeade we drank in the crypt that day, the clock on the wall began to strike, saying in its measured, mechanical way that this, too, would pass. But I was too thirsty, hungry, and frightened to look up and see what time the hands were pointing to. And I didn't need to look; the darkness outside the windows meant that it was very late. Those three, I thought, must be growing tired. They would soon conclude the investigation. Or if they didn't conclude it, because the picture they were trying to construct was incomplete, they would adjourn the questioning until the next day. And tomorrow was Sunday, I thought, so it wouldn't be the next day, it would be Monday. They couldn't lock us up here, they'd have to let us go home, and then . . . Then we could work out all the details between us, the exact place we burned the scrap of red dress, which was all that remained of Elka. And though in fact neither Elka nor Weiser had been torn apart by an unexploded shell, the headmaster, the militiaman, M-ski, and even the prosecutor would be satisfied, and Weiser would be satisfied, watching our trick with approval. Suddenly, with my eyes half closed, I saw the triangular eye of God wink at me from the clouds. It was just as in the picture Father Dudak showed us. "Remember, children," he'd say, pointing upward, "the eye of God sees everything, knows everything. It knows when you tell your parents lies, when you take your schoolmate's pencils, and when you don't cross yourself as you pass a church or wayside shrine. It forgets nothing and remembers everything, every good deed and every sin. And when your souls stand before Him, it will remind you of what you did on Earth." Yes, Father Dudak definitely had pedagogical talent, because often, when I told my mother a small fib or kept the change from shopping for myself, the triangular eye would give me no peace. And now, reminded of its existence, I trembled, because this was no small fib, it was a whole edifice of falsehood, lies built upon lies, for the benefit of . . . whom? Who were we lying for? For those three sitting behind the diamond-patterned leather-covered door? Or for ourselves? Or was it perhaps for Weiser, who made us swear we would tell no one? But if that was the case, if the lying was for Weiser, then what about the triangular eye that watched our every move and heard our every word from its place in the high heavens? Whose side was God on, then? I wondered. If He was on our side, that is, Weiser's, then we should be forgiven our sins. But what if He was on the other side? What if Weiser had bound us with a false oath? I became truly frightened, because it occurred to me, for the first time, that Weiser might be the spirit of evil, who had ensnared us in his net of temptations, putting us to the test.

Then I remembered what Father Dudak told us about Satan. "Oh, he doesn't always look fearsome. Sometimes a friend will say don't go to church, but that's Satan whispering, luring you away from duty with the promise of false pleasures. Sometimes, instead of helping your parents, you'll go to the beach, because a voice says going to the beach is more fun. And that"——the priest paused dramatically, as in a sermon——"and that is how the Devil leads even little children into sin. Remember, my dears, that nothing is hidden from God, and His wrath can be terrible. Behold the torments of the damned" ——practically shouting now——"of those who did not heed the voice of righteousness, who did not come to their senses in time! See how they suffer, and not for a hundred years, or two hundred, or five hundred, but for all eternity!" Before our eyes opened the pit of hell, drawn with consummate artistry, and shaggy devils were hurling naked sinners into it. We saw the bodies fall, saw them speared and writhing on pointed forks, and clawed by talons, and licked by flames that rose from the very bowels of hell to meet them. Thus did the priest paint damnation, and we believed the picture literally. Sitting now beside Szymek on a folding chair, I still couldn't decide whether or not the triangular eye would frown upon our lies when the time came for us to stand before it, like standing before M-ski or the militiaman, and nothing could be hidden any longer.

I realize now that these reflections were a symptom of my distress under the strain of the investigation. Perhaps, I thought, I should tell what happened that last day at the Strzyża. It didn't matter if they didn't believe me. It was Weiser's and Elka's business, really, no one else's. Let the truth be told, preserved, though no one would accept it. And I wouldn't have to reveal all Weiser's secrets. I would only have to tell, in order, step by step, what Weiser and Elka did when we stood ankle-deep in water, in the full sun, and Weiser said we should wait for them. Unless he had another kind of waiting in mind, something altogether different from waiting for a train, or for a shop to open, or for a vacation to begin. Through the closed door of the study we heard M-ski yell, then Piotr scream a moment after. They must have resorted to something extra special in his case, perhaps the plucking of the goose and the stretching of the elephant's trunk combined, or else something entirely new, unimaginable. Szymek shifted on his chair, and my leg got even more numb. I don't know why, but that song came to mind, the one we sang that year on Corpus Christi as we walked in procession behind Father Dudak and the monstrance: "Glo-ory to Thee, Jesus, So-on of Mary, the One True God in the Ho-ost." It wasn't so much the words that I remembered as the tune, the slow and stately melody that flowed in a narrow ribbon through my mind like a wisp of nostalgic, soothing incense.

We had a lot of time yet until six. Yellow Wings had been provided for, and he didn't need company. In our boredom, the oddest ideas entered our heads, all having to do with Weiser, naturally. What would he show us? Or do with us? Teach us to hover above the ground? Perhaps he'd change a butterfly into a frog, or vice versa. Should we ask him why he was dancing in the cellar of the abandoned brickworks? Piotr agreed that that would be good, but perhaps it would be better to ask him, instead, for another Schmeisser. If Weiser knew the whole forest, to Oliwa if not farther, he could have dug up plenty in the old German trenches. Perhaps he would consent to play war with us. Remember how he watched us that day in the Brentowo cemetery? After lunch, sitting on the moldy bench between the lines of laundry, we went back over his every gesture, his every word. Why didn't he go to Sunday school? Why did he need Elka? Who taught him to tame animals? Our discussion was interrupted by Mrs. Korotek's throwing her husband's clothes out the window. "Scum, drunkard!" she yelled. "Out, out, and don't come back! May my eyes never see you, my ears never hear you!" A shirt fell to the ground, a pair of trousers, shoes, then Mr. Korotek himself suddenly emerged from the stairwell. With an unsteady step, he went to the pile of clothes and began, as if nothing were wrong, to get dressed, because his wife's fury had driven him from the apartment in only his underpants. "Hey," he shouted up at the window, "and my socks?" But Mrs. Korotek knew no mercy and slammed the window shut, so we watched Mr. Korotek sit on the ground and put his shoes on his bare feet, watched him try to put the left shoe on his right foot and the right shoe on his left foot. At last he got them on correctly and left the courtyard, striding like a sailor, singing, "Adieu, adieu, my dear mulatto girl!" Mrs. Korotek was no mulatto; her husband was evidently singing just to keep his spirits up. Our conversation resumed, on the same theme. Where did Weiser learn to play soccer, and so well? Why had we never seen him play before? He always stood off to the side when the physical-education teacher divided the class into two teams. What reason did Weiser have to hide his talent? And who knew what else he could do, things, maybe, beyond our imagination? These questions gave us goose bumps, but the goose bumps made us want to ask more questions.

Above the roof of our building, swallows flitted, with their characteristic cry, a cross between a cheep and a whistle, and the sky, like all the skies that summer, was an expanse of bleached azure. Mr. Korotek returned from the Lilliput, inebriated to the limits of human possibility, but we were still deep in our discussion, whose main grammatical features were the conditional mood and the question mark. In a few days, July would be over, and half the vacation gone, but neither this fact nor the fish soup in the bay, let alone the excesses of Mr. Korotek, could distract us from the matter at hand.

At six o'clock exactly we were at the edge of the forest, where once warehouses had stood, belonging to the brickworks. The building, which at night had resembled a haunted castle, now looked as innocent as the tumbledown houses our Wrzeszcz and Oliwa suburbs were full of. The way to the entrance was across a yard overgrown with hogweed, couch and other grass, where not a single brick had lain for years. Inside, it was pleasantly cool. To our surprise, there was no one there. Piles of rust-eaten metal, some overturned wheelbarrows, a broken kiln—that was all. On the floor, empty paint cans, shreds of burlap, and pieces of wet, foul-smelling cardboard. Five minutes passed. It seemed like five hours. Piotr kicked at the cans, Szymek peered into the kiln, and I tried to right one of the wheelbarrows. I was beginning to doubt that anything interesting awaited us here, when behind us, at the entrance, we heard Weiser's voice: "You met the first condition—you're alone. Good. And now the second. Follow me."

Without a word we went down to the cellar, using the same steps that had caved in the night before, with the wooden floor. But there was no trace of damage; everything was whole—the trapdoor, the steps, the floor. Not one board showed the fresh marks of a plane; not one step had been fitted with new wood. We stood on the dirt floor of the cellar.

"You have to take an oath. Are you ready?"

Of course we weren't, but how could one argue with Weiser?

"What do we swear on?" asked Szymek. "If it's a crucifix, this has to be really important."

"You think it's not important?" After Weiser's question, there was an uncomfortable silence. What did he have up his sleeve? We didn't know.

"So, what do we swear on?" asked Szymek.

"You ask on what. Not why?" Weiser prompted.

"Well, it's obvious," said Piotr. "It's so we won't betray a secret. Oaths are always for that."

"Good," answered Weiser. "It's so you won't betray a secret. Tell me, do you three believe in life after death?"

We didn't know what to say. No one had ever asked us this point-blank. An obvious thing, when you're put on the spot like that, can become uncertain even for a man of experience, and what were we boys to feel, in the cellar of the abandoned brickworks, our hearts and minds feverish with anticipation?

"Sure," I answered for all of us. "Why shouldn't we?"

"Good," said Weiser. "Then swear on your life after death that you won't reveal to anyone what I show you here or anywhere else. That you'll tell people only what I say you can, if you're asked. If you betray the secret, you'll die without a future life. That will be your punishment."

We nodded. Weiser told us to lay our right hands on his left hand, and when we did that, he made each of us say in turn, "I swear!"

Then he went to one of the walls and pushed it, and a narrow passageway appeared. It led to a large room, a long hall made up of three or four rooms combined, the walls between them removed. Where the walls had been, you could see a few jutting bricks and stones. At the left of the entrance were two boxes, and beside them we saw Elka. The place was lit by two strong bulbs, which hung on wires from the ceiling. At the time, I paid no attention to this, but today I am convinced that Weiser installed them himself, running a lead from the Matemblew road, which would have taken more than ordinary know-how and skill. But who could bother with such details when Elka opened the first box and we saw the weapons? They were the real thing: three Schmeissers, a Russian PPS-42, two Walther 9 mm Parabellum pistols, two Stechkins, and a few more. Szymek whistled in awe. Piotr picked up a Parabellum and tried to pull out the magazine. "Not like that," said Elka, taking the pistol from him. "This way," and she showed him. "And it goes in this way, and here's the safety." We stood there like little children in front of a toy-store window, and though we were no longer little, our hungry eagerness to put our hands on everything was just the same. While we were touching these wonders, admiring the polished barrels, the olive sheen of the butts, and while we checked the triggers and firing pins, utterly absorbed, Weiser took clips of ammunition from the second box, and from a corner of the room he brought cardboard figures.

Elka pointed a finger at me. "You'll shoot first. We'll leave a Parabellum out. Wrap the rest in rags and put them away." We obeyed without a murmur. She loaded the pistol and told Szymek and Piotr to stand behind me. When Weiser came back from the wall at the far end, where he'd set up the cardboard figure, Elka handed me the Parabellum, with the safety off. "You can fire," she said, and it sounded like an order. If it hadn't been for all the war movies I'd seen at the Tramway Theater, I wouldn't have known how to stand, or what to do with my left hand, or the way to line up the sights. I knew all this, at least in theory, and wanted to do well, but when I lifted the barrel and aimed at the cardboard effigy, my arms and legs began to shake, and I felt beads of sweat on my temples and the back of my neck. In all the movies, the target was obvious: the resistance man shot at the Gestapo agent, the SS man shot at the Jew, the partisan shot at the gendarme, the Soviet soldier shot at the German and vice versa. But what I saw now was something completely unexpected and undefinable, and it frightened me as much as if I were shooting at a real person. In my sights were M-ski's head and shoulders, done in watercolor. And it wasn't the ordinary M-ski, that is, not the one we saw at school, in political parades, or in the forest. This cardboard M-ski had a droopy mustache, and the arch of the bushy brows and the way the eyes were set left no room for doubt about who he was supposed to resemble. Yes, although all those portraits, big as bed sheets, had disappeared from the streets and store windows of our town, I was overwhelmed with fear. And, as if that weren't enough, the man wore the cap of a Wehrmacht officer. Only Weiser could have thought of adding that touch.

"Are you shooting or aren't you?" said Elka in a mocking tone. So I fired—once, twice, three times, four times, until the magazine was empty. The bullets hit the wall above or to the side of the figure; only one, the last, drilled a hole exactly where the German eagle and swastika were on the high-crowned cap. "He got the bird!" cried Piotr. Weiser, as if in disbelief, went up to M-ski and put his finger in the bullet hole. "You hit the circle, the eagle wasn't touched," he said, coming back, as I straightened my fingers, which were cramped and tingling from all the recoil in the grip. The Parabellum, like any real pistol, was too heavy for a boy's hand, and Piotr and Szymek didn't do much better than I did. Piotr got the forehead only twice, and Szymek shot off a piece of M-ski's left mustache and put a crater in his right cheek.

Only Weiser—do I have to say it?—showed class. Who knows how many hours he practiced, here or in the forest, and how many cartridges fell to the ground before he achieved such wizardry? He fired twelve times, in quick succession, and on M-ski's face appeared two equilateral triangles, connected in such a way that they formed a star. Elka changed the cardboard effigy. It was M-ski again, but now in the uniform of an American general. Only one detail recalled the Wehrmacht officer: beneath his shirt collar, instead of a tie, the American M-ski wore an Iron Cross, just like the ones we'd seen in the movies. We took turns firing, but didn't do well this time either. Weiser again left us in the dust. He made two letters on the face, a U and an S, one on either side of M-ski's nose. As I summon up that evening, and the taste of the brick dust in my mouth comes back to me, and the ringing in my ears from the shots, and as I hear again the patter of cartridges falling on the dirt floor, I ask myself what Weiser's politics were. If he had any at all. Those effigies were the only indication of political views. But why combine M-ski, Stalin, and General Eisenhower in one person? It didn't make sense. Most likely, it wasn't meant to. Except, of course, putting the Iron Cross on Stalin.

But that wasn't all. While Elka removed the effigy, Weiser took a stamp album out of the ammunition box. A superb stamp album, with a real binding, and cardboard pages that had cellophane protectors running across them like beams of light. Anyone who collected stamps in those days, like Piotr, would have gaped at the sight of such a treasure. On almost every page, in neat rows, were stamps from the Occupation. There were two kinds: one showing Hitler, and one the courtyard of Wawel, the royal castle in Kraków, where Hans Frank, his deputy, lived then. The stamps had no postmarks, and Weiser had arranged them by color: first reddish brown, then brownish green, then green, and the steel-blue ones came last. There were more Hitler stamps than anything else; from every page, in even ranks, as if on parade, the dour face with the mustache looked at us. "They're Adolfs!" whispered Piotr. "You can get two zlotys apiece for those at the store." In fact, the philately shop in the Old Town was buying up Adolfs.

But Weiser's collection had another purpose, because after we'd gone through the whole album, he took out five of the reddish brown portraits of the Chancellor of the Third Reich, went to the far wall, licked each, and stuck them on the brick. "Great," said Elka, when Weiser came back. "The glue works like new!" He checked the magazine, then stood, planting his legs wide, the way they do in competitions. He didn't take more than three seconds to aim on each shot, so the whole thing lasted no more than twenty seconds. It wasn't easy, when we went up to the wall, to find the places where the Chancellor had been pasted. The bullets had destroyed the stamps completely; only here and there was a point of a jagged edge of stamp, a dot of colored paper smaller than a match head. Of the five Adolfs, not one remained. "He could be in the Olympics," said Elka with pride. Weiser put the Parabellum in the box and told us to go home. "In a few days—I'll let you know—you'll come back here. Until then, take this"—handing Szymek a booklet—"and this"—giving me a pistol.

Even before we went into the forest, we examined the booklet and the pistol. The booklet was a prewar instruction manual for small arms, and the pistol had neither magazine nor firing pin. Weiser hadn't said, "Learn to shoot, and do it so no one sees you." No, he'd made us swear an oath, then had given us a manual and a disarmed gun. Why? I couldn't figure that out as I sat in the main office, but today I think he did this to distract us from his real secret. I think that when we had watched him dance to the panpipe and rise in the air, witnesses of his trance, he hadn't expected us, hadn't intended to have any witnesses but Elka. What could he do in that situation? Put a toy in our hands, then other toys, and from time to time check to see how we were doing with them.

But what of the idea that he had been lying in wait for us from the start? How, then, could he *not* have expected us? Perhaps we tracked him down too quickly; perhaps that was meant to come later, in entirely different circumstances. And so he disarmed our curiosity, and sent it down an altogether different path. We never did ask him—or Elka, either—about that night and his mad dance. It never occurred to us that the pistol and the shooting gallery were designed to move us away from something more important. Because what was his marksmanship in comparison with his speech in an alien voice and unknown tongue, or with his levitation? Yes, from then on, Weiser was our leader and we his guerrilla band, and we could even think that it would end with an uprising—that was allowed—but we weren't to wonder how a human being could float half a meter above the ground. Weiser, you might say, had led us to the anteroom of his sanctum, but there presented a curtain as the final wall.

What did he wish to show us, or make us believe, we who were so unaware? I couldn't talk about this with either Szymek or Elka; that left Piotr, with whom the subject of Weiser had never been broached. Two years ago—two years and a month, to be precise, because, as I'm writing this, it's the end of October—I decided to have that conversation with him. Whenever I visit Piotr, I sit on the edge of his stone and am silent for a while. Each of us has to become accustomed to the presence of the other. It was the same, that September afternoon. I brushed the leaves, sand, and pine needles from the slab, and only then asked:

"Are you there?"

"Yes. Is it All Saints' Day already?"

"No."

"Why did you come? . . . You're not answering."

"Szymek was arrested."

"What happened?"

"He was printing leaflets. Now he's in jail. . . . You don't say anything. You don't care?"

"When someone gets into politics, he should take such things into account."

"Piotr, you talk like a stranger."

"I am a stranger."

"You talk as if you didn't care."

"There isn't much caring here."

"I don't believe it."

"You'll see."

"Don't try to frighten me."

"I'm not. These are obvious things."

"Not to me."

We fell silent. Above the cemetery, high overhead, an airplane droned, and somewhere there was funeral singing. Between the rows of stones, the wind blew dried grass and leaves.

"Why aren't we talking, Piotr?"

"Maybe because you came here for another reason."

"You're right."

"So, what is it?"

"You have to tell me about Weiser!"

"Have to? Why?"

"It's been bothering me more and more these last few years. Why did he need us? Why involve us in his affairs? Was it just to leave behind a maddening puzzle? You're not answering, Piotr. Now you're pretending you aren't there."

"You're supposed to come once a year and not ask any questions. Did you forget that?"

"I didn't, Piotr, but for my sake . . ."

"There are no exceptions. Go now, I'm tired."

Twenty-five months ago, that's what I heard from Piotr. Go now, I'm tired. It was the last conversation I had about Weiser, or tried to have. Later, I began to write, since there was no other way, only this, to find an explanation.

So we had a manual, a pistol without a magazine or firing pin, and all sorts of heroic plans and ideas. Weiser was no longer a worker of miracles. With the flighty foolishness typical of youth, our thoughts about him now tended more in the direction of Robin Hood or Major Hubal than toward Chaldean sorcerer or circus magician. It couldn't be helped.

Our practice was postponed, however. The next day, a week of prayer for the farmers began: services for the restoration of order to nature, that is, for rain. First, in every home, mothers carefully washed and dressed their children. Then husbands put on white shirts, and some, in spite of the heat, tied ties and got into black suits, their Sunday best. Finally, with a sprinkling of eau de cologne, which at ninety degrees did little to cover the smell of sweat, they led their families out into the street, where, on foot or by tram, all the faithful made their way to the Oliwa cathedral. The bishop would be present at the inaugural service, and everyone was curious to hear how he would address his weary flock. Further services were to be held in the various parishes, every evening at six. This I learned from my mother, early in the morning, and she didn't let me out for more than half an hour, afraid, no doubt, that I would wander off. Even before we entered the cathedral, I could hear the supplications, sung by a thousand voices. Then, when we were inside the cathedral, which was as long and narrow as a Viking boat, the chanting, the boom of the organ, and the smell of sweat, eau de cologne, and incense all merged into one mighty plea for rain, and that the barrenness of the fields and the bay might be turned aside. A delegation of farmers and fishermen knelt in the front row, all eyes upon them, as if their prayers had the greatest power.

"In pagan times," said the bishop, distant and lost among the golden garlands of the pulpit, "when there was a drought, our forefathers offered up sacrifices to appease their gods and ask for rain. But we, on whom God has bestowed His love and mercy in the persons of Mary and her Son, we, who profess the Gospel, are free of superstition and false belief. Christ, who shed His blood for us, made the greatest and final sacrifice, and it is He who hears our humble entreaty on behalf of the farmers, the fishermen, and us all!" The organ sounded a chord. "Lord, holy, holy, mighty, and immortal, have mercy on us," burst from a thousand throats. Everyone sang, and I was certain that the bishops, prelates, and nobles in the huge portraits on the walls were singing with us, too. "Beloved in Christ Our Lord," the bishop continued, "sin often leads us down the path of evil and away from God. And then He afflicts us, that we may come to our senses, return to the way of righteousness and grace, and cast off false prophets and all temptation." "From hunger, war, and untimely death, O Lord, spare us," echoed beneath vaults as high as the sky. "Let us now join in reflection," said the bishop, "upon the evil that has found a home in our hearts, and how this has angered the Lord, who afflicts us. How many of you have turned to Mammon, to idol worship, to iniquity? How many of you, hardened sinners, fools, have abandoned faith and God for—as you thought—a better life? How many of you, I ask?!" A deathly silence filled the cathedral. Lowered heads accepted the pastor's bitter words. "And I say to you, dear ones, that many of you, many of you have broken the Lord's commandments, have left the path of righteousness! Let us pray, therefore, with penitent hearts, let us pray to Mary, that she may intercede for us with the Son and with the Father, let us pray for a rain of mercy from heaven, and, if that is not lacking, the mercy of an earthly rain as well. Amen."

After the bishop's words, the organ roared with redoubled force, and the cathedral overflowed with "Hear, O Je-sus, how we do implo-ore Thee!" People furtively wiped away their tears, and I looked toward the back, where angels held horns, long and curved like sabers, and great stars revolved, and chubby cherubim faces blew puff-cheeked on fifes, and the organ bellows huffed, and bells and triangles rang; where all that was gold, silver, marble, and wood resounded, moved, and played in eternal praise.

That evening, a storm rolled in over the town, the first of the summer, and everyone saw in this God's hand, also proof of the holiness of the bishop. "Without him," people said, "not a drop would have fallen." But the downpour didn't last even half an hour, and the sky cleared immediately, and everything continued as before—the stinking fish soup in the bay, the stifling heat, the drought. Next morning, I was in Cyrson's, where my mother had sent me for potatoes, and overheard what some women in line were saying.

"My dear," one of them remarked, "if everyone observed the sacraments like that, it would come down in buckets for three days and nights."

"You can't trust people these days. They go to church, pretend they're praying to Our Lady," said a second one angrily, "but at home and at work they forget everything. On payday they get drunk as pigs, and if the Party secretary asks about their beliefs, they say the only thing they believe in is Marx. As if that's a more reliable faith for the workers than the Good Book!"

"And they call themselves Catholics!" a third woman put in.

"You'll see, flour will go up, eggs, potatoes," said the first. "In such a drought, there's nothing you can do."

"And there'll be war," groaned the second. "When prices go up, it always means war."

I stopped listening to them, because the thought hit me that it wasn't the bishop but Yellow Wings who should stand among the golden garlands of the pulpit; that instead of words of hope and love, it would be better for the congregation to hear the madman's awful prophecies. Because if the bishop, like Yellow Wings, had set before the assembly a gruesome picture of destruction and God's wrath, if he had spoken, like Yellow Wings, of blood, corpses, and retribution, surely more people would have fallen to their knees and beaten their chests and said, "I have sinned! I have sinned! Oh, how I have sinned!" But the question was: In whose name had the bishop spoken, and in whose name Yellow Wings?

The day before, Piotr had hidden the pistol in the cellar, and he had put the padlock key on the chest of drawers in the hall of his apartment. As bad luck would have it, his father, leaving for work, took the key by mistake. Now we had to wait for Piotr's father to come home, and sat bored to tears in the withered patch of garden next to our building. Around two, I saw Mrs. Korotek with a basket of laundry. "Ay-yiy," she said to herself. "What next? Men are a plague." She put the basket on the ground, took some clothespins out of her bosom, and started hanging underpants, shirts, and dishrags on the line. "A plague," she repeated. "He'll get drunk again, won't bring home his pay." And suddenly, for the first time in our lives, we sided with Mrs. Korotek, and with all the wives and mothers in our building, because today was payday!

"He won't be back at four," said Piotr. "And he could lose the key. Last time," he explained, "he lost his wallet and all his papers."

"You don't have another key?" asked Szymek.

"If I had another cellar key, you idiot," Piotr snapped, "do you think we would be sitting here all day?"

It was hopeless. We knew that Piotr's father, like my father or like Mr. Korotek, could easily come home at six o'clock, or midnight, for that matter.

"The whole day's wasted," I said. "What do we do now?"

Help came our way, unexpectedly, from Mrs. Korotek. Her basket empty, she stopped as she was leaving and asked:

"What are you up to, boys?"

"Nothing . . . just sitting around."

"Had your lunch yet?"

"Yes, ma'am."

"You have nothing to do now?"

"No, ma'am."

"What about later?"

"Later, ma'am? How much later?"

"Oh, three, three-thirty."

"Nothing, really."

"Perhaps you boys can do something for me."

"Sure, ma'am. What do you want us to do?"

"Not much, it's a little thing. Go to the Lilliput, you know, where they sell beer. You'll see my man, he's always sitting there. Go up to him, take him aside, tell him I'm sick, the ambulance came and took me to the hospital. You'll do that for me, you little imps?"

"Yes, ma'am."

"So what will you tell him?"

"That you got sick and the ambulance came, and they took you to the hospital, and Mr. Korotek's to come home right away."

"Ah, you boys are gold," she said with a broad grin. "You won't forget, will you?"

"No, ma'am, we'll go," we said, and in our thoughts planned how we could get the key from Piotr's father without his suspecting anything. He would be there with Mr. Korotek, of course.

The Lilliput was right next to the Prussian barracks, opposite what was once the garrison chapel but after the war became the Protestant chapel, which was closed that summer and being converted into a new movie theater. Every day, from morning on, particularly when it was hot, the bar's little courtyard was packed with groups of men drinking, and on a day like this one, the murmur of voices could be heard from quite a distance. The Lilliput was the kind of establishment women didn't enter. Vodka wasn't sold; the customers brought their own, in satchels or jacket pockets or tucked under belts. They'd order a couple of steins of frothy beer and strengthen it as desired with the colorless stuff. All the men in our part of Upper Wrzeszcz stopped there after work at least once a month, and in a short time they freed themselves from the troubles of daily existence, thoughts of the future, and un-pleasant memories. Those who worked at the ship-yard were already three sheets to the wind when they arrived at the Lilliput. On the way, right by the second gate, the Chestnut Bar waited for them, and from there they'd go to the Lilliput, taking the No. 2 tram or the electric train.

It was three-twenty when we saw the faded yellow sign. The chicken-wire fence bulged like the side of a barrel, from all the bodies inside. Noise. Arms waving. In a corner, by a lilac bush, stood

Mr. Korotek, and with him were Piotr's father and mine and two other men, each with a stein in his hand.

"They shit," Mr. Korotek was shouting, "they shit on us! Let the foreman cut the speeches and share the bonus!"

"Right!" one of the men agreed. "What's right is right!"

They all clinked steins and drank. My father took a bottle from his satchel and poured a little vodka into each stein.

"Before they get drunk," Szymek suggested, "let's listen to what they're saying."

We crept up to the lilac bush on the street side, and in its shade could eavesdrop. But the subject had apparently been exhausted, because Mr. Korotek turned in our direction, unbuttoned his fly, and pissed into the bush, a powerful yellow stream. Then he turned back to his companions, but neglected to button his fly. We didn't see this, but what happened next demonstrated to us the consequences of such carelessness.

One of the bricklayers working to turn the Protestant chapel into a movie theater called to Mr. Korotek:

"Hey, button up, mate, or your bird will fly away!" And everyone laughed.

Mr. Korotek emptied his stein, wiped his mouth on his sleeve, and answered:

"And you, asshole, your hand will wither."

"And why?"

"Remove a cross from a holy place, and your hand will wither sooner or later."

The subsequent discussion, joined by other voices, proceeded at a fast pace.

"It's a Lutheran church, German!"

"Lutheran, not Lutheran, the cross is the same."

"You do what you're told, too."

"Listen to the philosopher!"

"They pay you, you do it!"

"You'd eat your own shit for money. A cross to you is nothing!"

"Watch it!"

"Oh?"

"Keep your dick in your pants, comrade, or you'll lose it!"

"Excuse me, it's a comrade we're talking to. Listen, everyone, to the comrade!"

"You don't like the Party?"

"Is that where you learn to respect your elders?"

"You have something to tell the Party?"

"Whether I do or not, you I could teach some manners!"

"Go ahead, please!"

"Maybe I will!"

"Hey, we have a dickless defender of the faith here, boys! Ha, ha, ha!"

"Say that again!"

"And then what?"

"The Blessed Virgin herself won't be able to help you, you son of a bitch!"

"The Blessed Virgin's dickless defender—" But the bricklayer couldn't finish the sentence, because Mr. Korotek hurled his stein at him. It flew over the enemy's head and struck someone else. For an instant, there was silence. Then all hell broke loose. The friends of the man struck went after the bricklayers, because they were nearest, and the bricklayers, defending their colleague, waded into the wrong crowd. Chest hit chest, fist hit fist, steins broke on heads, and legs kicked at others. The soldiers from the nearby barracks took off their heavy belts and beat left and right. Soon the battle was raging inside the bar, too, judging by the pieces of table that came flying out the windows, taking panes and frames with them. Passersby slowed down and looked, wondering, but the combatants themselves couldn't have explained why they were fighting or for what. The crush of bodies pushed against the fence, the rusty chicken wire split apart like paper, and a dozen men tumbled into the street. "The militia! The militia's on its way!" someone shouted. "Run!" And as the growing wail of a siren came from the direction of Grunwald Avenue, we watched Mr. Korotek crawl out from under the pile of bodies, then Piotr's father, then mine, and they left as quickly as they could, to avoid getting caught. Thus, thanks to his unbuttoned fly, Mr. Korotek was home before four, though with a black eye and blood on his shirt, and half an hour later we had our pistol and could begin practicing.

In the beginning, there was a cloud of incense, and out of the cloud came Weiser. Why, instead of continuing the story, do I keep retreating, returning, repeating? There are sentences, simple and clear, that after a little thought suddenly become puzzling, complicated, then altogether incomprehensible, sentences uttered by various people that unexpectedly come to mind and give you no peace. What, for example, does "My kingdom is not of this world" mean? Father Dudak explained it more than once, and I've heard it since from men wiser than he. But all the wise commentaries in the world are no help. When I read it aloud or under my breath, mouthing the words, and think about it yet again, terror overwhelms me, and despair. Because this sentence is not simple or clear, and the more I contemplate it, the more the black, bottomless hole of uncertainty opens beneath me. It was the same with Weiser—is the same. His brief appearance, then departure, is exactly like such a sentence, clear and easy to understand only at first. I don't mean to suggest a religious analogy—Weiser never spoke about religion in our presence. Nor about his inner life. But if Weiser is such a sentence, I must repeat that sentence over and over, in the hope that what is impossible to understand will at last, after the hundredth time, become breathtakingly simple.

Where did I leave off? Yes . . . half an hour later we had our pistol and could begin practicing. But as fate would have it, we weren't to open the instruction book even once that day, or to practice standing with the pistol or aiming. A few minutes after five, as we were leaving for Bukowa Hill, Piotr's mother called out from a third-floor window: "Where are you boys going? Back in the house! Get washed, dressed, there's a Mass at six, did you forget?" There was nothing we could do; we had to obey Piotr's mother, because she was speaking for all our mothers. Yes, there existed then, and still does, a conspiracy of all the mothers in the world, just as there's a conspiracy of all drunken fathers on payday. I won't go into detail about the Mass, because Father Dudak performed that day like a mirror image of His Eminence the bishop. When the prayers and hymns were done, and the final chord of the old harmonium mixed with the organist's hoarse falsetto had died away, we went outside and gathered on the sandy road that came straight from the forest. Elka approached us out of the crowd.

"Enjoying yourselves?" she asked.

We weren't sure what she meant—our practice with the pistol, which hadn't happened yet, or the fact that the service was over.

"What do you want?"

"I have something for you." A cunning smile.

"Then give it to us and scram. We're busy," said Piotr nonchalantly.

Elka laughed, showing her gleaming row of white squirrel's teeth.

"Dopes! I have a message for you."

"From Weiser?"

She nodded. "Be in the hollow behind the firing range tomorrow at five, and bring"—and she made a pistol with her fingers. "Understand?"

We understood, but didn't know what Weiser was going to show us, or have us do. The first month of the vacation was behind us, and none of us had any idea that our acquaintance with Weiser would end in just a few days.

At the cemetery the next day, we found that Yellow Wings was gone. "He left . . ." "They got him . . ." "Not here, there're no footprints . . ." we said. Szymek took command: "Let's get to work."

And immediately we were all business. Don't stand like that. Arm higher. No, no propping! Sights, trigger, good, again. You're taking too long to aim, fire as soon as you get the target in line, that's it, good. My turn now. The sun had long since passed its highest point, but we practiced without rest, assuming the correct stance, preparing to fire, exhaling, and squeezing the frozen trigger of the disarmed pistol. Every now and then Szymek would stand on top of the crypt and sweep the terrain with his French binoculars, because all this was in preparation for real combat. Later, we practiced firing from a kneeling position, from the hip, and prone, exactly as it showed in the prewar manual. "We could rob a bank now," said Piotr, "if we had bullets." Szymek said that partisans didn't rob banks, but I reminded him of a movie in which the resistance men emptied safes, weapons in their hands, to get money for their cause. "Yes, but that was during the Occupation, and they were taking it from the Germans, but now . . ." Szymek argued, then stopped. "Now, who would we take it from?" His question remained unanswered. Weiser would decide; we would leave it up to him. After lunch we returned to the cemetery, because there was plenty of time yet before five.

We didn't practice for long. Down the railroad embankment, heading toward Brentowo, came

M-ski, but without his butterfly net or his folder for plants. If it hadn't been for the absence of these permanent attributes, we wouldn't have followed him, but his empty hands and quick walk piqued our curiosity. He proceeded along the embankment all the way to the blown-up bridge, where the unused tracks crossed the Rembiechowo highway. Once he passed the asphalt, he didn't go back on the embankment, which was high there, but took a path that went along the slope farther down. He reached the spot where the Strzyża flows under the embankment through a narrow tunnel, and continued upstream, not once looking behind him. "Aha," said Szymek, pointing, "someone's waiting for him!" And in fact, some three hundred meters farther, in a small clearing near thickets of hazel and alder growing on the bank, M-ski stopped and talked to a person. We moved closer, crawling the last twenty meters on our stomachs. M-ski now sat on the grass beside a dark-haired woman, who looked like a housewife interrupted in the middle of cooking or ironing. The nature teacher's hand was reaching under her apron.

"No, not now," said the woman. "I told you not to come here anymore! We have to meet somewhere else."

"Then why did you come?" asked M-ski, who had removed her apron. His hand stroked the woman's thigh like a windshield wiper, back and forth. "One more time," he begged. "Just one more time!"

"No, no," said the lady, but she unbuttoned M-ski's trousers. "The same?" she asked, more quietly.

"The same," he said.

The lady got up, and M-ski got up, too. She took off her dress, and M-ski dropped his trousers and the funny white underpants he had on, and then she smacked him in the face, hard, and again, backhanded, hard.

"Uhh," we heard a groan. "More!" The woman smacked him without stopping, and we could see his mole-flecked shoulders rise and fall with each blow. "More, more," he panted, so the woman changed hands and went on smacking. Suddenly M-ski stood bolt upright, stiffened, a shudder ran through his body, and we saw his buttocks quiver. "Uhh," sighed the teacher.

"That's that," said the lady, and put on her dress and then her apron, while M-ski, still standing, pulled up his underpants and trousers. He took out a rolled-up banknote and handed it to her the way you give a ticket to the conductor on the train.

"Next time," said the lady, "don't come looking for me here."

"Where, then?" asked M-ski placidly.

"Where we met last time."

"And you'll be there?"

"I'll be there, I'll be there," she said, and walked off, upstream, from where she must have come. M-ski straightened his shirt and trousers, and without saying good-bye left in the other direction.

"Weird," said Szymek, as we hurried toward Brentowo. "Why couldn't he feel her up the normal way? And he didn't even get on top of her."

"On top of her or not, it was disgusting!" said Piotr, indignant.

"Pooh," Szymek went on. "You should have seen what Jacek's sister did with her boyfriend in our attic, then you'd know how it's really done!"

"Why didn't they go into the woods?" I asked. "Why do it in the attic?

"It was winter, birdbrain!" said Szymek, poking me in the ribs. "But we'd better move, it's almost five!"

We ran up the slope at an angle, and only the grass, high as our knees, slowed us. To the left, far below, was the firing range; to the right, beyond the wall of forest, was the distant bay, blue as a painting. "You sound like a herd of elephants," Elka growled when she saw us. "And you're fifteen minutes late!" We didn't give the reason for our delay. "Now," said Elka, "you'll see something that should teach you respect." For whom or what? Elka didn't tell us. "Teach you respect" was all she said. Weiser turned the crank of the magneto, and we, on our stomachs at the edge of the hollow, saw the first explosion, which I've already described, a vertical swirling column of azure blue. Yes, that was the first one Weiser showed us in the hollow behind the firing range. Running to meet him at the appointed place, we had not imagined anything like this. We were expecting, perhaps, a shooting examination—but once again Weiser stunned us. When he set the next charge, and the air was again torn by the roar of an explosion, and a two-color cloud lifted and a few moments later dissolved like morning mist, we were ready to swear not one but a dozen oaths to Weiser and do whatever he asked. But he said nothing; he was in no hurry. Elka took the manual and the disarmed pistol, and that was it. Tomorrow's meeting would be at the brickworks in the early afternoon. We stood there uncertainly, waiting for more.

"You can go home," said Weiser. "That's enough for today."

"And tomorrow we'll do some shooting, right?" Szymek ventured. Weiser didn't answer, but Elka snapped:

"Don't bother him!" As if Szymek had overstepped himself. "He has more important matters than your shooting. You're to listen and not ask questions. Understood?"

What more was there to say? In the evening, for lack of anything better to do, we knocked a tin can off the top of a garbage can with a slingshot, and the following conversation, roughly, took place:

"I tell you, he's planning something big."

"What?"

"I don't know—the kind of thing the whole town will talk about, and we'll be in the papers!"

"That's stupid. They don't write about kids in the papers."

"They will!"

"What do you think he's planning?"

"If they catch us, it's prison."

"For what?"

"Possession of a gun is nothing? And the magneto, and the explosions?"

"They're not ours."

"Doesn't matter. We're accomplices!"

"But what do you think he's planning?"

"An uprising!"

"Come on, uprisings are done in a city. There have to be barricades."

"Guerrilla warfare, then."

"With just us? Five people isn't enough."

"How do you know it's only us? He could have

other groups, and for secrecy they don't know about each other."

"Right!"

"Maybe he'll blow up the zoo gates and let all the animals go free!"

"Think of it, a lion on Grunwald Avenue!"

"Charging innocent mothers and children. But we run out and *blau,* got the lion, *blau,* got the tiger, *blau,* got the panther!"

"Save the panther for him."

"We take care of the animals, and they put our pictures in the paper. Students from school No. 66 save citizens from wild beasts."

"I bet it's for a ship!"

"A ship?"

"Once he's trained us, we'll seize a ship at the dock!"

"Not at the dock, out in the bay."

"Fine, the bay, and he'll take over the bridge, and we'll be in charge of the cabins and the hold, and off we go to Canada!"

"Africa!"

"No, Canada!"

So between a guerrilla war and pirating a ship to Canada we spent the rest of the day shooting the rusty tin can, and the stones piled up at the base of the garbage can as we pulled harder and harder on the bicycle-tube slingshot, until dusk fell and it was time to go home. But why didn't we discuss M-ski? Why didn't we talk about the dark-haired woman by the river, and puzzle over the sight of our teacher, trousers and underpants lowered, being smacked in the face, this same M-ski before whom we trembled in nature class and during breaks, when he came down the crowded corridor? But Weiser was closer to us than any of M-ski's secrets.

That night I had a dream, which I remember to this day; it was in color, like a Disney film, and extremely upsetting. I was standing on the seashore, probably at dawn, and animals came out of the water one by one. You wouldn't find such creatures in a zoo or in any book on foreign lands. First was a winged lion, dripping wet, and on the sand behind it emerged a bear, growling and with bones in its mouth. Then from the green sea came a four-headed panther with bird's wings along its back. The procession ended with the strangest monster of all: a cross between a rhino and a tiger, with enormous fangs of steel and several horns, ten, maybe twelve, like the antlers of a deformed stag. The animals charged the homes of the fishermen nearby, broke down the doors and shutters with their paws, tore apart the men as they were waking, pulled out the women's hair with their claws, and the children, who couldn't run, were smashed against the white walls. This went on for a long time, and my fear wouldn't let me wake up and wrench myself from the nightmare. Then in the east, in the rays of the sun, I saw a boy dressed in white. It was Weiser coming. With an outstretched hand he pointed at something or someone I couldn't see in the tangle of quivering bodies and twisted corpses. Weiser went first to the lion and ripped off its eagle's wings. The beast fell lifeless to the ground, its tail lashing. Next Weiser pushed the bear with his hand, and the animal rolled over on the sand, unconscious. Third was the monster with the horns. Weiser pulled them out like weeds, and the monster crumbled to its knees, then to its belly, and the steel fangs fell out of its jaws and turned into round ten-zloty coins. Finally Weiser faced the four-headed panther with the bird's wings along its spine, and this was the strangest and most terrible thing of all, because all four pairs of eyes, and all four noses, and all eight ears belonged to M-ski. Each of the four heads of the beast was the head of M-ski. I'll never forget how dreadful they looked. Weiser, just as at the zoo, transfixed the panther with a stare, and the animal became like a frightened kitten, and cringed and licked the hand of its tamer. I didn't catch what Weiser said to the surviving fishermen and their families; the crashing of the surf drowned everything out, drowned out even the

No. 4 tram, which always squealed horribly when it took the Jelitkowo loop. Weiser nimbly jumped aboard and rode off, as if he were a tourist coming back from the beach, and the sunlight reflected on a window in the second car blinded me, and suddenly I felt my sheets damp with sweat and knew I was in bed and all this had been only a dream.

The sun came through a crack in the blind and tickled me. Through the door to the kitchen, I could hear my father leaving for work. Near me, my mother still snored, exhausted by yesterday's marathon of laundry. Above the bed hung a picture of the Black Madonna of Częstochowa in a Biedermeier frame, and through the open window came the clatter of a cart on its way to the Oliwa market. There was no sea, no animals coming out of it, no Weiser dressed in white, no fishermen torn to pieces. Instead, I heard steps in the hallway, a neighbor shuffling to the toilet. In these apartments, with thin walls dividing the old German rooms into tiny cubicles, you could hear everything—the neighbor now shaving with steady strokes of the razor, and then his diarrhea, from yesterday's drinking. But what about my dream? I left nothing out, I added nothing. Perhaps it came because of the discussion about M-ski that never took place.

The dream frightened me so much that even when I knelt at the grille of the confessional for the last time, and Father Dudak still seemed as important as the Pope or the Society for the Propagation of the Faith, even then I couldn't talk about those indelible scenes. This was in January 1971, when I knew exactly what had happened to Piotr and what his funeral had been like. I didn't come to confess my sins, but knelt, as humble and penitent as ever, before the august figure.

"Calm yourself, my son. The decrees of Providence are not for us to fathom," said the priest, and I could smell his sour, old man's breath. I was filling with rage and despair.

"Does that mean, Father," I asked, "that God wanted his death?"

"One should never speak like that, never," he said in one breath, and I asked:

"But Father, everything happens by the will of God. So that death, too, was necessary to Him, wasn't it?"

"All that take the sword shall perish with the sword," came the voice through the grille.

At that, I could no longer hold in my bitterness. Shouting almost at the top of my voice, which made all the devout old women listening in gasp, I said:

"No, Father! Piotr wasn't fighting anyone, he didn't even pick up a stone. You know what happened, it was by accident."

Father Dudak cut me short. "There are no accidents in God's world. What is it that you wish? Would you have Him reveal His secrets to you, who are but dust? You sin, my son, with the sin of pride, and that is a grievous sin. Better men than you have asked, and He did not answer. Read the Book of Job. What is your suffering compared to Job's, that you dare to question and feel anger? A spirit of humility is required, my son, humility and patience are required of us all!"

"Father," I said more quietly, "why do the wicked triumph, and mock the righteous? Can't that be changed?"

"Your reward will be in heaven. Do not seek it in politics."

"Piotr didn't!"

"It is the Lord, not you, my son, who decides what justice is. Do you have other sins?"

"No, Father. I came only to ask why there is less and less faith in me."

"So you have sinned," he interrupted again, shifting in his seat, "not only by pride, but also by doubting. Think no longer of your friend, and pray."

"I can't pray. The more I think, Father, the less faith I have."

"Repent of your sins!"

"I can't!"

"Ask God for His forgiveness!"

"I see no sin in myself."

"Satan lies in wait for you, my son! Pray for forgiveness!"

"I can't! I can't!"

And I ran from the church, shouting, because again before my eyes was the subduer of wild animals on the Jelitkowo beach.

Weiser had returned to me—in the confessional. Was it another trick to distract my attention, this unexpected invasion into the most private area of my life?

Anyway, there I lay, on the pullout bed, after my nightmare, with my mother snoring, exhausted from yesterday's laundry, and the sound of the toilet flushing. Today, I thought, Weiser would check to see what progress we had made in the art of firearms, and the prospect of visiting the abandoned brickworks filled me with happiness.

Meanwhile—again meanwhile—the door of the headmaster's study opened for the hundredth time, and from the jaws of the tobacco-smoke-breathing Leviathan the skinny figure of Piotr was ejected. The fact that he had screamed disconcerted him— that we had heard him crying. But he kept his wits about him, because when the militiaman called Szymek, Piotr gestured to us: the striking of a match.

That meant that during his interrogation he told them that we had burned the piece of Elka's dress: to satisfy those three, and the public prosecutor, too, who wanted the case closed. We nodded. But where had that wretched piece of dress been lying? Where were we supposed to have found it? They'd be sure to pull out the map and tell us to show them where exactly, to the meter. And where we lit the fire. We hadn't decided on that, and unfortunately none of us was telepathic. The militiaman slammed the door behind Szymek, and silence filled the main office, where I had counted the squares of the parquet floor up, down, and across, silence and the steady tick of the clock. I fought sleep. Ever since that dream, I was afraid that when I closed my eyes, evil thoughts would come. That the same thing might appear. I was afraid all the days after, to the end of the vacation, and in the main office now I was afraid. Why hadn't I told Szymek or Piotr my dream? Why had I hidden that image of strange beasts crawling from the sea at the Jelitkowo beach? Why hadn't I stood up like Yellow Wings and revealed to them my truth? It was only then, as we sat on our folding chairs in the light of the single lamp on the janitor's table, that Piotr let his head sink in resignation, and I saw the welts on the palms of his hands. It was only then that I began to understand the accident that followed my dream, when we were shooting the Schmeisser in the hollow behind the firing range. But, in order.'

At the appointed hour, we were at the brick-works. Without a word, Weiser took twelve mold-green Adolfs from the album, stuck them on the brick wall, handed us a loaded Parabellum, and said, "Four Adolfs each. Shoot till you hit them all." Elka was to count the used cartridges and refill the magazine. I remember exactly: Piotr turned out to be the best shot, using only six bullets to hit his four Chancellors; Szymek was second, using eight; and I was third—it took me eleven bullets to get my four Adolfs. My ears were ringing. "Not bad," said Weiser. "But you"—he turned to me—"need more practice." Then he said we'd go to the hollow, since we hadn't disappointed him—that's how he put it—and as we were walking through the nettles, ferns, and broom, and passed the thicket of spruce trees, dark even in daytime, I waited for him to fall behind, a little away from the others, and then I told him my dream, like the greatest secret. I told him about the monsters that came out of the sea, and how he had subdued them and saved the unfortunate fishermen. I don't think I was trying to butter him up because I had shot the worst, and he didn't take it that way, either. He listened to the end, didn't interrupt, then said—I remember what he said—"All right. Don't tell anyone else."

And it wasn't a threat. After a moment he added, "You'll change the targets. That's an important job." And off I went, delighted, as if a special favor had been bestowed on me despite my bad shooting.

If today I write that Weiser was someone who was totally different, I have good reason, but it doesn't mean he wasn't also our leader, our general. Who but a general would have thought of shooting right next to the army firing range, under the noses of entirely real soldiers? The brickworks cellar was too small for playing with an automatic. But where could we shoot without the sound sooner or later coming to the attention of people living in the vicinity, or of those out picking raspberries? His idea was simple: If shooting practice was going on at the army range, we should have our own at the same time, next door. On the other side of the high rampart there, the hollow began, where the thicket, tall grass, and dense shrubbery could provide cover if we needed to flee. Also, the hollow led to a gorge two kilometers long and overgrown with pine trees; it would take fifty soldiers to close it off. All this, Weiser had planned, provided for. We watched with amazement as he told us to take our positions, loaded the gun, and waited for the sound of shots to come from the other side of the rampart. "Now I'll show you," he said, ready to squeeze the trigger, "how to do it." And as soon as we heard a volley on the other side, which rumbled between the walls of trees, Weiser fired the same short volley, a repetition of the first. "They'll never know," he said. "Over there, it'll sound like an echo, as long as you shoot right after."

So we fired with the soldiers, fired on opposite sides of the same earthwork, except that on the real firing range they had automatic Kalashnikovs, while we had a German Schmeisser, found by Weiser. It wasn't easy, though, following their rhythm. The volleys, short, usually in series of three, didn't keep to the same pattern. *Pow, pa-pow, pa-pa-pow* was the most frequent—one shot, then two, then three in rapid succession. But there were other sequences—for example, three, two, two, one, or two, three, two, or one, one, three, then an extra one, unexpected.

"They're shooting like they're low on ammunition," observed Szymek. "I don't understand it."

Weiser, leaning over the open magazine, smiled in his way, faintly, and said:

"A soldier's supposed to shoot like he's low on ammunition."

Piotr asked why.

"How many bullets would you carry into a battle?" said Elka in a know-it-all voice. "A hundred? Two hundred?"

After this question, which no one answered, we were certain that Weiser was preparing us for something big, and suddenly we felt like Fidel Castro's men, who, a year before, December second, had landed in the Oriente Province and fought the hated Batista, lackey of the imperialists. M-ski had entertained us with this account through one entire nature lesson.

"It's a shame," Szymek whispered as we lay in the ferns, because they were taking a break now on the other side. "If only we had a Batista here!"

"What?" asked Elka.

"We'd really give it to him," Piotr explained. "We land on the beach, attack the barracks, and revolution sweeps the country, a real revolution with guerrilla warfare and everything!"

Elka burst out laughing, so loud that even Weiser gave her an admonishing look.

"What dopes you are," she said, trying to stifle her laughter. "How can you have a revolution twice?"

But there wasn't time to explain our desires to Elka. Weiser ordered me to the rampart, and they prepared for the next round of shooting.

Our target was not Batista, unfortunately. It was M-ski, with a mustache, done in black paint on packing paper, and like the last time in the cellar, it resembled—perhaps a little less—the huge faces we had carried in second grade in the May Day parade. Then it happened, the thing I didn't grasp at the time, but that in the school's main office somehow began to seem no accident. As I anchored the sheet of paper with the final stone, shots range out from the firing range. *Pow, pa-pow, pa-pa-pow* echoed through the forest. A one, two, three series. "Hurry!" Elka shouted. "Move, we're starting!" I realized that I had to get out of the line of fire before the next volley, because it was Weiser's turn now and he was waiting impatiently for the shooting to begin again on the other side, which would be in less than ten seconds. I had ten seconds to get off the rampart and run the length of the narrow path along the edge of the hollow back to the others. I went as fast as my legs could carry me, but halfway down the path the shooting started. Could Weiser tell if I was far enough from the target, that he, the best shot, could fire now? I was thinking this when I felt a pinch below my left ankle, just above the heel. A thistle or stone, I thought, but a moment later I was on the grass, and the pain wouldn't let me get up or take a step. The others ran out from the ferns, leaving the gun behind.

"A ricochet," Weiser shouted. "Don't move, don't move," and then they were around me.

Elka removed my sandal, and Weiser lifted my

foot and took a look. A ricochet, all right. The bullet had torn out a small chunk of flesh, but hadn't lodged there.

"Good," said Weiser, "the bone wasn't touched. It has to be dressed, or it'll get infected."

"We're too far from home," said Elka, "and we don't even have peroxide."

I watched a trickle of blood make bits of dark mud in the dry sand. Szymek and Piotr helped me walk by supporting me on either side.

"The brickworks," Weiser ordered, taking command, and we indeed felt that we were in a war. From the other side of the rampart came a rumbling volley, and the whine of bullets before they hit their targets and buried themselves in the earth, but I was wounded for real, and my foot hurt badly. Weiser led the way, then we three came hobbling, and Elka brought up the rear because Weiser had told her to gather up the used targets and the gun, which was now wrapped in an old piece of burlap.

It was cool in the cellar, and for a moment my foot hurt less, but only for a moment, because when Elka touched my heel, I screamed, "What are you doing?" She backed off, partly frightened and partly out of respect for my wound, from which blood still flowed. They laid me on top of one of the big boxes.

"Got dirt in it," said Weiser, meaning the hole in my foot. "Not good. Water," he said to Elka, and when she left, he opened the other box and took out a Primus stove. "We'll wash it first," he said to no one in particular. "Then it has to be cauterized." He took a broken German bayonet from the box, another of his finds. Elka brought some water in a tin can and used a handkerchief to clean the hole.

"Hurt?" she asked. I said nothing. My eyes were on Weiser the whole time. He put the Primus on two bricks, lit the burner, and bathed the blade in the bluish flame, constantly turning it.

"It's the only way," he said, not removing his gaze from the burner, "to stop gangrene. This is all we have here."

Szymek pressed my ribs to the box, Piotr gripped my right leg and also pressed it so it couldn't move, and Weiser held my left calf, under the knee, like a real medic, and with the red-hot blade began to operate. He had to lift my foot into the light, and as he dug the point of the bayonet into the hole, I could see his hand. "That Schmeisser," he said quietly, digging, "is worthless. I knew it was off a little, but that much is unacceptable." That's how he put it: unacceptable. And he added, as the blade went deeper into the hole, "We'll scrap it, take out the lock, magazine, firing pin." Who was he speaking to? We were all silent, and the smell of burned flesh filled the cellar. "Good," he said, putting down the bayonet. "Now bind it, and you two can take him home."

Elka gingerly tied a piece of wet cloth around my foot, though she didn't have to be so careful, because from the moment Weiser took the blade from the hole, I felt nothing, as if I had no foot, or it wasn't mine, made only of wood. "I'll stay here a while," he said. "You"—turning to Elka—"go with them." When we were on the creaking steps, he stopped us for a moment. "They'll make you stay home," he said to me. "And if they ask what happened, tell them you walked into barbed wire. Yes, some rusty barbed wire," he said calmly. "Now go!"

I don't remember exactly what route we took home, perhaps the usual way across the hill above the firing range, or maybe through the field dotted with boulders, which we called the quarry. Even then, what Weiser had said seemed strange to me. The gun we'd used hadn't been off at all, since even I, on my turn before the accident, had managed to hit M-ski five times with it. and if it was off, then by the principles of gunsmithing it should have been off above or below the target, not to the side.

"They'll make you stay home." I recalled his words, sitting in the main office, and suddenly I realized that that had been the whole point, that was what Weiser intended, to prevent my being with them for the next few days, so I would have to find out everything from Szymek or Piotr. Weiser had deliberately removed me, and not because of my poor shooting. Perhaps it was to warn me. Warn me of what? In any case, to the end of the vacation my foot gave me a lot of trouble, and even now, as I write this and look at my sock, I know that two centimeters below my anklebone is the scar from Weiser's ricochet and cauterization. And when the wind from the bay changes direction, I'll feel a slight twinge in my left foot, a permanent reminder of what happened in the hollow behind the firing range, of Weiser, of all the days of that sweltering summer, when drought ruined the fields, the bay was filled with fish soup, the bishop, priests, and their congregations asked God for rain, people saw a comet in the shape of a horse's head, Yellow Wings escaped from the insane asylum and was chased by the militia, the bricklayers converted the Protestant chapel into a new movie theater opposite the Lilliput, and the men in our building loved the speeches of Władysław Gomułka and said that the workers had never had such a leader, nor would again. Everything my eyes saw then, and my hands touched, is contained in the scar above my heel, a centimeter long and half a centimeter wide, the scar I finger when I lose the thread sometimes or wonder if all *that* was as real as our cobblestone street, and Cyrson's, and the stinking butcher's, and the barracks next to the soccer field. Or when doubt comes and tells me that it was only a boy's dream about his childhood, about the terrible nature teacher M-ski and that strange, obsessed grandson of Abraham Weiser the tailor. That's when I bend down and finger the scar, my left foot, my right hand, and then I know that Weiser existed, that the explosions in the hollow were real explosions, and that nothing in this story was invented, not one sentence of it, not one moment of that summer and that investigation. And again I see Father Dudak and his golden censer, and smell the burning amber, and hear, "Glo-ory to Thee, Jesus, So-on of Mary," and see Weiser emerge from the gray cloud, which is redolent of eternity and mercy; I see the way he regards all this with unblinking eyes, and then the chant "Da-vid Wei-ser doesn't go to chu-urch." His checked shirt is thrown into the air, Elka fights like a lioness, and still we understand nothing. But is there any point in this story where one can say, "I understand"? Do I understand, for example, why Weiser removed me for a while? Or how Piotr, resting in the earth, is able to talk with me? No theory will help. All I can do is continue telling.

227

So. If Weiser, for reasons of his own, wanted me out of the way, his goal was achieved. The next day my foot swelled up like a balloon, and pus collected in the hole. My mother dragged me to the doctor, who cleaned the foot and recommended compresses and as little walking as possible. Now I had to spend the whole day peeling potatoes, watching the noodle pot, and hearing my mother complain about my father and all men, because she was the good, complaining kind of mother. My foot, in her opinion, was a punishment for disobedience and constantly running around outside. On top of that, the radio was on all the time, and as I peeled the potatoes or rolled out the noodles, which I hated because it was lousy woman's work, the Opoczno and Łowicz folk choirs took turns howling in the kitchen, or else it was arias from *Boris Godunov* and *La Traviata,* long and boring, interrupted now and then with some overture. I was sorry we didn't have a radio like Mr. Korotek's that could get different frequencies. Ours had only one station; the most the black rubber knob could do was turn down a folk soprano's screech or the blast of a Russian baritone. My mother wouldn't let me turn the radio off, because once in a while they played dance music, or even a little American jazz. Then she'd turn the black rubber knob up all the way, take the rolling pin or the potato knife from my hands, and do all my work for me, tapping her feet, singing along, and beaming. My mother loved to dance, but as far as I can remember, my father never took her anywhere with him. After dinner, he usually fell asleep under his paper, tired from work, and on Sundays, when we came back from church, he'd get into bed, and could nap the rest of the day, unless one of his friends or a neighbor dragged him off to the Lilliput. So I was bored to tears, and the only book in the house, aside from the cookbook, was *The Doll* by Prus, which I gave up on after the first chapter. I was dying to know what the others were doing, but my mother wouldn't let me stick my head out the window, so I couldn't even call to Szymek or Piotr when they crossed the courtyard. For two days, nothing—as if Weiser had forbidden them to come to our apartment. On the third day, in the morning, Piotr knocked at the door. He and I had to whisper, because the apartment had only a living room and a kitchen, and my mother went back and forth between the two, ironing and cooking at the same time.

"Yesterday he showed us a new trick," said Piotr, with no great enthusiasm.

"What was it?" I asked, frantic. "What did he do?"

"Nothing much, a trick with coals."

"Coals? What kind of coals?"

229

"We made a fire."

"Where?" I interrupted.

"Near the brickworks. In a field by some hazel trees," Piotr said.

"What was the trick?"

Prodded by my questions, Piotr told me that first they'd shot in the cellar with a Soviet gun, which was harder than either the Parabellum or the Schmeisser, because it kicked like hell and was way off. Then Weiser said they should meet in that field, in the evening, and they went, and then he said that the time we saw him in the cellar dancing and floating in the air, we might have thought he was crazy. He wasn't angry about that; in our shoes, he would have thought the same. But he wasn't crazy at all, because, he explained, he was planning to join the circus.

I couldn't believe my ears.

"Planning to join the circus," Piotr repeated, eating the cherries my mother had brought us on a china plate. "As soon as he's worked out a few super tricks, he'll quit school, and any circus manager will welcome him with open arms, even without a seventh-grade certificate, and Elka will be his assistant."

"And the firing range? And the explosions? And the guns? And what about the ship and the uprising and the guerrilla war?"

"We asked him about that, too," said Piotr, spitting cherry pits into his cupped hand, "and he said the shooting was only for fun, but he might use it in one of his tricks, he hadn't decided yet. And he showed us," Piotr went on, "the trick with coals. Out of the fire we made, he took coals, put them on the ground, and stood on them barefoot. Then he walked back and forth on them, nothing to it, and when he showed us his feet, there wasn't one burn. Any more cherries?"

From the kitchen I brought a colander filled with cherries, the last of the year.

"And did Elka play music while he did it?"

"No," he said. His full mouth kept him from talking fast. "She jabbered the whole time, probably because she'd seen it before."

"He didn't say anything else?"

"What else was there to say? We were standing with our mouths open. That's a trick only fakirs can do, but he can do it, too."

"Then why doesn't he go to the circus now? He can do so much, they'd take him right away. Remember the panther at the zoo?"

"Umm." Piotr was spitting pits one after another, this time into the plate.

"Maybe he's working on another trick."

He shrugged. "How would I know? Circus artists themselves don't know what they're going to do next." Finished with the cherries, he said good-bye and left, without even telling me what they were doing tomorrow.

I sat all evening and pictured Weiser in a tail-coat, a whip in his hand, taming lions or panthers, bowing in the spotlight to thunderous applause. And Elka, in a costume covered with sequins sparkling like diamonds. She would hold the flaming hoop, or put her head in the mouth of the most ferocious lion, frightening the audience to death and making all the old ladies faint. Weiser had outwitted us again, completely, because we believed him, taking this latest trick of walking on coals as proof that his circus plan was true. True, and not a clever fraud. I'm not talking about his bare feet on the coals—that part was undoubtedly genuine. I mean the way he turned our eyes in a completely differ-ent, new direction, so no other ideas would occur to us.

The clock in the main office struck eleven. I regained my sense of time. The door of the head-master's study opened suddenly, and I heard M-ski pronounce my name.

"Sit," barked the militiaman. "And you," he said to Szymek, "go back to your place!"

"We'd like to know," M-ski came straight to the point, "why only Korolewski wrote in his state-ment that you three burned a scrap of red dress.

Why didn't you, or your other friend, mention that?"

"I was afraid, sir."

"You were afraid?"

"Yes."

"Well, then, tell us where you found this unfortunate piece of material."

"In the hollow behind the firing range, sir, where Weiser did his explosions."

"That we already know," said the headmaster in a milder voice. "What we need is the precise location. Tell us that, and everything will be all right." Saying this, he played with the end of his tie, which now resembled not a Jacobin jabot or a wet rag but a noose with a knot that could slide up or down.

"Try to remember," the militiaman said.

"Near the ferns."

M-ski laughed dryly.

"Indeed! There are more ferns there than trees!"

The militiaman spread out the map of the hollow on the desk.

"Come here," he said, "and show us exactly where."

What was I to do? I had no idea which spot Piotr had shown them, or Szymek after him. I chose a spot near the cross that marked where Weiser had laid the charges.

233

"You're lying!" shouted M-ski. "Again you're lying, and your friends are lying, you're all lying, but I'll . . ." He started toward me, to grab me by the ear, but the headmaster quickly stopped him.

"Wait, let's ask him where the fire was, where they burned the scrap of cloth."

"It wasn't a scrap," I said, and they froze in surprise, waiting to hear what I'd say next. "It wasn't a scrap, sir, it was a whole piece of a dress."

"Korolewski clearly wrote 'a scrap,'" said the militiaman, leaning so close that I could see the trickles of sweat on his temples. "And now you're telling us it was a whole dress!"

"No, sir, it wasn't a whole dress, definitely not, it was a piece as large as . . . that map," and I showed in the air how large it was, though no one had ever seen it, because Elka hadn't been blown up at all. The militiaman came even closer.

"If that's so, then there must have been pieces of body, too. But Korolewski didn't mention that, nor did either of you two."

"Were there pieces of body?" growled M-ski. "Don't lie!"

"There was only that piece of dress, sir," I replied, satisfied that I had confused them. But they didn't let themselves be taken in; they returned to the first question.

"Large or small," said the headmaster, "you

haven't told us the most important thing: where did you burn it?"

"Near the railroad embankment."

"What embankment?"

"The one no trains run on."

"Where exactly?"

"By the blown-up bridge."

"You're lying," said M-ski, now dangerously close. "There are several blown-up bridges there. Which one?"

"The one behind the Brentowo church, sir, where the tracks cross the Rembiechowo highway."

"Enough!" shouted M-ski. "Enough lies. Your friends tell a different story." And he grabbed me by both ears at once and pulled up, making me levitate like Weiser in the cellar of the abandoned brickworks. "How long will you three keep lying? There was more than the dress, wasn't there? Where did you bury the remains of your classmate?" He lifted me, dropped me, lifted me, but I couldn't answer, I only cried, "Let go, sir, please let go!" until finally he did, because his hands hurt. He shoved me to the wall, where I could rest a moment. "Paws out," he panted. "Maybe this will help your memory." And from the drawer he took a length of rubber hose, which he used to maintain order in his nature classes. "Come here," he said, but I didn't budge. "Come here," he said, with a glance at the

235

headmaster and the militiaman. "Are you afraid?" I stayed by the wall.

"Are you going to tell us or not?" asked the militiaman.

"I told you everything, sir," I whimpered, tears running down my face, but the sight of them only infuriated M-ski, who came up to me, grabbed my hand, opened it as if I were a little child, and dealt five blows that sounded like horse's hoofs on asphalt.

"Tell us."

"It was the same place, sir, where we saw you at the Strzyża!"

"Where's that?" asked the headmaster.

"At the Strzyża. It's the river that flows under the railroad embankment."

M-ski froze, but only for a moment. His cheeks reddened.

"I hunt butterflies there sometimes," he said, turning to the others. "But that has nothing to do with this." He grabbed my hand again, but I kept ahead of him.

"You didn't have your butterfly net that time," I said, "or your folder for plants!" The rubber hose hung in midair, didn't fall on my open hand. M-ski glowered at me, but there was fear in his glower.

"You're sure of that?"

"Yes, sir." And I smiled brazenly, because the

cards had been put on the table, at least some of them, though the militiaman and the headmaster suspected nothing.

"Very well," he said, "we'll think it over." And to the other two: "Let's break for tea."

When I went out into the main office, for the first time experiencing the nauseating taste of blackmail, mixed with tears, the janitor jumped up from his chair. "All done, then?" he asked the militiaman. "That's it?" "No" was the answer. "A pot of water, please, and as for you"—to us—"no talking!" The janitor vanished with the pot, and we could hear him limping down the empty corridor. The door to the headmaster's study was kept ajar, to make sure we didn't talk. Everything they said could be heard, if we listened carefully, but this time we didn't avail ourselves of the opportunity.

"We—found it—by the old—oak," Szymek whispered. "Burned it—that evening—at the quarry. Seven o'clock—out of fear." Before the janitor came back down the corridor, which smelled of silence and floor wax, the most important things were established. Szymek had made up good details, and they were plausible, too. The old oak tree in the hollow was hard to miss. Had Elka been blown up, a piece of her dress could easily have settled there. Finding the piece, we didn't know what to do with it. And at the quarry, forty min-

237

utes on foot from the hollow, there was in fact a spot designated by the ranger for campfires. So we went there, a natural choice, and there fire claimed the piece of red cloth. The janitor returned with the pot of water and took it into the headmaster's study.

"I found it—at the roots," Szymek whispered. "You put it—in your pocket," meaning me, "and Piotr—threw it on the fire. Then home."

The janitor was with us again, the door was closed—and as I recall that scene today, I think it was the finest stage whisper I ever heard. One thing puzzles me: Why was the janitor sent for water then and not one of us? Left unguarded, even with the headmaster's door ajar, we could quickly put together a story that had no holes in it. Was it because they wanted to get the investigation over with? Was this M-ski's idea? I thought about M-ski through the long break, as they drank tea and we went on sitting in the main office on the folding chairs, which hurt our behinds.

M-ski was faced with a problem now; he understood what had happened, that was clear. So the game of the investigation had become a game between M-ski and me, and although I never told the boys about my act of blackmail, the first in my life, this game went on for years and years, after graduation, after Piotr's death, and it is continuing today, I think, in another time and place. When I finished school, M-ski was still teaching nature, was still the assistant headmaster. Later, after 1970, when two heads of state signed the agreement that both Polish and German newspapers called historic, and many people left for the land of Georg Wilhelm Friedrich Hegel, I learned that M-ski was among them. At the time, I shrugged, never expecting to see him again. But I did. During my visit to Elka, which was a game, too, as I've written, involving Weiser, M-ski reappeared, incredibly, as if nothing could happen without him.

From the large sitting room where Elka lay, I had made my way up to the bedroom. My arms were no longer the wings of an Ilyushin 14, and the rest of my members in no way resembled the silver fuselage that lifted her red dress. Beside the bed was a small portable TV. Depressed, I switched it on and got into Horst's pajamas, paying no attention to the program. Then, on the screen, I saw the face of M-ski, smiling, plump. He was answering a reporter's questions.

"Why did you decide so late to return to the Fatherland?" asked the reporter.

"Och, that's not simple," said the face. "I would say, in general, for political reasons."

"What did you do in Poland?"

"Scientific research," said the face. "And I had to teach school."

"Why had to?"

"My research, which focused on the uniqueness of the flora and fauna of the forest surrounding Gdańsk"—a frown—"was ignored."

"Did you publish the results of your scientific work upon your arrival here?"

"Unfortunately," said the face, showing a certain annoyance, "my manuscript was confiscated at the border."

"Why?"

"Also for political reasons, I'm afraid." Without batting an eye.

"What are you doing at present?"

"At present," the face said, hesitating, "I teach vocational subjects at a school of horticulture."

"Are you able now to continue your research unhampered?"

"Oh, yes." A smile like a Coca-Cola ad. "Unhampered!"

"What are you working on now, may we ask?"

"I am studying"—on the face, great gravity—"a near-extinct species of butterfly in Upper Bavaria."

"Will the results of your work be published?"

"Yes," replied the face, "quite soon."

I was about to turn off the television and the face, when the Chancellor appeared on the screen, Herr Willy Brandt. He was making a speech to the Bundestag, against the Greens. "You have no idea, Mr. Chancellor," I said aloud, since there was no one in the room, "the kind of ally they have now." And I switched off the set, afraid the face would jump at me from the screen, the face of many years ago, with a mustache painted by Weiser.

This discovery depressed me completely, and the next day I was on my way to Munich, to my uncle, who had a beautiful house, lawn, car, and nothing else. I thought about the woman who had looked like a housewife and slapped M-ski in the face. Even today that memory gives me mixed feelings, because if M-ski goes after near-extinct butterflies in Lower or Upper Bavaria in the summer, he's sure to rendezvous with some Bavarian lady. Just as by the Strzyża, he'll stand above a mountain stream, which will drown out the resounding smacks of the sturdy German female.

What happened next? We believed Weiser's story. If he didn't want to be a general or a pirate, why shouldn't he be a circus artist? My dream—I reasoned at the time—only confirmed this: Weiser was a born animal tamer. Except why did he need the pyrotechnic explosions and that arsenal he'd amassed in the cellar of the abandoned brickworks? That, I couldn't understand, because the two things didn't go together. So I believed, but not completely, not a hundred percent, and kept my doubts to myself when I went to the next explosions in the hollow behind the firing range. Each time, the hole in my foot started oozing again; my mother yelled, and kept a closer watch on me than ever, so I wouldn't go out. I won't describe the explosions, I did that already. I don't think I left anything out. And Weiser? Besides the explosions, he went on teaching Szymek and Piotr how to shoot, in the cellar and the hollow. They were having fun, and I had to sit at home bored. I didn't dare go out, either, not because of my mother, but because if my foot got worse, I wouldn't be able to sneak out for the next explosion, which I always knew about a day in advance from Szymek or Piotr.

Time passed, and one day I looked up at the sky and saw the first clouds. Their high stretched-out feathers promised no change in the weather, but now I could sit at the window, my chin in my hands, and watch them slowly change shape against an aquamarine sky. The news brought by Szymek and Piotr was the same: the fish soup in the bay had thinned a little, stinking heaps of carrion no longer covered the sand, but forget about swimming. One kid who put his foot in the water on a dare pulled it out immediately in disgust. Sea gulls were dying, too, and sanitation men had collected their bodies into huge piles, which from a distance looked like hills of snow. They were carted outside town with the fish and burned at the public dump. The Jelitkowo fishermen appealed to the authorities for compensation, but no one had said anything definite yet. In Brentowo, Yellow Wings had turned up again. People said he was parading about in a rusty helmet—ours—near houses, frightening everyone. He still wasn't caught. He wasn't sleeping in our crypt, either, so he must have had another hiding place. Also, in the valley on the other side of the embankment, just beyond the cemetery, there were men with poles measuring the ground and putting up barbed-wire fences. In the fenced-in areas, other people were putting up sheds and little houses out of planks, old plywood, and tar paper. They didn't like strangers hanging around. Maybe because they had hoes, spades, and rakes in those sheds, or maybe because they were simply nasty, unpleasant people, which is what Piotr thought.

In Gdańsk, at Long Market, a historical tram had been put into operation, drawn by two horses, but a ticket cost fifty groszy. Piotr and Szymek went for a ride on it, but not with Elka and Weiser, who that day had disappeared somewhere. I asked where they could have gone—the airfield? the brick-works?—but apart from the fact that Elka took the music instrument with her that morning, the one she'd played when Weiser danced, they couldn't tell me a thing. Szymek's guess was that Weiser was preparing a new trick and would be showing it to us soon. Today I know that Weiser wasn't preparing any trick, because he had never intended to join the circus. But we believed then, and, be-lieving, could admire his arsenal or go for a ride, like Szymek and Piotr that day, in a historical tram for fifty groszy. What other news? Not a drop of water was coming out of Neptune's Well, and Mr. Korotek was fined for not crossing the street at the intersection where they'd recently installed the town's first traffic light. He called the militiamen names, too, and they almost took him to the station. What else? On the next street, Karłowicz Street, there were electric lights; all the old gas lamps were going to be scrapped. The Lilliput was closed for three days, after the last fight between the bricklayers and some soldiers who didn't have passes. The new movie theater was going to be called the Torch, and they said it would have a panoramic screen, which our local Tramway didn't.

Weiser never once visited me, and when I went to his explosions, he didn't say a word about the hole in my foot and what had happened afterward. Time passed slowly and uneventfully for me, as for everyone in our district that hot summer, when the dust of June, the grit of July, and the grime of August were not once washed from the leaves by longed-for drops of rain. Having nothing else to do, I drew pictures in a notebook, of whatever came into my head. Yellow Wings standing on a roof in the Old Town. Behind him, slender pines. And above the town, above the heads of those gathered on the sidewalk, airplanes, airplanes in flocks, like cranes. Another page was filled with Weiser. Weiser flying over the bay on a black panther. The fishermen fall to their knees and their wives hide their heads in fear. There was also Mr. Korotek, rolling across the courtyard a bottle of vodka big as a barrel, and mice run out of it and make for the nearest garbage can. I drew M-ski, too, and Father Dudak, whom I gave butterfly wings and put in the nature teacher's net. And there was a landscape, a view from the hills toward the airfield, with an airplane in the shape of a censer flying by. We were all inside it, and over the town, the bay, and the cemetery instead of the sun there was a giant triangular eye, and it sent its rays in all directions. My mother didn't like it when I sat hunched over the paper, because she saw me drawing not flowers and trees but crazy stuff—that's what she called it—and she interrupted by making me see to the potatoes again or the noodles.

Until one day—I think it was after the fifth explosion, and my foot was almost healed—Szymek knocked at the door of our apartment. In his hands he had a scroll of paper.

"Know what this is?" he said from the doorway. "Guess, guess!"

"A flag? A wanted notice? An advertisement?"

"Better," he said, grinning. "It's a poster!"

"Oh," I said.

As Szymek unrolled the colorful paper on the couch, he said excitedly: "The man who sticks things on the bill posts, the one with the old bicycle, gave it to me. See what a beauty it is!" I saw a lion, jaws open wide, and beside it a woman in a tiny spangled dress. Underneath, the caption read: COME TO THE CIRCUS.

"Nice," I said.

"Nice? You don't understand." He gave me the happy news. "We're going to the circus! Tomorrow!"

"We don't have tickets."

"Elka's buying them, for you, too."

"And the money?"

"Don't worry about that. You'll pay it back when you can."

"How much?"

"Ten zlotys for adults, five for us."

"Where did you get that much?"

"I'll tell you the whole story." Szymek moved the poster aside and sat on the couch, because all the chairs in the room were piled with laundry. "Piotr went to Gdańsk this morning, to the hardware store, to buy some nails for his father. At the square he saw circus wagons. Well, he didn't go to the store. Instead, he got off at the stop there and had a good look at everything, the wagon the clown lives in, the wild-animal cages, the horses, the acrobats. He even saw the magician's top hat, because when the men were carrying things, the hat fell out and rolled on the ground, and the magician, who looked like an ordinary man, shouted and called the men stupid. Piotr saw and heard all this, and he watched the circus people put up the tent, too, pulling the cables and then hammering stakes into the ground with huge hammers. Then he remembered the nails for his father, bought them, and came back and told us the news. Half an hour later—it could have been an hour—this comes to our bill post." Szymek put his hand on the garish poster.

"But the money. Where did you get the money?"

"That part's amazing," he went on. "We were standing by the bill post, watching the man putting

247

on the glue and pressing out the posters one after another, because he was covering the whole post with the same poster, and we were standing there and saying how great it would be to go to the circus if we had the money. I had enough for a ticket, and Piotr, too, but Elka probably didn't, and Weiser, who knows, and then there was you. Anyway, Mr. Korotek came up, completely sober, and it turned out he had heard us. 'How many are you, then?' he asked. 'Five,' we said, because with you we're five. He took out his wallet and give us thirty zlotys. 'There,' he said. 'When you sell some bottles, you can pay me back. But you don't have to.' Elka went to get the tickets. She's buying them for tomorrow, because tomorrow's when it starts. Super, huh?" He rolled up the poster again. "I'm hanging it over my bed," he added. "Unless my mother throws it out, because the lady doesn't have much on."

Szymek left, pleased with himself, and my mother, who had heard a little, said she'd give me five zlotys for a ticket. I didn't need, she said, to take advantage of Mr. Korotek's bigheartedness.

Next day, from morning on, time went at an insufferable crawl, because the show we had tickets for didn't start until four o'clock. I went outside to see the posters. The concrete bill post looked wonderful, plastered from top to bottom and all around with lion's jaws and women in tiny dresses. Usually it was a drab thing, with nothing new on it for months and months, just a patchwork of tattered notices, obscene graffiti, and last year's military registration orders. I stood spellbound and wondered if the lion I'd see at the circus would be as ferocious as the one on the poster. I stared at the gaping jaws, the rows of enormous, shiny fangs, and suddenly felt a light poke in my side.

"You're walking." It was Weiser's voice. "The foot's not swollen?"

"No," I said. "And it doesn't hurt anymore, either. So?" In my "So?" was hope and anticipation, because if Weiser came up behind me and asked a question, he must be thinking of something.

"Come," he said. "I'll show you how to catch grass snakes."

"What do you want grass snakes for?" I asked. "Are you training them?"

He shrugged. "If you don't want to come, don't. I thought you'd like to see it," he said slowly, as if he didn't care.

I did want to see how grass snakes were caught. We went up the street.

"But what do you want them for?" I asked again.

"You'll see," he said. "Here's the sack we put them in," he explained, "and in the forest we'll find a stick."

We passed a row of small, almost identical houses with slanted roofs and half-circle attic windows that looked like automobile headlights turned off during the day. Weiser, as we climbed a path through the larches, said nothing. Ten minutes later, panting, we stood on a hilltop, with a view of the airfield and the bay on one side, and to the south, far below, Brentowo and the hills in front of the firing range.

"We're going there," he said, pointing south, "where those fences have been put up, for garden plots."

We went down the slope now, as if on skis—left, right, zigzagging to keep from running too fast. Different scents met in the air: the sweet smell of faded lupine mixed with clover, the cool fragrance of mint and the tang of wild thyme.

"Will you sell them? Or take them to M-ski? But one snake would be enough for him, wouldn't it? Why does he need more than one?" I asked when we reached the valley bordered by the cemetery and the embankment on which no trains ran. Weiser didn't answer. First he looked for and found a stick a meter long and forked, the kind used by snake hunters in the Bieszczady Mountains. Then he turned to me.

"See that thicket?"

I nodded.

"A lot of them there. Go and shake the bushes. But gently," he added, "so they don't all come out at once."

Not a difficult task. I walked carefully along the edge of the thicket, and with a stick stirred the clumps of tall grass, the nettles, the raspberry bushes, the black broom, and the ferns. The grass snakes slithered out from under my feet, first slowly, then more quickly, and without a sound fled in Weiser's direction. He immobilized them with the forked stick, then gingerly grasped them with his fingers and threw them into the sack.

"Again," he said when I finished the flushing. "They don't all come out the first time."

I did it again, exactly as before, and to my surprise almost as many snakes slithered out the second time. Weiser closed the sack with a tight knot.

"Good," he said. "Now let's cross those damned gardens and take them to the other side." He said "damned gardens"—I remember that, because Weiser never said more than he had to. He said it again as we passed the people working there, stubbornly digging the desert-dry soil and even more stubbornly nailing together planks and plywood with holes in it to make their shacks. On these shacks, for some reason, they painted smiling elves, lost fawns, or daisies with girls' faces, which looked awful, even indecent.

"What do you have there, boys?" a fat, sweaty man asked us, looking up from his hoe. "What are you doing here?"

"Nothing, mister," I answered first. "Just picking grass for our rabbits. There's a lot here."

Weiser slowed down but didn't stop, didn't even glance at the fat man, and I followed him, my eyes on the sack, which swung in time to his steps.

"From now on," called the fat man, "you get your grass somewhere else. I don't want to see you here again, understand? This land belongs to people now." The fat man went on shouting, but we were soon out of earshot. The path led down to the embankment.

"Good thinking," said Weiser. "You can be relied on."

My heart almost burst with pride. I didn't notice how we reached the cemetery, the upper part of it, where he stopped me with a motion of his hand.

"We'll let them out here," he said, untying the sack. "They'll be all right here."

I watched as the grass snakes crept out of the open sack, some quickly and some, perhaps more frightened, so slowly that Weiser had to prod them with a finger. The snakes scattered among the gravestones. Their gray-brown bodies slid, curving, into the dense underbrush of nettles and hogweed, and after a moment there wasn't one in sight. No, that isn't true, there was one. I saw a snake on a gravestone, in flickering sunlight, sunlight filtered through a dome of beech leaves as through the green stained glass in our church during High Mass. The snake was more than a meter long, and hardly moved; it only raised its head, as if to the light, then lowered it again onto the stone. The symmetrical yellow near its snout shone whenever a ray of sun broke through and hit the slab. "Look," I whispered to Weiser, "it's not afraid of us." And indeed, when I put out my hand and touched the snake, and felt the cold of its flattened snout, cold like a dog's nose, it didn't wriggle away, it only recoiled slightly. After a while, it turned its snout from us and disappeared into a nearby clump of fern, which swayed lightly from its passage.

"Something's written here," I said to Weiser. "Can you read it?"

He leaned over the marker and read:

"Hier ruht in Gott Horst Meller. 8 VI 1925–15 I 1936." And further, syllable by syllable: "Werst unser Slieb alle Zeit und Hliebst es auch in Snigkeit. I don't know German," he said, "but the first part means Here Lies Horst Meller, and the second's a poem, because it rhymes. See?" He put his finger on the carved gothic letters. "Zeit, and the second line, Snigkeit. Eit-eit, it's definitely a poem."

"He was eleven when he died," I said. "Our age."

"No, he was born in 1929, not 1925," said Weiser, putting his face to the inscription. "It's a nine, not a five."

"You talk as if you knew him." For the first time, I argued with Weiser. "That's a five, not a nine. He was born in 1925, and was eleven when he died."

"Either way, we don't know who he was," Weiser cut me short, and on the way home he told me that the garden-plot people killed the grass snakes because they couldn't tell a grass snake from an adder. The moment they saw something crawling they ganged up and hit it with hoes and rakes, so the snakes had to be moved to the old cemetery or to the field with the boulders. That way, some of them might survive.

And Weiser was right. The next year, when the garden plots took over the whole valley behind the cemetery, on the other side of the embankment, and there were rows of carrots, peas, and cauliflower instead of tall grass, you hardly ever saw a grass snake, only the remains of one, with ants busy around it. Three or four years later, there were none anywhere—not in the old cemetery, either, or in the quarry, where Weiser also took them in his sack. I never really found out why he did this.

He certainly didn't have M-ski-like fondness for them, and his own explanation, to this day, doesn't satisfy me. Nor did I ever learn who Horst Meller was, buried in 1936, on whose gravestone my hand once touched a grass snake. I'm certain, however, that Weiser never had Piotr or Szymek help him evacuate the grass snakes, and on that day, the day we were going to the circus, he may have taken me along with him by chance, on the spur of the moment. Unless he felt that grass snakes were not for just anyone.

M-ski came and stood in the open doorway of the headmaster's study, looked first at me, then at Szymek and Piotr, then at the clock on the wall, and said, "Enough!" He examined our faces, as if to read his own thoughts in them. "Enough," he repeated after a long pause. "No more of this! You have one last chance, and if you don't take it, the prosecutor and the militia will attend to you! Do you understand?"

There was no reply.

"Korolewski"—Szymek's name rang out—"you're first!"

In my mind I rehearsed the details of our "funeral," and as the door slammed shut behind Szymek, I wasn't sure I would remember everything.

Was M-ski's threat real? I doubted it, but even if it was, it didn't frighten us. Because what more could frighten us? The clock said half past eleven. In the darkness outside, raindrops beat against the metal windowsill, and those three, clearly, also had had enough. How long can a person go on asking the same things?

The show began gloriously. An orchestra composed of a few brass instruments and a bass drum played a fanfare, and the ringmaster ran into the arena, dressed in a green tailcoat and a white shirt that had a profusion of lace in the front and at the wrists. He announced the first act, but before he could finish, a wrinkled dwarf in an elf's hood came up behind him and tugged at his tails. Then a dove flapped out from under the coat, and the ringmaster, not turning around, kicked the dwarf like a horse, and the dwarf, screeching, rolled off into the wings with somersaults. A hurricane of cheers, an avalanche of laughter accompanied their exit, and three acrobats entered the ring. First they paraded around it, showing off their muscles, taut and as big as melon halves. Next they lined up by height and jumped one on top of the other until they made a pyramid two stories high. The smallest one, at the very top, did tricks—stood on his hands, then on one leg, then sprang into the air, and went head over heels and landed on his partner's shoulders again.

"That's the oberman," Weiser whispered to Elka, but loud enough for us to hear. "What?" asked Szymek, uncertain. "The oberman," Elka repeated. "The one at the bottom's the unterman, the one in the middle's the mittelman, and the one jumping now, he's the oberman, the highest and the most important." "He might be the highest, but he's not the tallest," whispered Piotr, but there was no time for further argument, because the oberman did his last somersault, a double, and landed on the sand beside the unterman, then the mittelman jumped down, and now all three were bowing in all directions. The man in the green tailcoat came back and announced the act with the horses and the lady bareback rider. At the entrance to the wings, the dwarf was waiting for him with a tight-stretched rope—a trap for the ringmaster, except that the rope brought down, not him, but the dwarf, who then hopped like a frog after his exiting enemy.

After the horses' plumes and the brightly colored stockings and the rearing up and the rolling over, and then after a pair of acrobats in skintight outfits, Green Tailcoat announced the magician, whom he called an illusionist, but everyone was looking for the funny dwarf, wondering what he'd do this time. Suddenly the ringmaster clutched his stomach, made a twisted face, and a trombone in the orchestra produced a note that sounded like a fart. Then, from under his coattails, which bulged a little, though no one had noticed that until now, the dwarf, curled up in a ball, fell to the crash of the drum. Everyone doubled up with laughter, while the ringmaster summoned the clowns to clear the mess. Holding their noses, they kicked the offending object away, and the audience howled with delight, particularly when the ringmaster walked off bowlegged, as if his trousers were full. Only Weiser didn't laugh; he looked completely uninterested.

Szymek now took his binoculars out of his pocket. "Watch the hands and the sleeves carefully," Piotr told him. The magician was dressed like the ringmaster, except that his tailcoat was black. He wore a top hat, of course, and black patent-leather shoes polished like mirrors, and he did all his tricks in white gloves. First his lady assistant gave him an umbrella. In the blink of an eye the umbrella became a fishing rod, complete with reel and line and a hook at the end. The magician put a finger to his lips: Silence, please, because fish don't like noise. He leaned forward, as if over water, and cast the rod, and on the hook appeared a live, gleaming fish, and, what's more, completely golden. Piotr couldn't contain himself. "Do you see anything, do you see how he did it?" He nudged Szymek in the side. "Let me look." But Szymek kept adjusting the focus and said nothing. The fish was put in a bowl set on a small table by the lady assistant. You could see it swimming like a normal fish in a normal fishbowl. The magician cast again and reeled in another, and another, God knows from where, and each time a fish appeared on the hook, out of thin air, and then was swimming cheerfully in the bowl.

The magician put down the rod and took off his top hat. "Now," Piotr whispered feverishly, "now watch!" Out of the hat the magician pulled a long chain of colored scarves, then shook them, turning them into one big scarf, and with it he covered the bowl full of golden fish. With two shakes the rod became a magic wand, and with the wand he tapped the covered bowl. A drum roll and cymbals as the assistant removed the scarf. Instead of the fishbowl and the fish, on the table sat a white rabbit, twitching its ears, obviously alarmed by all the clapping. "He doesn't let me see a thing!" Szymek shouted over the din.

I glanced at Weiser, but he didn't seem to take any part in Szymek's and Piotr's excitement. He sat straight, his eyes fixed on some point in the ring, as if the whole thing bored him and he was sitting there only out of politeness. During the intermis-

259

sion, Elka and Piotr went to get some orangeade. Sitting beside Weiser, I didn't have the courage to ask him anything, even though he knew all about the art of the circus. The orchestra played enthusiastic marches and waltzes while people walked between the benches, exchanging a nod or a mumbled Excuse me. In the ring, two clowns were punching each other in the face, kicking each other in the behind, and throwing buckets of water at each other. Weiser, I thought, would love to be out there in a magnificent costume, bowing to the thunderous applause. I thought this, seeing his look of concentration and his pointed aloofness, as if to say, "I can do that better," like all unrecognized artists. That's what I thought then and long afterward, but today—reaching this point in the story— I think otherwise, especially in light of what happened in the second half of the show. I mean, of course, the incident during the lion taming.

After the intermission, I kept a careful eye on him during each act, watched his face, hands, fingers, which today tell me something quite different from what they told me then, when I believed, like Szymek, Piotr, and maybe Elka, that he wanted to join the circus. Weiser was very calm, applauded limply, and was not at all amused by the antics of the dwarf and Green Tailcoat between the acts. It was the same with the elephant parade, the fire eater, the hoop jugglers, the dogs' basketball game, the trapeze act, and the magician's second appearance. The magician this time pulled all sorts of things out of the air: a glass of milk, a squeaking balloon, an enormous bouquet, doves, a rabbit. Then from his top hat he took a bottle of champagne and two goblets, and finished by drinking a toast with his assistant, and the audience was delighted when the cork, flying up, turned into a dove. While everyone else was craning his neck and hopping in his seat and making loud remarks, Weiser didn't move. It was only when the finale came, and Green Tailcoat announced the evening's main attraction, the wild-animal act, that Weiser sat up straighter and folded his hands on his knee in impatience.

Down a tunnel leading to the cage that filled the ring ran two lions, a lioness, and a black panther. The panther was just like the one at the Oliwa zoo. Behind them came the tamer in high boots and a white shirt with a mandarin collar. The whip he held was a little shorter than a horsewhip. His wife and assistant in the same person—as Green Tailcoat introduced her—wore a skintight outfit trimmed with sequins. She had high boots, too, but they were white, with fringes at the top. The animals squinted as they prowled the ring, as if not sure what they were supposed to do.

"Herman! Brutus!" yelled the tamer. "To your

places!" The lions hesitated, then jumped onto stools. "Helga!" This was the lioness. "To your place!" She nimbly got onto her stool. It was the black panther's turn. "Sylvia! To your place!" The panther, just like the lions, in one bound was on her stool. The man cast a vigilant eye from animal to animal. "Herman! Brutus! Stand!" The lions rose on their hind legs, presenting their chests. "Helga! Sylvia! Stand!" The she-cats obeyed together, and now all four were standing, on their haunches, like dogs begging for a piece of sausage. The tamer bowed to the audience, there was loud applause, and the animals resumed their former position. The tamer approached them, cracked his whip, and when his assistant had put an extra stool in place, he yelled, "Herman, jump!" Herman jumped from his stool to the empty one. "Brutus, jump!" Brutus did the same, occupying the stool vacated by the first lion. "Helga, jump!" yelled the tamer, but Helga for some reason held back, didn't want to jump. "Helga, jump!" he yelled again. It was only at the third command, with some prompting from the whip, that Helga obeyed. The panther, however, didn't wait to be told, but jumped the moment the lioness left her stool. There was applause now without the tamer's bow. He went up to Sylvia and stroked her muzzle with the end of his whip. "Good Sylvia," he said aloud, "nice Sylvia," stroking her luxuriant whiskers. The panther responded by lifting her head and purring, a deep, throaty sound. The audience loved this and applauded again.

The tamer's wife put a large leather ball in position. "Herman, jump!" Herman jumped onto the ball, rolled it a few meters by moving his paws, then returned to his place, tossing his head in a comical way. Brutus did the same, then Helga. The panther, once again not waiting for the command, finished the trick, leaving the ball at the far end of the ring. There was loud cheering, but when I looked at Weiser, I saw he wasn't clapping—only drumming his fingers on his knee. The tamer's wife now brought out a hoop covered with something papery, and she set it on fire with a match. A murmur of excitement ran along the benches.

"Herman, jump!" yelled the tamer, and cracked his whip. The lion made a fabulous leap through the burning hoop and stood on the far side of the ring. "Brutus, jump!" He cracked the whip again, and the big cat's leap thrilled the crowd. "Helga, jump!" And again: "Sylvia, jump!" And both she-cats stood with the lions. The trick was repeated in reverse; the animals jumped back through the hoop of fire and landed on their stools, as the woman, her sequins glittering and shimmering, swept the hoop in the right direction. Again all four cats sat on their stools, and again the tamer bowed and received his applause.

Then something happened that no one would have thought could happen. The tamer's wife put out the fire by giving the hoop a quick shake; then, turning away from the animals, she went to the next prop—a seesaw, which stood by the bars of the cage. She had taken two, maybe three steps when she tripped in the sand. That was enough for the panther to make a lightning leap at her, and they hit the ground almost together—first the tamer's wife, and on top of her, striking her head with a paw, the panther. Two horrible sounds—a double thud and a short, strangled scream from the woman—then silence. No one in the audience moved.

"Sylvia!" The tamer took a step toward her. "Sylvia, to your place!" But the panther, instead of returning to the stool, clawed at the woman, in the area of her shoulder blades, as if to say to the tamer, "No closer, this is mine!" The lions shifted uneasily on their stools. Brutus swayed from foot to foot, and Helga gave a long, deep growl. From the wings two helpers came with a fire extinguisher, but the tamer motioned them to stop, because at that very moment the woman moved. Sylvia spat in anger and hit her mistress in the lower back, tearing the costume with her claws. On the sand fell sparkling sequins, and across the woman's bared buttock red lines of blood began to flow. Someone in the upper benches sobbed, but was quickly silenced.

Weiser sat straight, his head motionless, but his fingers kept drumming on his knee. Dear Christ, I thought, let him go down there and show them what he can do, because he can, he can. Let him look the panther in the eye the way he did at the zoo, and tame her, subdue her, crush her rebellion as he did with that other one, and reduce her to a timid little dog, and let him do it, please, before it's too late.

Herman jumped from his stool and lifted his head, smelling an exciting smell. The tamer signaled to the orchestra, and the musicians began to play, at half volume, the exit music. The lions stirred, restless. "Herman! Brutus! Helga! Here! Here!" the tamer said. "Here! Here!" The lions reluctantly went toward the tunnel; then slowly, as if half asleep, they went through the opening, and a helper closed the gate behind them.

The tamer had only the panther to deal with. Both her forepaws rested on the woman's still body, and her tail flicked in agitation, left, right. "Sylvia," he said more quietly, "good Sylvia, to your place, Sylvia!" But the panther, aware of her advantage, gave a warning snarl. Her eyes followed the man's every move. "Sylvia"—he took one step forward—"to your place!" But Sylvia had no intention of surrendering her trophy. From her throat came a rumble, and she raised her paw, threatening to strike. Weiser's fingers still drummed on his knee, and for the first time I was furious with him. If it hadn't been for the horror of the situation, I would have screamed at him and gone at him with my fists. Why didn't he move, why didn't he go down there and show his ability, now, as the red puddle grew larger on the sand? How could he sit there so quietly, as if he were watching the bareback rider or the clowns? Dear Christ, I thought, do something to make him move, give him a shove, he'll do the rest himself, he can, he can, just make him . . . But Weiser sat like a statue, head and face of stone, legs of stone, except his long fingers, which kept drumming in three-quarter time.

The tamer didn't know what to do. He couldn't step forward, he couldn't step back; he stood as one hypnotized and kept on speaking to Sylvia, more and more softly, repeating the same words. "To your place! Good Sylvia, to your place!" And this was more frightening than the possibility that the panther would attack him. One of the helpers moved around the outside of the cage, slowly, so as not to attract attention, with a fire extinguisher under his arm. A second man came from the wings with an air rifle. Drawing closer and closer to the panther, they both crouched. I didn't know then that the fire extinguisher contained a drug and that the air rifle shot tranquilizer darts. The men looked ridiculous, like small boys with a wooden sword and a slingshot stalking an African buffalo. The panther pawed at the woman, but without conviction. The man with the fire extinguisher knelt, aimed, and released a powerful stream into the animal's face. The panther sprang to her feet. The blast pushed her head back, but her large paws remained in place for a second, so that when she abandoned her prey, she dragged it a meter, maybe two, in the sand. Then, snarling at her invisible enemy and pawing the air, she drew back to the other side of the cage. Hit by a dart from the rifle, she shuddered in a brief epileptic dance and fell. The tamer was now at his wife's side; he took her in his arms and carried her out. Three helpers threw the panther onto a canvas sheet, which they dragged to another exit.

That was the end of the show. I wept. I was sorry for the pretty lady and her costume with the sequins, but I was sorrier, bitterly sorry, about Weiser. Because I knew one thing: either he couldn't do everything, or he had refused to help. It seemed more likely that he had refused to help, and this was horrible—refused to rush down there, squeeze through the bars, and stand eye to eye with the black panther. The audience hadn't gasped with fear, then with joy when the boy approached the beast and humbled it with a stare mightier than all the darts and fire extinguishers in the world. No, nothing like that had happened, because Weiser felt that he didn't need to do all that for the tamer's wife in her skintight outfit trimmed with sequins. Who, then, would he do it for? Elka, perhaps, I thought, or one of us. If he'd done what he should have done, besides saving the woman he would have been rewarded—recognition, fame, maybe even an instant invitation to join the circus, then travel, public appearances, and even greater fame, a fame beyond our town and the whole country. Vienna and Paris, Berlin and Moscow—all at the feet of the eleven-year-old wild-animal tamer who doesn't need a whip. Headlines in the papers, standing room only. He had thrown all this away, drumming his fingers on his knee one-two-three, one-two-three. Today, I know that Weiser never intended to become a circus artist. Anyone who levitates and shoots at the Chancellor of the Third Reich can't be in the circus. That sentence is illogical, but let it stand, because everything in this story is illogical. So let it stand.

The next day, we went to the big top to find out if the lion tamer's wife was alive. We were also curious about what they were doing with the panther. All we heard was that the woman was in the hospital and the wild-animal act would take place without the panther. The ticket lady said they hadn't decided yet what to do with the animal. Maybe in a few days she'd be back in the show, or maybe the circus would sell her to a zoo. For two hours we walked around in the Old Town, but it was boring, and we had no money, so we went home. As we passed the bill post on our street, I saw Weiser coming in our direction with a sack under his arm. He was returning from the forest, had clearly been catching grass snakes again and transporting them to the cemetery or the quarry. Elka was nowhere around. "What do we do today?" Szymek asked him. "Any ideas?" "I don't have time today," said Weiser. "Tomorrow, come to the hollow behind the firing range. There'll be an explosion." Instead of going inside, we went to the Prussian barracks, but about twenty army boys were kicking a ball on the field in a cloud of dust, so there was nothing for us there. In the afternoon, we headed for the cemetery across Bukowa Hill, to drop in at the crypt, perhaps, and play war, though no one was particularly enthusiastic about that. I learned now from Piotr that while I was sitting at home with my swollen foot, Weiser had twice refused to lend them the old Parabellum, and didn't even want to hear about the Schmeisser. Running around with a stick and shouting "pow pow," when you'd held a real gun in your hand wasn't the same. But there was no arguing with him—if he said no, it was no. Szymek kicked the pinecones that lay on the road, and I chewed a long blade of grass with a spray of seeds on its end. The rise was behind us now, and around a bend in the descending road we could see the cemetery. On this side all the gravestones were broken, and the rusted crosses, like the jutting masts of sunken ships, were overgrown with couch and nettles. As we passed Horst Meller's grave, farther down in the cemetery, the bells began ringing.

"Yellow Wings!" we cried in one voice, and Szymek, the quickest, said, "To the crypt! They'll be after him again!" Which wasn't the best idea, because even if you stood up on the crypt, you couldn't see the belfry. But we ran as if we and not the escaped madman were being pursued. For about three minutes the bells echoed between the walls of the trees—then silence. "Someone came," whispered Piotr. "They're chasing him." And indeed, a moment later, there was a crackle of twigs and the rustle of branches pushed aside, and we saw Yellow Wings hurrying in our direction. He had remembered the crypt. But when he came close enough to see three faces watching him intently, he bolted toward the embankment and the valley where the new garden plots were. Perhaps, too absorbed in his flight, he hadn't recognized us and was frightened. In any case, instead of diving into the crypt, where an entire division of militiamen and orderlies wouldn't have found him, he kept running, chased by the limping sexton and a man we'd never seen before. Sand flew from Yellow Wings' feet. The grass bowed before him. The bushes parted to let him pass.

The problem was—perhaps he didn't know this, or had forgotten it—the valley was not the valley it once was, where the grass grew high as your knees, and there were clumps of thistle and broom, and on sunny days grass snakes quietly slithered by, and partridges burst up from underfoot like rockets with wings. He tripped on the first barbed wire, got up, pulled it down with his hands, and ran on. But those men with the hoes, rakes, spades, boards, and brushes in their hands had seen him, seen him fleeing, and like dogs they caught the scent, and with music in their hearts and wicked satisfaction in their eyes they moved to block his path, to surround him. We ran after the sexton and the man, not wanting to miss what happened next. Yellow Wings, seeing people coming at him, stopped, turned, ran back, toward the sexton. The man accompanying the sexton—he did it well, too—put out a foot at just the right moment, and Yellow Wings went crashing down at the sexton's feet. Had he jumped up at once and run in our direction, he would have escaped, but it didn't happen that way. He got up slowly. The man had time to jump on his back, and for a while they rolled like snarling dogs. Then Yellow Wings broke free, and off he ran, but again in a bad direction, because the garden-plot people had now made a half-moon and were closing in.

That's when we saw a completely new side to Yellow Wings. He didn't run now, but stood in the middle of the circle and lowered his head a little, like a wrestler, waiting. The men stopped, not certain what to do next.

"Someone run to the phone at the rectory," shouted the sexton. "Call the militia, or the hospital!"

A fat man, the one who had threatened me and Weiser when we were moving the snakes, put down his hoe and ran to the cemetery. At the same time, two more courageous garden-plot men stepped toward Yellow Wings.

"Easy," said one. "We won't hurt you."

"Yes," said the other, "you'll be all right if you come quietly."

But Yellow Wings was of a different opinion. He leaped at them, knocked the stick out of the hand of one and felled the other with an elbow to the stomach. Both quickly retreated, and Yellow Wings now stood like a samurai encircled by enemies. Holding the stick high in both hands, he looked noble, magnificent.

"He's dangerous," said one of the men. "Let's wait for the militia."

"Are there too few of us," growled someone else, "to take care of one crazy man?"

Then came the most beautiful part of the show—because all this was a kind of show, after all, with those grown men, our fathers' age, holding hoes and rakes, and Yellow Wings in the center, like the hero of a legend or a story. The men began to close in, and Yellow Wings stood with his legs apart.

"He must have been a swordsman once," said Szymek, craning his neck. "Look at that!"

And, in fact, Yellow Wings could not only bring down fire and brimstone on the Earth and the inhabitants thereof; he was also worlds better than they at stick-fighting. He leaped, he spun in all directions, parried with lightning speed, and the blows he dealt were all on target. The crack of snapping tool handles mingled with the yelps of the attackers. At one point it looked as if they had him, had cornered him with their gardening weapons, but it was only an illusion. They withdrew, black-eyed, battered, with scratches all over. Yellow Wings stood triumphant. The garden-plot men went into a huddle and conferred. Again they charged, more vigorously this time, but didn't get him, and emerged from the encounter much the worse for wear.

A stone flew at the victor. Another stone. A third. Yellow Wings dodged them nimbly, and some he hit with his stick, but there were more and more of them, and they came harder and from all sides. One got him in the neck. The second hurt more— it hit him in the wrist, and for a while he could hold the stick with only one hand. Then in the head, in the neck again, then in the head again, and after that it was hard to see, because the stones fell like hail, and the men closed in and finally got to him, though he still defended himself, but all we could see now were sticks rising and falling and twisted faces and bared teeth. How much time passed before the siren wailed from the Rembiechowo highway? I only remember an eternity of sticks, spades, and hoes rising and falling. And I remember that when the ambulance, red cross on its door, came lurching in the sand of the embankment on which no trains ran, and the orderlies in white jumped out, I was running to the cemetery, Szymek and Piotr shouting behind me, running to the wooden belfry, and that I freed the ropes from the blackened beam, tied there by the sexton, and pulled on them with all the strength of my arms and legs,

pulled jumping, pulled standing, pulled like a lunatic, because I felt, for the first time in my life, like
a lunatic, and I pulled and wept, and wept and
pulled, and wept until Szymek and Piotr jumped
on me and tore me from the ropes, which had become a part of me, and dragged me away and into
the woods on Bukowa Hill. I also remember that I
said nothing to them, and went by myself to the
beach at Jelitkowo. I sat there by the stinking brown
water until night fell. Now and then a fisherman
walked along the beach, and with a long pole tested
the fish soup near the shore. The Brzezno light-
house started turning, and the ships at anchor in
the bay switched on their lights. Far away, toward
Sopot, someone lit a fire on the beach. Even if Weiser
himself had approached me then, and requested
something, I wouldn't have answered.

Szymek came out of the headmaster's study. He
winked. That meant: I said what we agreed on. I
heard my name. The militiaman, I noticed, had
buttoned all his buttons, and the headmaster had
straightened his tie, which now didn't resemble a
Jacobin jabot or a wet rag. It was an ordinary tie,
bought at the department store in downtown
Wrzeszcz.

"Well, then," asked M-ski, "have we remembered something, or do we prefer to be arrested and talk to the prosecutor?" He ended louder.

"I remembered something, sir."

"Go on," said the militiaman with a sigh, "tell us what you know."

"The whole thing from the beginning?"

"No," interrupted the headmaster, "just the part about Wiśniewska's dress."

"But it wasn't a dress, sir, it was only a piece of one."

"Fine, a piece, then. Where did you find it after the explosion?"

"There's an old oak there, sir. That's where we found it."

The militiaman pushed the map at me.

"Where?"

"Here, the oak is here, and here"——I pointed——"was the piece of dress."

"Who found it?" M-ski asked quickly.

I paused, as if dredging up this detail.

"It was Szymek, sir."

"All right," said M-ski, his face betraying nothing, though I knew he was pleased. "And where did you burn it?"

"At the quarry, sir."

The militiaman grew impatient at this. "There are no quarries around here. What are you talking about?"

"No," said the headmaster, and explained to the militiaman for me. "It's the field with the boulders. Everyone here calls it that."

"When was this?" M-ski continued.

"That same day, that evening, sir."

"And it was you—wasn't it?—who took the piece of dress there."

"How did you know, sir?"

M-ski smiled complacently. "You see, there is little that escapes us. What time was it?"

"I don't remember exactly, sir. After seven, I think."

"Yes. And what did you do then?"

"Nothing, sir. We went home."

"Why didn't you tell your parents?"

"Because it was so awful, sir, their being blown up, so awful I don't know if I could tell it even at confession," I poured out in one breath.

M-ski smiled again.

"But now you've told it, and not to the priest, either, but to us."

"Do you come from here?" the militiaman asked unexpectedly.

"Excuse me?" I replied, because what could he mean by such a question?

"Are your parents from here?"

"Yes, sir, they are, my father was born in Gdańsk and my mother, too."

"Very well, then," M-ski concluded the questioning. "And you found nothing of Weiser?"

"No, sir, the explosion was so huge, we didn't even look for pieces. It was only by chance that we found—"

"You can go. Call your other friend," the headmaster cut me off. "What are you waiting for?"

For the first time since the investigation began, I felt confident.

"Piotr, your turn," I called from the doorway, and as we passed each other, I winked, just as Szymek had, to tell him that everything was going smoothly, which is what those three had wanted from the start. I sat on my folding chair and nodded to Szymek, and he nodded back. The janitor yawned and yawned, revealing a row of rotten black teeth, and I remembered what had happened next.

The following morning at Cyrson's, I'd overheard the women talking.

"Did you hear? They caught the madman who was running around Brentowo and terrifying people."

"Not a madman, my dear, a pervert."

"Jesus and Mary, a pervert, you say?"

"Of course, a pervert. What kind of madman runs around in a cemetery ringing bells? And puts a helmet on his head and goes through the streets? A madman, my dear, thinks he's Napoleon or Mickiewicz."

"My sister-in-law, who lives there," another woman said, "claims it wasn't a madman at all, but a holy man, inspired, and once he stood on the roof and spoke like Scripture!"

"Like Scripture?"

"Well, almost. All about God and punishment for our sins."

"No, it's a madman. We have a priest for that. And on the roof, you say?"

"On the roof, and even the militia came, but he got away."

My turn in line came, so I didn't get to hear any more. When I ran out of the store, I saw Szymek.

"Are you over it?" he asked, not angry.

"Yes."

"Then read this," he said, putting under my nose the newspaper he was taking home. "Here," he said, pointing at a headline: PUBLIC-SPIRITED ACTION.

"What's it about?"

"Just read it," he said, impatient.

The story told of the capture of a dangerous lunatic, who had been taken thanks to the assistance of the proud members of the Rosa Luxemburg State Garden Cooperative. It was signed with the initials K.Z.

"So?" I asked.

"They write about him, but nothing about us."

"You want them to write about us?"

"In this case, no. It's better no one knows we helped him."

"Yes," I said. "It's better no one knows."

We crossed the cobblestones to the other side of the street. From the butcher's behind Cyrson's came the sickly sweet smell of entrails. At our gate we met Weiser and Elka, who were just leaving.

"Come earlier today. We'll be having a picnic," said Elka cheerfully.

"The usual place?"

"The usual place." And she started to run after Weiser.

"Wait!" Szymek stopped her. "If it's a picnic, we have to bring food, don't we?"

"No," she said, and pointed at the basket in her right hand. "I have everything."

The two of them went uphill toward the forest.

"An explosion picnic." Szymek laughed at his own joke. "Not bad, huh?"

But the picnic was completely unexplosive. When we went down into the hollow, Elka and Weiser were sitting under the oak with a tablecloth spread before them.

"Where'd you steal that?" asked Piotr. "From Father Dudak's altar?"

"Just don't get spots on it." She gave us a look. "See how white it is?"

It had all been done with class—Elka was no slouch. There were sliced tomatoes, cucumbers, between them a saltcellar, butter in a little china pot, and yellow cheese, also cut in slices. We sat cross-legged. Szymek took five bottles of orangeade from his string bag. We had bought them in order not to come empty-handed.

"Well," she said, salting the tomatoes, "you brought something, too."

When everything was ready, she took a loaf of bread and a knife from the basket, gave them to Weiser, and he cut thick hunks and distributed them to us, going clockwise.

"Not a bad idea, this picnic," said Piotr, chewing bread and tomato. "Eating in the woods instead of at home. Why didn't we think of it sooner?"

I asked Elka what the occasion was for the picnic. She hadn't said anything about it.

"You dopes." She laughed, showing her squirrel's teeth. "We're saying good-bye to the vacation."

That made us sad. It was true: the day after tomorrow we would have to stand in the gym in white shirts and dark shorts and listen to the headmaster tell us that summer was almost over, we were all rested and tan, and he was happy to welcome us back within these walls that we should love and respect. With other summers, you could feel the end approaching in everything around you— in the cumulus clouds that moved across the bay like angels' wings, in the sharp air of the last days of August, in the gusts of wind, not cold yet but salty, smelling of the sea. You could feel the summer dying when the vacationers began to leave Jelitkowo and more and more beach chairs stood empty. But now, in the silence around the white tablecloth, it was different: the summer seemed to swell and bud in the warm, vibrant air. The dust of three months covered the leaves and ferns, and not the faintest puff of wind disturbed the stillness between earth and cloudless sky. The drone of an invisible plane. Crickets playing their monotonous melody. And, at our feet, amazing ants with tiny membrane wings, who would disappear in two weeks, then return in a year, at this same time.

"Christ, what I would give to have another month," said Szymek, breaking the silence. But no one felt like talking. Weiser opened the first bottle of orangeade and poured the fizzing liquid into a glass that Elka held for him. The glass went from hand to hand, and I wondered why all the fuss, since we always drank from the bottle. "Red," observed Piotr. "The red is better than the yellow." But still no one felt like talking, and we all knew, anyway, that red orangeade had more gas in it and smelled nicer than the yellow. When we were done eating and drinking, Elka put everything back in the basket. Weiser pulled the magneto out of the bushes and hooked up the wires, and we moved from the oak to the other side of the hollow.

I've already written that the last explosion, though we didn't know at the time that it would be the last, was unlike the others. I wrote that the dust, pieces of earth, and torn grass formed a giant funnel cloud, dark, almost black, narrow at the base and widening upward, and I said what it reminded me of many years later. The funnel—this I didn't write before—traveled almost the length of the hollow like a top, a top released by an unseen hand, and it sucked up twigs, dead leaves, pinecones, even small stones. It swept up the basket, which had been left under the oak tree, and hurled it a dozen meters. The basket fell upended, so that everything inside it, including the orangeade bottles, was strewn with a clatter on the ground. But the white table-cloth came down slowly, gently swinging left and right.

Then Weiser and Elka left, but not as if it was anything special; they just said, "See you," as they usually did, and walked up the hill together. I don't know whether they held hands or not, but considering what we learned the next day, that's a detail of little significance. Szymek would have said they were playing doctor. I'm not so sure. Perhaps they spent that night in the cellar of the brickworks, and she played the panpipe while he danced, fell, spoke in an unknown tongue, and levitated. Or perhaps they wandered in the forest all night and at dawn sat on one of the hills and watched the sunrise. Anything was possible.

In the morning, the first person I met on the stairs was Weiser's grandfather.

"Where's David?" he asked sharply, and I was frightened, because Mr. Weiser hardly ever came out, and when he did, he always glowered.

"I don't know," I said.

He leaned so close to me, the tape measure hanging from his neck touched my nose. "You must know," he said, enunciating carefully. "Who would know if not you?"

Fortunately, Mrs. Korotek came by, on her way back from shopping, and, having good ears, she overheard and interrupted.

"You don't know, then, Mr. Weiser, that he went with Elka to Pszczółki?"

"Where, ma'am? Who with?" Mr. Weiser looked at her over his wire-framed glasses.

"Pszczółki, Mr. Weiser. It's out in the country, toward Tczew. Half an hour by train."

"What's that you say?"

"Half an hour by train."

"Half an hour?"

"By train. Elka's visiting her granny for the day. She spent the night."

"And David?"

"David, you ask. He's after her all the time." Mrs. Korotek smiled, showing every tooth she had left. "Sees nothing but her. You didn't know?"

This explanation did not satisfy Mr. Weiser. He straightened his glasses and took the tape measure off his neck.

"David tells me everything. Why didn't he tell me?"

"Ask him when he gets back." And Mrs. Korotek went on upstairs.

Soon after that, I heard Mr. Weiser knocking at Elka's door, heard him asking, and Mrs. Wiśniewska saying yes, Elka had asked if she could take a friend along, and Mrs. Wiśniewska had said why not, there was more room in the country than here, and she even packed them something to eat for the trip, because from the station there it was three kilometers to walk, if not more. When I went down to the courtyard, Szymek and Piotr already knew everything; they had eavesdropped at the back door. We knew Weiser and Elka hadn't gone to Pszczół-ki, but that was all we knew. They weren't at the brickworks, and the secret door there that led to the shooting room was locked. They weren't in the hollow or at the cemetery or at the quarry. They weren't anywhere. Finally we took the railroad embankment as far as the Rembiechowo highway, where on the broken arch of the bridge you could sit and watch the occasional car go by, ten meters beneath your feet. But instead of sitting, we stood on the concrete parapet, as at the edge of a cliff, and sent down spit bombs whenever a car went past.

On the other side of the highway, the blown-up bridge continued, and the embankment, after curving slightly for fifty meters, went into a tunnel where the rise began. On the left was the fence of the insane asylum; just before the fence, the Strzyża. To get to the stream, you didn't have to follow the railroad tracks but could walk along the bottom of the embankment, where there was a narrow path, the one M-ski took to meet the housewife. The path stopped at the water, so to go upstream, south, you had to push through underbrush, as we did when we followed the teacher. To the left of the embankment, the Strzyża flowed into a pond, and from there it fed, through a stone-framed grate, into the town's sewer system. I see this all perfectly, as if drawn on a map, and in a minute I'll shout, "There!" and point to where the river meets the embankment, and we'll run down from the bridge to the road and run, single file, stepping on each other's heels, along the narrow path, because it was there, where the Strzyża flows into the tunnel beneath the railroad tracks, that I saw Weiser and Elka, just a moment ago, saw them sitting at the water, doing nothing, only dipping their feet, and we'll run to them again, over and over in my mind, yelling and jubilant, as if we'd found, in an amber room, the treasure of the last king of the Incas.

How did it end? I don't mean the story—this story has no end—but the investigation, which concluded three minutes to midnight, after Piotr was questioned and M-ski called all three of us into the headmaster's study. We stood in front of the desk, the janitor behind us. The air stank of smoke and sweat, and the September rain drummed on the windows as one by one we took the militiaman's yellow ballpoint pen and signed our statements, and the report, too. We signed twice, with carbon paper, each of us leaving four signatures attesting to what happened. We were witnesses of the last explosion in the hollow behind the firing range. Weiser and Elka were blown to bits. All that remained was a piece of her red dress, which out of fear we burned that evening at the quarry. We had no knowledge of explosives other than those discovered in the cellar of the abandoned brickworks. Weiser possessed a rusty old German automatic, and let us touch it once, but that was all. The whole truth. First Szymek made his signature, which was crooked because he was left-handed. Piotr was next, signing in letters as large as two-zloty coins. I was last. As I wrote the final letter of my name, the clock struck twelve. "You can go home now," said M-ski. "The sergeant will escort you." The headmaster got up and buttoned his jacket, and the janitor dumped the ashtray butts into the wastepaper basket. At that moment, M-ski would not have failed to deliver some high-minded, solemn statement, some maxim like "He who fears not the truth need fear nothing," but just then there was a pounding at the school's front door, and someone roared over the rain: "Open up! Open up! Open up!"

The janitor turned on the outside light, and in the driving rain I saw my father and, behind him, Mr. Korotek and Piotr's father, and behind them, Szymek's mother and mine. My father burst in and, before anyone could say anything, seized M-ski by the lapels and bellowed, "They found her! They found her!" Then he released M-ski, and everyone started talking at once, the way they do at a party or the marketplace, so for the first minute you couldn't understand a thing. Elka had been found by the pond, just beyond the tunnel, where the stream broadens among thick rushes. She was alive, but still unconscious. They had taken her to the hospital. How she got there, no one knew, since they had combed the area, but only as far as the firing range. No one had any idea what had happened to Weiser. The militia was now searching for him in the place Elka was found. M-ski looked at us, and in his eyes we saw the same stupefaction as when someone gave a correct answer at the blackboard or got everything right on a test. "In that case," he said, "the investigation must go on, and we'll turn this matter over to the prosecutor!" "Fine," said my father in an even louder voice, "but not today!" This with a very dark look. Had M-ski, the militiaman, or the headmaster tried to keep us, even for a moment, my father would have punched one of them for sure, and there would have been a fight even worse than the one at the Lilliput, because Mr. Korotek and Piotr's father were right beside us and glaring just as fiercely.

But the investigation wasn't resumed on Monday, or ever. Because when Elka regained consciousness and was questioned, she remembered nothing, not even her own name or where she lived.

Her amnesia, attributed to shock, was expected to be temporary. After three weeks, she did know where she lived, but she said she was a boy and that her name was Weiser. She couldn't find the words for certain things, would say to the nurse, "Give me a post," when she meant a bowl of soup. She got everything confused. It was only at the beginning of October that she recovered her balance; but still nothing about him, not a word. The last time she'd played with Weiser, she said, was mid-August, and she didn't recall much of that. Mr. Weiser was dead by now, and aside from the prosecutor, who interrogated us one more time during the first school holiday, no one asked about David. We told the prosecutor that of course no burial of a piece of dress had taken place. After the explosion in the hollow, Weiser and Elka went up the hill, and that was the last we saw of them. The case, finally, was closed.

The official explanation was as follows: the air from the blast threw Elka into the thick ferns. We panicked, fled. We couldn't see Weiser, because he had been blown apart, or Elka, because she was lying in the ferns. Fear and our imagination made us think we saw them walking off, up the hill. We didn't. It was only the imagination of bad boys playing with unexploded shells, who made up this story out of fear. When Elka came to, at least partially, she tried to walk home, but she took a wrong turn by the Strzyża, and there collapsed in the rushes while circling the pond, unless she fell from the embankment and the current carried her into the rushes before she could drown. Our lies were forgiven, because Weiser, after all, had been the ringleader in our dangerous games, and the blame was mostly his. But M-ski, in nature class, continued to give us suspicious looks, to the end of school, though that may have been only because we knew something about his secret life.

Is that everything? Everything except for that day by the Strzyża, when we ran toward the stream and Elka turned to us and shouted, "You'll scare away the fish!"

She was joking. There were no fish in the Strzyża, and they didn't have a rod or a net.

"What are you doing here?" panted Szymek. "They're looking for you."

"Looking for us?" she said in surprise. "Who is?"

"Not sure," he said to Weiser. "Your grandfather, at least. He's worried."

"I told him I was going to Pszczółki with her."

"You're lying," Szymek yelled at Weiser, for the first time. "We heard your grandfather asking everyone about you—he didn't know anything. And you two didn't go to Pszczółki anyway." In his anger there was a note of admiration, and curiosity.

"What," bridled Elka, "did you come to spy on us?"

"All right, let's forget it," said Piotr, peacemaking. "But what are you doing now? There aren't even minnows here."

Elka looked at Weiser, who now was standing mid-calf in the water, watching it pour over a concrete sill.

"We're not doing anything," he answered for her, and after a moment of hesitation added, "Only a little planning."

He paused, knowing that we would wait for him to go on.

"For a special explosion," he explained. "We have to do all the calculations first."

I looked upstream, where the Strzyża meandered between alder and hazel bushes, and understood immediately what he had in mind. It was an extraordinary idea. If a charge were set in the tunnel under the embankment, the explosion would fill that narrow section with earth, turning the culvert into a dam seven to eight meters high, and where we were standing now, and farther up, there would be a regular lake, all the way to the trees.

"That's brilliant!" whispered Szymek. He loved the idea of a dam. "We'll be able to swim here."

He pointed at the meadow on the Rembiechowo highway side. "That'll all be covered with water!"

"Right," said Weiser. "But we have to calculate the mass of earth needed, the force of the explosion."

Piotr was the only one who didn't like Weiser's plan. He said there was already a pond on the other side, and that could be used for swimming. But we didn't let him finish, because the pond was overgrown and had scum on it, and the very thought of getting into it was revolting.

"We'll have to measure the tunnel," said Weiser. "Who volunteers?"

I was first to jump forward.

"Good," he said to me. "Count your steps carefully and watch out for the bottom."

The tunnel wasn't high; the highest point of its arch came up only to my eyes. I crouched and stared into the darkness. "Ho!" My shout echoed back at me: Ho . . . ho . . . ho . . . I entered, stooping, my hands on the damp, slippery walls. Eleven, twelve, thirteen. I stepped cautiously, and under my feet felt rotting weeds, ooze that had collected over the years, and pieces of brick. Twenty-one, twenty-two, twenty-three. In my nostrils, the smell of swamps and decay, sharp, cold, and penetrating. Thirty-one, thirty-two, thirty-three. It was like the smell of the crypt in the Brentowo cemetery, or of the cellar in the abandoned brickworks, but it didn't frighten me, nor did the many cubic meters of earth above my head, because at the end of the tunnel and the darkness surrounding me—forty-two, forty-three, forty-four—I could see a point of light, the opening, and it grew larger and brighter before me, until the cold stopped—fifty-nine, sixty, sixty-one—and I stood in the sunlight, blinking, straightening my neck, because I had made it to the other side.

"Four minutes," I heard Piotr say. "Can't it be done faster?" He was standing at the entrance, in the full sun, and at first I couldn't look at him directly.

"Of course it can," I replied, "but I didn't want to lose count."

We climbed the slope to the top of the embankment, which looked like a deserted road, and there Piotr pointed to the insane asylum, visible in the distance, behind the crowns of the trees.

"You think he's there?" he asked.

"Yes," I said, "definitely, because they didn't kill him."

I remember that when we started to descend on the other side of the embankment, I tripped on something. It was a railroad tie, hidden in the grass. At the bottom, Elka and Szymek had their feet in the water; Weiser stood on the bank. He held a stick and was drawing on the ground, where the grass was thinner.

"What's that?" I asked, but Elka quickly told me not to bother him.

It was a square, divided into smaller, equal squares, in which he had written, erased, and written. He asked me how many steps.

"Sixty-one," I told him, and he wrote something else, and erased it, as if it were a multiplication table or an abacus.

"Come here," Elka called to me. "Can't you see he's busy?"

I joined them, but had managed to count all the squares in the large square—there were thirty-six, six by six. Piotr said that if the explosion worked, the water could cover the meadow and eventually reach the road.

"What then?" I asked, but Elka was not at all worried.

"The firemen will come, and the army, and they'll drain it and build a new tunnel. But we will have had our swim by then," she explained, as if describing an outing to Jelitkowo. "We won't be here then."

"But we'll come and look with the other people," Szymek added, "and no one will know who did it."

"And if a train was going over," added Piotr, "that would really be something!"

Weiser rubbed out the squares with his foot.

"All right," he said. "It works out."

"Now what?" I asked, impatient.

"I have to see where to set the charge. There's no glass there?" he asked me, and I understood that he was going into the tunnel.

"No glass," I said. "Can I go with you?"

"Stay here."

Elka went up to him.

"I want to see it, too." And they went to the entrance, ducking and disappearing into the dark passageway, just as I had done a while ago, and Piotr ran up the slope to wait for them on the other side. I stood, my hands on the concrete arch, and watched the bent silhouette of Elka, who followed Weiser. I listened to their voices growing fainter as the splash of their steps merged with the gurgle of the stream. Then I saw a blurred shape where the light was, at the end, and in the light the shape lost its contour completely and vanished. How much time went by? How long was it before I heard Piotr shouting overhead, "What's happening? Where did they go?" Szymek said it was eight or nine minutes, but I wasn't sure about that, not then, and even less now, as I write this. Piotr had waited on the other side, waited and counted,

counted and waited, until he got tired and looked into the tunnel. Not seeing them, he figured they had turned back, that they had found a good place for the charge. So he ran up and down the embankment again, to our side, and saw me standing by the tunnel and Szymek wading in the water, but no one else. I thought he was joking when he said, "They didn't come out there," and he thought I was teasing him, trying to frighten him, but we soon realized that the joke was not his or mine— only Weiser's. "It's impossible," I said. "There's no place, no alcove in there where they could hide." Yet they were not on this side and not on that side of the embankment. For an hour, Szymek and I waded in the tunnel, tapping every stone, every brick, every piece of cement. "Weiser," I shouted, "Weiser, no more tricks. Where are you?" But other than the sound of the water and the drumming echo, there was no answer. We sat at the Strzyża until evening, one at either end of the tunnel and Piotr on watch at the top of the embankment—to no avail. We went home with lowered heads, for though we didn't think that anything bad had happened, though we were certain that tomorrow morning they'd be at school, at the assembly that marked the start of the academic year, there was still something abnormal about this disappearance, almost as if Weiser had thumbed his nose at us, a thing he hadn't done, ever, from the time we met him. When the Brentowo cemetery was behind us—we went by the embankment—and we could see the roofs of our district from the top of Bukowa Hill, and beyond them the airfield and the bay, a gust of wind came from the north, from the sea, the first of the fall, a cool and invigorating wind. At the houses, where the forest ended, I felt drops of rain, drops as big as grapes. They fell, and the ground instantly drank them in, but more drops followed, faster and faster, and in a moment the street, the town, the entire world was immersed in a gray sheet of rain.

This is where the story ends. All my thoughts about Weiser disturb me, they disturb me so much that I won't write any more of them. Let them stay in my memory, in my heart. But there is still Piotr. I wrapped my manuscript in brown paper, for him; I stuffed it into a crack in his stone.

"Is that you?" he asked.

"Yes," I said.

"Why did you come? It isn't All Souls' Day."

"I know, Piotr, but I've brought something for you. Read it, and I'll come tomorrow, or in a couple of days, and we'll talk."

He said nothing. That meant he agreed.

———

I don't know how it happens, but instead of taking the bus, I go on foot. First I pass Bukowa Hill, where the clearly marked lanes have nothing to do with the past. On the left should be the Brentowo cemetery. Here. A big square. No tombstones with gothic letters. The trees have been cut down. A bulldozer, beside the small brick church, is making a pile of stones and broken markers. It's digging the foundation for a new, much larger church. The hole is several meters deep and the size of a small soccer field. I walk on. Where the empty crypt once stood, there's a four-story building with three stair-wells. The new tenants are putting up curtains and cleaning the windows, after the painters, even though it's cold out. Now I am on the railroad embankment. Where you could once see, beyond the trees, the hills around the firing range, there are now high-rises, as yet without plaster. One, two, three, and behind them a fourth. The top of the embankment is in worse shape, rutted by the trucks and cars of the garden-plot people. I take it to the Rembie-chowo highway, which doesn't look at all like a highway. It's an ordinary street with sidewalks, streetlights, and, again, a lot of cars. I'm weary, as if I were old. I regret not taking the bus. But per-haps, I think, it's good that I've taken a look. Piotr likes to begin with what's going on in town. He'll want to know every detail. So I look around one more time and head for his cemetery. No more reflecting; I take a street down, turn right, go up, and there I am. To the right of the cemetery gate is the road to the insane asylum. If I went that way and passed the buildings with barred windows and surrounded by an old park, I would come to the place where I saw Weiser for the last time. But it wasn't for that that I made this journey. I have to talk with Piotr now. I take a seat on the cold stone and pull up my scarf.

"You read it?" I ask, though I don't know if he feels like talking.

"Yes," he says.

We are silent for a while. I pull the manuscript from the crack and put it in my bag. But Piotr doesn't begin with his usual "What's new?" Our conversation today will have a different character. I can tell this from the first sentence:

"You didn't say which dress Elka was wearing."

"When?"

"At the Strzyża."

"The red one, of course."

"That should be mentioned."

"It was the same dress she had on at the airfield."

"And what about the guns Weiser had hidden away? The official report says only that explosives were found. Not a word about guns."

"Because all they found was TNT and some detonators. Weiser must have hidden the guns before they went looking for him at the brickworks. Remember, the secret door that led to the shooting room was locked."

"I remember."

"You see? Weiser had everything planned."

"Another point. M-ski is well done, true to life. But he never would have made an error in nomenclature or classification."

"It wasn't *Arnica montana,* then?

"It was *Arnica montana,* of course, the mountain tobacco plant. But you have M-ski putting it in the subfamily *Liguliflorae,* the tongued flowers, which includes such plants as *Scorzonera hispanica* and *Taraxacum officinale* . . ."

"You've lost me."

"*Scorzonera hispanica?* It's the black salsify, the oyster plant. And *Taraxacum officinale* is the common dandelion. They belong to the *Liguliflorae,* but not *Arnica montana.*"

"I'm losing my mind. How do you know these names? M-ski never taught us all that."

"*Arnica montana* belongs to the subfamily *Tubuliflorae,* like *Achillea millefolium,* the yarrow."

"Does it really matter?"

"To M-ski, certainly. And another thing. Horst Meller. Did you ever find out who he was?"

"For God's sake, who today is going to care who Horst Meller was?"

"You see, you put in some unimportant detail, and the action stops. The ants with wings. The smell of the butcher's behind Cyrson's."

"The ants and the butcher's are just as important as what subfamily *Arnica montana* belongs to."

"The next thing you'll say is that everything matters."

"Yes, everything or nothing."

"Then why didn't you write that I was afraid of the dark? Afraid of dark corridors, dark cellars? Even at the Strzyża, I wouldn't go near that damned tunnel. I waited and counted, but I never looked inside. Why didn't you write that?"

"I was at the other end!"

"You didn't see my silhouette, did you?"

"I saw Elka's back, that's all I saw."

"One more thing. What's this headmaster business? In elementary school, it was always the director."

"Yes, but after you died, the name was changed to headmaster."

"So?"

"If you think it's important, I'll make him the director. He's not likely to complain—he retired long ago."

"Other than that, everything's the way it was."

"That's all you have to say?"

"What more did you want? I read it and I've made my comments."

"And Weiser?"

"Weiser?"

"What about Weiser? He didn't really plan to join the circus. He was tricking us. Where is he now?"

"You wrote all this, and you don't know?"

"I know more than I did, but not everything. That's why I came. I have to know the truth."

"I kept my promise, but still you ask."

"What happened to him?"

"We've talked enough."

"What happened to him? Why aren't you saying anything? Why don't you answer, Piotr?"

So again you'll take that path from the cemetery, first down, then up, then finally down again. You'll stand over the rushing water, where the river flows into the low, arched tunnel. You'll step in the cold water and stand at the entrance, your hands on the wet concrete. You'll take a deep breath, then shout, as if shouting in the mountains, "Weiser!" The echo answers in muffled syllables, but only the echo answers. The water that gurgles over the sills of cement is the same as it was in years past, and if the sky were not cloudy, you would think that you were back. "Weiser," you shout, "I know you're in there!" and you hurl a rock into the black opening. The only answer will be a splash. "Weiser," you'll shout again, "I know you're in there. Come out!" In the noise of the water, there will be no answer. "Weiser, you bastard, come out! Do you hear me?" And you'll put your head in the tunnel, and crouch down in the water, and on your knees go through the ooze, slimy weeds, and stones toward the point of light at the other end. "Weiser!" you'll shout. "Stop playing tricks, you son of a bitch, I know you're there!" Above you, a hollow reverberation, like the rumble of a train, but that is not an answer. You emerge from the tunnel. Soaked, covered with mud, you sit on the riverbank and, shivering, remember the words of that chant: "Da-vid Wei-ser doesn't go to chu-urch." You'll look up at the sky, where behind leaden clouds drone the engines of an invisible jet. And instead of saying anything, instead of swearing and cursing, you'll think how all that your eyes once saw and your hands once touched has long since turned to dust. You'll stare without seeing, and no longer hear the water, or the wind that ruffles your matted hair.